Frederick Ryland, John Locke

Locke on Words

An Essay Concerning Human Understanding

Frederick Ryland, John Locke

Locke on Words
An Essay Concerning Human Understanding

ISBN/EAN: 9783337365950

Printed in Europe, USA, Canada, Australia, Japan

Cover: Foto ©Andreas Hilbeck / pixelio.de

More available books at **www.hansebooks.com**

AN ESSAY

CONCERNING

HUMAN UNDERSTANDING

BY

JOHN LOCKE, Gent.

BOOK III.—OF WORDS

WITH INTRODUCTION and NOTES

BY

F. RYLAND, M.A.

LATE SCHOLAR OF ST. JOHN'S COLLEGE, CAMBRIDGE

LONDON
W. SWAN SONNENSCHEIN & CO.
PATERNOSTER ROW
1882.

LONDON:
WOODFALL AND KINDER, PRINTERS,
MILFORD LANE, STRAND, W.C.

PREFACE.

No apology seems to be needed for presenting the "immortal Third book" of Locke's Essay in a separate form. All who know it admit that it may be read with great profit by those who have neither time nor inclination to study the rest of the work in which it forms a kind of episode. While it affords the student an admirable example of all that is most characteristic in Locke's style, method and opinions, it has also a real and substantive value of its own. As Hallam remarks, " Among many excellent things in the Essay on Human Understanding, none are more admirable than much of the third book on the nature of words, especially the three chapters on their imperfection and abuse."

The present is a reprint of the seventh edition, published in 1715–16, with, however, a few unimportant corrections of typographical errors, and the omission of the long and uninteresting note added by Locke to Chapter III. in reply to the criticisms of Stillingfleet.

The Introduction and Notes have been put together chiefly with a view to assisting " the man of very ordinary capacity," the average reader, who as a rule knows little Logic and less Metaphysics.

CONTENTS.

—◆—

CHAPTER I.

Of Words or Language in General.

CHAPTER II.

Of the Signification of Words.

CHAPTER III.

Of General Terms.

Chapter IV.

Of the Names of Simple Ideas.

Chapter V.

Of the Names of mixed Modes and Relations.

CHAPTER VI.

Of the Names of Substances.

Chapter VII.

Of Particles.

Chapter VIII.

Of Abstract and Concrete Terms.

Chapter IX.

Of the Imperfection of Words.

CHAPTER X.

Of the Abuse of Words.

CHAPTER XI.

Of the Remedies of the foregoing Imperfections and Abuses.

INTRODUCTION.

I.—*Chief Events of Locke's Life.*

Born ... ... Aug. 29th 1632

Goes to Westminster School under Dr.
Busby; with Dryden and South among
his schoolfellows 1646

Commences residence at Christ Church, Oxford 1652

Takes the degree of Bachelor of Arts ... 1656

Senior Censor of Christ Church 1664

Goes as Secretary to Sir W. Vane, Ambassador to the Elector of Brandenburg ... 1665

Enters the family of Lord Ashley, afterwards
Earl of Shaftesbury, where he lives in the
capacity of doctor, friend, secretary, and
tutor to the son, and afterwards to the
grandson, of his patron 1667

Secretary of Presentations to the livings in
the gift of the Crown 1672
(This he lost next year in consequence
of Shaftesbury's fall.)

B

Of the Conduct of the Understanding, written
    about   1697
          (Not published till 1706.)
Dies   ...   .   Oct. 28th 1704

II.—*Locke's Place as a Philosopher.*

. John Locke's is probably the most important
name in the list of English philosophers. Locke is
to us what Descartes is to France, or Kant to
Germany, the founder of a school destined to influence all subsequent national thought. Two rival
claims have been advanced to this unique position—
on behalf of Bacon and of Hobbes. But Bacon
was an isolated thinker, whose writings seem to have
had singularly little effect on his contemporaries, or
on his successors for two centuries. There was
never a Baconian philosophy, nor was there any
pretence of one until the nineteenth century. Notwithstanding his magnificent project of a complete
Reformation of Science, parallel to that which he
had witnessed in Religion, Bacon's direct and
tangible contribution to the great revival amounts to
little more than a series of disconnected hints on the

B 2

methods of discovery. Locke himself owed nothing
to Bacon, nor did any other English thinker, until
within the last sixty or seventy years. We may,
perhaps, say that Bacon is to Hobbes and Locke what
Wicliffe is to Cranmer and Latimer: with broader
and more revolutionary conceptions, he yet left
much less important traces of his own immediate
influence. The claim of Hobbes to pre-eminence
in English philosophy is thus stronger than that of
Bacon. He was the source and origin of all future
discussion in Ethics. But his influence, although
remarkably powerful, was almost wholly effected by
way of antithesis. The Leviathan led to the development of the two great rival schools of the
Intuitionists and Utilitarians, but in both cases the
development came through contradiction of the
system, not by expansion of it. And it cannot be
said that in other fields, such as Metaphysics and
Psychology, Hobbes made any marked impression
or left many fervent disciples. Certainly Locke owed
little or nothing to him ; perhaps he had never even
read the Leviathan.*

---

* Mr. Fox Bourne appears strangely to exaggerate when
he says that Locke "had learnt quite as much from his
[Hobbes'] 'Treatise of Human Nature' and his 'Leviathan,'
as from the 'Discours de la Méthode' and the 'Meditationes'
of Descartes."—*Life*, ii. p. 89.

Although Locke cannot claim the same supreme importance in the history of philosophy as Descartes, from whom he derived a great deal more than English writers have, as a rule, cared to acknowledge, he is in every sense an epoch-making thinker. His intellectual descendants are so numerous and so widely spread that it is difficult to classify them. His Essay gave rise directly to the line of metaphysical speculation which was developed and extended by Berkeley and Hume ; and indirectly, by way of negation, to Kant and German Idealism ; while it finds its most recent exponent, as one born out of due season, in John Stuart Mill. It gave birth to the great Psychological school, whose favourite doctrine is the "Association of Ideas,"— represented in the last century by Hartley and Hume, and in our own time by the Mills, Spencer and Bain, while it contains more than traces of the modern comparative and pathological methods of research. Locke's theological works were the origin of the rationalistic theology of the eighteenth century ; Collins was his friend and executor. His little book on Education, "our one classic" on that subject, occupies a position in the science of Pedagogy almost as notable as his Essay does in the sciences of Psychology and Metaphysics : he first made the road, as it has been said, which the great educational reformers followed. His influence on the development of modern theories of Politics and Economics, if less important, has yet been decidedly marked. It is hardly an exaggeration to say that in France nearly every important thinker, from Voltaire to Victor Cousin, may be called a disciple of Locke. The Encyclopædists and their followers, and even the leaders of the reaction against them, were influenced almost to a man, though of course in different degrees, by the teachings of the great Englishman. The psychological theories of Condillac, Cabanis and De Tracy, the political theories of Turgot and Rousseau, and the educational theories of the last, can be traced more or less directly to this one source ; while probably all the apostles of the eighteenth century Illumination could trace to him the first suggestion of their metaphysical and theological scepticism.

Nevertheless, perhaps, Locke's fame depends less on the way in which he impressed a bent on the course of subsequent philosophical thought, than on his popularity amongst men "not accustomed to abstract speculation," but yet desirous to "raise themselves above the alms-basket, and not content to live lazily on scraps of begged opinions." Like Socrates, he essayed to bring down philosophy from the skies. He writes "for the man of very ordinary capacity." He has firm trust in the common sense of the normal British citizen, even while his analysis seems to threaten its authority. Honest, impartial, and never run away with by enthusiasm—here lies the secret of his wide influence in England, where the national mind has always been ostentatiously practical. Locke's manful disregard of mere consistency, his readiness to qualify statements which seemed extreme, and his loyalty to common sense, explain how it is that he enjoyed, especially during the realistic eighteenth century, so general a popularity. Berkeley and Hume were too rigidly logical, and too ready to indulge in paradoxes offensive to the man of ordinary capacity, to gain the same wide audience. Locke's reliance on common sense is seen even in places where he appears most at variance with it ; while Berkeley and Hume are never more divergent from the thoughts and feelings of the vulgar than when they claim to be their advocates and exponents. To take an example : Locke's doctrine of perception, although it may strike us now as artificial and paradoxical, was doubtless put forward by him as an honest statement of the plain, natural, and non-metaphysical belief held by unsophisticated people. He abandoned as far-fetched the thories of such writers as Cudworth and More, who make a broad distinction between thought and feeling, and who recognize even in external perception an act essentially intellectual, due to the synthetic activity of thought, and not to mere passive reception of ideas on a *tabula rasa*. Such a view seemed to him to savour too much of mystery and metaphysics to satisfy the " large, sound, round-about sense" for whose approval he always sought.

Another characteristic feature of Locke's writings is his earnest and evident desire to arrive at truth ; and to arrive at it fairly and honestly. He will allow no hypothesis of his own, and no tradition of the elders, to stand in the way. He feels a hearty enjoyment in the pleasures of intellectual exercise ; and this enjoyment prevents that over-anxiety to come up with the game which leads sometimes to hasty theorizing, and sometimes to the supine acceptance of antiquated beliefs. He is ready to allow "law" to the knowledge of which he is in pursuit. Both by precept and example he teaches his reader to think for himself. He represents in glowing colours the value of truth, the pleasure of seeking it, and the necessity of striving lawfully for it. As he tells us in his own manly way, he who " sets his own thoughts on work, to find and follow truth, will (whatever he lights on) not miss the hunter's satisfaction ; every moment of his pursuit

will reward his pains with some delight, and he will
have reason to think his time not ill-spent even when
he cannot much boast of ' any great acquisition."
His books are thus eminently energizing and stimu-
lating to the mind. However unlike in other
respects, he resembles Plato in this. Few authors
serve better the purpose of a mental tonic.

It is of course not necessary or possible to deny
that Locke has his faults. Leaving out of consideration the acknowledged inadequacy of his philosophy
as a positive system, there are other defects in his
writings which one would willingly have missed.
One of these, for instance, is the tone of ironical
contempt wherein he speaks of his predecessors in
metaphysical speculation, not only of Plato, Aristotle
and the Schoolmen, but also of Descartes, to whom
he owed so much. Though not altogether unpleasant at first, it jars on the ear through repetition.
When Bacon criticizes gravely and with moderation,
Locke too often sneers. His sympathies with alien
modes of thought were indeed very limited. What
did not seem reasonable on the face of it repelled
him so completely that he too often regarded it as
unworthy of further consideration. New or uncouth
technical terms, a hint of what he suspected to be
mysticism or verbal jugglery, was generally sufficient to repel him from a fair examination of

doctrines which in themselves were reasonable enough.

Yet, after all, this intolerance of verbiage is not by any means an unmixed evil, if only applied impartially all round. The theology, philosophy and science of to-day would perhaps be none the worse for the criticism of a nineteenth-century Locke, with the seventeenth-century Locke's jealousy of undefined, and perhaps undefinable, terms. Possibly Evolution, Culture, Welfare, and sundry strange words ending in -plasm and -geny might attract his attention, instead of Substantial Forms and Intentional Species, and be none the worse for the scrutiny. We may still be permitted to think with Locke, that "it is not without all reason supposed, that there are many such empty terms to be found in some learned writers, to which they had recourse to etch out their systems where their understandings could not furnish them with conceptions from things."

III.—*Locke's Doctrine of Ideas.*

" Philosophy is much indebted to Mr. Locke for his observations on the abuse of words. It is pity he did not apply these observations to the word *idea*, the ambiguity and abuse of which has very much hurt his excellent Essay." (Reid, Intellectual Powers, Essay VI. Chap. iii.)

Knowledge, says Locke, consists in the "perception of the connection and agreement, or disagreement and repugnancy, of any of our ideas." (Essay, Bk. IV. Chap. i. sec. 2.) Thus the first step towards understanding Locke must be to get a notion of what he means by the word Idea.* He defines it as "whatsoever is the object of the understanding when a man thinks," or "whatever it is which the mind can be employed about in thinking." And as Locke, following Descartes, uses the words *think* and *thought* for all the operations of consciousness, *idea* is equivalent to *direct object of consciousness.* It includes what are now distinguished as Sensation, Feeling, Perception, Conception, Image, Representation, and even Emotion. It includes what Hume calls " impressions " —that is, directly and immediately known feelings, as well as what Hume calls " ideas "—that is, remembered impressions.

It is tolerably evident that a word used to denote so many different things cannot have a very clear and definite meaning. But Locke adds to the confusion by also using the word to denote the attributes in external things which are supposed to produce impressions or sensations in us, as well as to denote the impressions themselves. The term may

---

* On the history of the use of this word, see Hamilton's Reid, note G, p. 925.

thus express a merely personal or subjective phenomenon in my mind, or something which would still
exist if I were unconscious or dead. "A snowball
having the power to produce in us the ideas of white,
cold, and round, the powers to produce those ideas in
us, as they are in the snowball, I call 'qualities'; and,
as they are sensations or perceptions in our understandings, I call them 'ideas'; which ideas, if I speak
of them sometimes as in the things themselves, I
would be understood to mean those qualities in the
objects which produce them in us." (Bk. II. Chap.
viii. sec. 8.)   Instances of this use will be found in
Bk. III.   It leads to ambiguities such as those mentioned in the note to Chap. x. sec. 17.

All ideas come to us from experience ; there are
no ready-made notions in our minds, no "innate
ideas." But experience is not confined to external
things ; we have experience also of states of consciousness. "Our observation, employed about external sensible objects, or about the internal operations of our minds," Locke tells us, "supplies our
understandings with all the materials for thinking."
These two " fountains of knowledge " are called
Sensation and Reflection, the faculties of external
and internal perception. By an *idea of sensation*, or
sensible idea, Locke means what we call a sensation,
or what we call a perception, or the remembrance of

them. By an *idea of reflection* he means the result of
an act of introspection or self-consciousness, "that
notice which the mind takes of its own operations,"
or the remembrance of it. Thus *red, solid, hot,* whether directly perceived or not, are *ideas of sensation.*
If I am looking at a poppy, I have what we call a
sensation of red ; and if I shut my eyes and picture
the poppy to myself, I have a remembered sensation
of red ; Locke calls them both *ideas of sensation.* If
I am actually conscious of remembering, or of willing,
or am imagining one of these mental states, I have
an *idea of reflection.*

All that the mind can do with regard to the ideas
it thus becomes possessed of is to recall, compare,
and unite them. It cannot originate any ideas. "All
those sublime thoughts which tower above the clouds
and reach as high as heaven itself take their rise and
footing here : in all that great extent wherein the
mind wanders in those remote speculations it ·may
seem to be elevated with, it stirs not one jot beyond
those ideas which sense or reflection have offered for
its contemplation." (Bk. II. Chap. ii. sec. 24.) The
mind gives birth to no entirely new idea; but it combines, separates, and compares the ideas which come
to it from inward or outward observation.

Our ideas come to us from distinct and definite
objects. This particular poppy gives me an indi-

vidual idea, or perception; that particular stick of
sealing-wax gives me another individual idea, or perception.　They are, as Locke says, "particular ideas
received from particular objects."　But I can leave
out of sight the points wherein the poppy and sealing-
wax differ, and retaining in my mind the point
wherein they agree, I can form the general abstract
idea of *red*. It is general, because it applies to a large
number of distinct objects.　And it is abstract, because it is formed by a process of drawing off (*abstrahere*) the attention from the points of difference,
in order to concentrate it on the point of resemblance.　General ideas are thus abstract ideas, and
Locke is quite right in calling them so.　But it must
be noticed that the names of general ideas are not
abstract terms. An abstract term is properly opposed
to a concrete term, and signifies the name of an
attribute, in contradistinction to the name of a
thing. Poppy is a concrete term; redness an abstract
term.*

Another division of ideas is that into *simple* and
complex.　By *simple ideas* Locke means "uncom-
pounded appearances," that is, unanalyzable elements of knowledge, whether furnished by Sensation
or Reflection.　Not all ideas given by experience are

---

* Cf. note to Chap. viii. sec. 1.

simple; but only those which are found to be incapable of further analysis. Flower is to Locke a complex idea ; but fragrance, redness, softness, smoothness, are simple ideas ; because, while we can split up the idea of a flower into these and similar component ideas, we cannot break up our idea of redness or fragrance into still simpler elements. Locke's list of simple ideas embraces many which we have learnt to consider extremely complex; such, for instance, as Solidity and Extension.

Locke divides *complex ideas* into three classes, which he calls *Modes, Substances,* and *Relations.* His treatment of the last of these, ideas of Relation, is not very clear or consistent, and fortunately they may be left out of consideration by the reader of Bk. III., in which practically only the two former kinds of complex ideas are discussed.

By *Modes* Locke means "such complex ideas which, however compounded, contain not in them the supposition of subsisting by themselves, but are considered as dependences on or affections of substances; such are the ideas signified by the words ' triangle, gratitude, murder.'" (Bk. II. Chap. xii. sec. 4.) They are composed of groups of simple ideas more or less large and more or less varied. The less complicated groups, "which are only variations or different combinations of the same simple idea," are called *simple modes*. The more complicated groups, which involve several simple ideas, are called *mixed modes*. The ideas of triangle and circle are modifications of the one simple idea of space, and belong to the former class; the ideas of gratitude and murder, involving notions of states of consciousness, external actions, the obligations of law and morality, etc., belong to the latter. (Bk. II. Chap. xxii. sec. 1.)

Ideas of substances resemble mixed modes in being compounded of simpler ideas of different kinds; but they differ from them in being "taken to represent distinct particular things, subsisting by themselves, in which the supposed or confused idea of substance, such as it is, is always the first and chief." (Bk. II. Chap. xii. sec. 6.) On the other hand, mixed modes are not thought as answering to "real beings that have a steady existence," but merely as groups of "scattered and independent ideas put together by the mind." By ideas of substances Locke means ideas of groups of attributes, together with the supposed metaphysical basis, or substratum, in which they are said to inhere. When we fully analyze our idea of a concrete external thing, we discover a more or less numerous set of simple ideas, such as those of space, solidity, colour, temperature, etc.; and further, we are obliged to assume what we can never discover, an "unknown support of these qualities we find existing," the substratum or metaphysical substance of the thing, of which we can have only an obscure and confused idea. Thus our idea of an orange consists of ideas of roundness, yellowness, juiciness, a given size and weight, a peculiar taste, etc., *plus* an indeterminate idea of a "something to which they belong and in which they inhere." The word 'substance' is used by Locke to denote both the concrete thing itself and the metaphysical basis or substratum.

It is not necessary here to examine the validity of the doctrine of ideas propounded by Locke. An able discussion will be found in Reid's Essays on the Intellectual Powers (Essay VI. Chap. iii.), where it is pointed out that Locke's theory would make impossible all knowledge save that of our own states of consciousness. If all we know be our own ideas, we can never have any actual knowledge of external objects, but only of our own ideas about them. We remain shut up in the vicious circle of our own ideas. This line of argument is developed in Prof. Green's admirable Introduction to Hume's Treatise of Human Nature, probably the most subtle piece of metaphysical criticism in English.

Although even a brief summary of this discussion would be out of place, the reader must be reminded, that great as was Locke's advance on previous thinkers in clearness of style and directness of

C

thought, in practical breadth of view and in exhilar-
ating freedom from pedantry, he here took a step,
and a long step, backwards. In his theory of
knowledge he left little room for the part played
by the intellect in combining the raw material of
knowledge given us by the senses. It is not that he
fails to recognize the deliverances of what has been
called the Internal Sense, for, as we see, he places
"Reflection," at any rate theoretically, on a level
with external sensation as a source of ideas. It is
not that he rejects a doctrine of "innate ideas,"
which probably no philosopher ever seriously
advanced, and thus became the coryphaeus in a
long, tiresome and unnecessary series of logomachics.
But it is, that he always tends to neglect, and never
fully appreciates, the supreme importance of the
intellectual factor in experience—the synthetic
activity of thought which brings into relation and
gives meaning to the unrelated, and in themselves
unmeaning, feelings yielded by internal and external
sensation. This fundamental defect set English
metaphysics travelling on the road to absolute
scepticism, a road which ends in an impracticable
subjective idealism, as unsatisfactory to the philosopher as it is revolting to the plain man. We know
nothing, according to Hume and Mill, but our own
states of consciousness, and these we do not know

as our own ; we know neither ourselves nor the universe ; everything is reduced to an incoherent flux
of phenomena. Thought itself becomes a series of
isolated and unmeaning states of feeling.

But, it may be objected, to say this is only to say
that Locke did not anticipate Kant. If so, the
indictment is manifestly unfair. In point of fact,
however, Locke, made a distinct step backwards.
Historians of philosophy have not sufficiently
noticed that in his contemporaries, More and Cudworth, as well as in the despised Schoolmen, the
factor which he so fatally left out of account is
clearly and unambiguously affirmed. Kant's work,
like that of many other great reformers, was after
all only a restatement, though with fuller consciousness of its meaning and implications, of an old
truth ; the truth, that knowledge is not merely a
passive reception of ideas, but a synthesis of impressions by the active energy of thought.

The Scholastics distinctly laid down that the
intellect is not a *tabula rasa,* written on from without, although they at the same time allowed that,
prior to experience, the mind has no content of
ideas. It is thought and not sensation that really
produces the record of experience. A parallelism
was recognized between Biology and Psychology ;
for, just as the living organism builds itself up by

assimilating dead matter from without, so does the
fabric of knowledge build itself up by the integration of the "forms" of external things.*

Cudworth (1617–1688), whose daughter, Lady
Masham, was Locke's greatest friend, thus sums up
and appropriates the scholastic theory : " Knowledge
is not a passion from anything without the mind,
but an active exertion of the inward strength, vigour
and power of the mind, displaying itself from
within." He makes a clear distinction between
this synthetic activity of consciousness and the
internal sense ; and shows that even in perception of
external objects the intellect actively exerts itself.
"Things are never perceived merely by their own
force and activity upon the percipient, but by the
innate force, power and ability of that which perceives. And sense itself is not a mere corporeal
passion, but a perception of the bodily passions
proceeding from some power and ability supposed
to reside in a sensitive soul, vitally united to that
respective body." It is the intellect that gives us
the relations of whole and part, equality and
inequality, priority and posteriority, cause and
effect; and consequently that gives us objects at

* See, for instance, Kleutgen, La Philosophie scolastique
(Paris), vol. i. pp. 34 *sey.* Cf. also his correction of Frosch-
hammer's misrepresentations, p. 144.

all. At the same time, Cudworth makes it clear that this objective idealism does not do away with the reality and actuality of our knowledge, as the theory of subjective idealism derived by Hume and Mill from the teaching of Locke certainly does.*

Henry More (1614–1687) remarks that "relative ideas" prove that the soul has "active conception proceeding from herself, while she takes notice of external objects." And he gives the following instances: "Suppose one side of a room whitened, the other not touched or meddled with, this other has thus become unlike, and hath the notion of *dissimile* necessarily belonging to it, although there has nothing at all been done thereunto. So suppose two pounds of lead which therefore are two equal pieces of that metal; cut away half from one of them, the other pound, nothing at all being done unto it, has lost its notion of equal, and hath acquired a new one of double unto the other. Wherefore the ideas of equal and unequal, double and sub-double, like and unlike, with the rest are no external impresses upon the senses, but the soul's

---

* Treatise concerning Eternal and Immutable Morality, Bk. IV. chaps. i. ii. It may be as well to say that though this work was not published till 1731, the same views are taught in The Intellectual System, published in 1678.

own active manner of conceiving those things which are discovered by the outward senses."*

The ultimate effect of the negative thought of Locke and Hume was a more distinct enunciation of the forgotten factor ; we may say that it helped to solve the problem by a *reductio ad absurdum.* In itself it was a retrogression. It obliterated one-half, and that the more important half, of the truth in order to bring into higher relief the other, and less important, half. But the metaphysical speculations of the great English philosophers were not wasted ; because the new solution offered by Kant and Hegel is incomparably fuller and more complete than that of St. Thomas Aquinas, or More, or Cudworth. And that new solution was only rendered possible by Locke's doctrine of Ideas.

IV.—*Locke's Doctrine of Species.*

In the sixth chapter of this Book of the Essay, Locke expounds, at considerable length and with great ingenuity, his theory of the nature of Species. He lays down that Species or natural classes of things

-----

* Antidote against Atheism, Bk. I. chap. vi.

are arbitrary in their origin, that they are relative not absolute, and are not made by Nature herself but by the understanding of man. They "depend on such collection of ideas as men have made, and not on the real nature of things." This somewhat paradoxical statement has been a stumbling-block and rock of offence to many of Locke's warmest admirers. It seems important, therefore, to point out in advance the true sense in which classification may be said to be "arbitrary," and also to explain Locke's general position with regard to the subject.

It is obvious that any property may be taken as a foundation for the division of things into classes. An artist classifies things by forms and colours, while the man of science classifies by less easily recognized attributes. The statesman, the theologian and the poet classify men and things in very different ways. The special interest determines the principle on which the classification depends. (Cf. Chap. ix. sec. 14, and note.) In this sense classification is arbitrary. Objects are, indeed, made by Nature to resemble each other, but the classes are made by the mind, which selects such points of resemblance between things as interests it most, and "sorts" them in conformity therewith.

This, however, is not the whole of the truth. A little reflection serves to show that some particular classifications are more likely to be generally useful than others, viz., those which are founded on points of resemblance that involve other points of resemblance. A grouping founded on such attributes as these will be more serviceable than others founded on attributes which do not imply further similarities. It is, however, by no means an easy matter to discover these attributes. To use the words of Mill, though in a sense slightly different from his own, "this, of course, supposes a comparison of the things, feature by feature and property by property, to ascertain what attributes they agree in, and not unfrequently an operation, strictly inductive, for the purpose of ascertaining some unobvious agreement, which is the cause of their obvious agreements." (Logic, ii. p. 221.)

We see, then, that classes are, broadly speaking, divisible into two sorts, (1) those which are distinguished by the possession of only one or two principal common attributes and the derivative attributes dependent on these, and (2) those which are distinguished by an immense number of common attributes more or less independent and unconnected. These latter are called by Mill Real Kinds, or Natural Kinds. While we can sum up in a moment the points of resemblance between the members of the class of "white things" or "heavy things," there is no likelihood of our ever discovering all the properties common to specimens of the Natural Kinds "sulphur" or "man." . "There is no impropriety in saying that, of these two classifications, the one answers to a much more radical distinction in the things themselves than the other does. . . . The differences, however, are made by nature, in both cases; while the recognition of those differences as grounds of classification and of naming is equally, in both cases, the act of man." (Logic, i. pp. 138–9.) The recognition of a Real Kind is not a matter of mere "convenience;" it cannot be "arbitrarily" fashioned by the mind. To frame a good definition, or a good classification, is "not a. matter of choice but of discussion, and discussion not merely respecting the usage of language, but respecting the properties of things."

In the notes it will be pointed out that Locke, although his language is somewhat inconsistent, has yet said sufficient to show that he did not consider classification of things into their species as entirely arbitrary. (Cf. especially Chap. vi. sec. 30 and sec. 36.) But at the same time (cf. sec. 38 of the same chapter) he shows that he does not discriminate between classes based on few and slight resemblances, and those more fundamental ones which Mill calls Natural Kinds.

The value and originality of Locke's treatment of the subject of species consists in his statements that (1) species are not absolute but relative, and are due immediately and directly to our own minds; that although Nature makes resemblances, it is man that selects them as a basis of classification. (2) The boundaries of species are not immovable. Not only are our definitions always more or less unfixed and vague, but Nature from time to time produces objects which fall into no recognized class (cf. secs. 23, 27). The recognition of this tendency to variation is a step towards the modern theories advocated by Mr. Darwin and Mr. Spencer. Locke's statements are, however, too strong; and a grave defect in his view is the consequence. He overlooks the important connection between inheritance and classification. He adduces the existence of mules, and other crosses, to show that the pedigree is of little or no value in determining species. This is going too far. He is quite right in drawing attention to the easily forgotten fact, that Nature does not keep the "supposed real species distinct and entire"; that is, does not make the progeny always exactly resemble the parents; but he errs in under-estimating the part played by the forces of heredity, or inheritance from ancestors, which tend to preserve the species unaltered. The doctrine of evolution takes into consideration both the forces which resist, and those which bring about, variations of kind. (3) Species depend on names. Locke recognizes the influence of language on classification (sec. 39). To name a thing is to class it; much that is beautiful in poetry, as well as much that is misleading in philosophy, is due to the effect of these implicit classifications.

It may perhaps be advisable to quote here the following passages from the correspondence of Locke and his friend Molyneux, bearing on the question of the nature of species. Molyneux, writing on December 22, 1692, remarks that : "What you say concerning *genera* and *species* is unquestionably true ; and yet it seems hard to assert that there is no such sort of creatures in nature as birds : for tho' we may be ignorant of the particular essence that makes a bird to be a bird, or that determines and distinguishes a bird from a beast; or the just limits and boundaries between each ; yet we can no more doubt of a sparrow's being a bird, and an horse's being a beast, than we can of this colour being black, and t'other white ; tho' by shades they may be made so gradually to vanish into each other, that we cannot tell where either determines." To this Locke replies as follows : " In the objection you raise about *species*, I fear you are fallen into the same difficulty I often found my self under, when I was writing on that subject, where I was very apt to suppose distinct *species* I could talk of, without names. For pray, Sir, consider what it is you mean, when you say, That *we can no more doubt of a sparrow's being a bird, and an horse's being a beast, than we can of this colour being black and t'other white*, etc., but this, that the combination of simple ideas, which the word *bird* stands for, is to be found in that particular thing we call a sparrow. And therefore I hope I have nowhere said, *There is no such sort of creatures in nature as birds ;* if I have, it is both contrary to truth and to my opinion. This I do say, that there are real distinctions, and differences in those real constitutions one from another ; whereby they are distinguished one from another, whereby we think of them, or name them or no ; but that that whereby we distinguish and rank particular substances into sorts or *genera* and *species*, is not those real essences or internal constitutions, but such combinations of simple ideas, as we observe in them. This I design'd to show in *lib.* iii. *c.* 6. If, upon your perusal of that chapter again, you find anything contrary to this, I beg the favour of you to mark it to me, that I may correct it, for it is not what I think true. Some parts of that third Book concerning words, though the thoughts were easie and clear enough, yet cost me more pains to express than all the rest of my Essay. And therefore I shall not much wonder if there be in some places of it obscurity and doubtfulness."

OF

HUMANE UNDERSTANDING.

BOOK III.—OF WORDS.

The Commonwealth of Learning, is not at this time without Master-Builders, whose mighty Designs, in advancing the Sciences, will leave lasting Monuments to the Admiration of Posterity: But every one must not hope to be a Boyle, *or a* Sydenham; *and in an Age that produces such Masters, as the Great——*Huygenius, *and the incomparable Mr.* Newton, *with some other of that Strain; 'tis Ambition enough to be employed as an Under-Labourer in clearing Ground a little, and removing some of the Rubbish that lies in the way to Knowledge; which certainly had been very much more advanced in the World, if the Endeavours of ingenious and industrious Men had not been much cumbered with the learned, but frivolons Use of uncouth, affected, or unintelligible Terms introduced into the Sciences, and there made an Art of, to that Degree, that Philosophy, which is nothing but the true Knowledge of Things, was thought unfit, or uncapable to be brought into well-bred Company, and polite Conversation. Vague and insignificant Forms of Speech, and Abuse of Language, have so long passed for Mysteries of Science; and hard or misapply'd Words, with little or no Meaning, have, by Prescription, such a Right to be mistaken for deep Learning, and heighth of Speculation, that it will not be easie to perswade, either those who speak, or those who hear them, that they are but the Covers of Ignorance, and Hinderance of true Knowledge. To break in upon the Sanctuary of Vanity and Ignorance, will be, I suppose, some Service to Humane Understanding: Though so few are apt to think, they deceive or are deceived in the Use of Words; or that the Language of the Sect they are of, has any Faults in it, which ought to be examined or corrected, that I hope I shall be pardon'd, if I have in the third Book dwelt long on this Subject; and endeavoured to make it so plain, that neither the Inveterateness of the Mischief, nor the Prevalency of the Fashion, shall be any Excuse for those, who will not take Care about the Meaning of their own Words, and will not suffer the Significancy of their Expressions to be enquired into.——*
THE EPISTLE TO THE READER.

OF

HUMANE UNDERSTANDING.

BOOK III.—OF WORDS.

CHAPTER I.

OF WORDS OR LANGUAGE IN GENERAL.

§. 1. God having designed Man for a sociable Creature, made him not only with an *Man fitted to form articulate Sounds.* Inclination, and under a necessity to have Fellowship with those of his own Kind; but furnished him also with Language, which was to be the great Instrument, and common Tye of Society. *Man* therefore had by Nature his Organs so fashioned, as to be *fit to frame articulate Sounds,* which we call Words. But this was not enough to produce Language; for Parrots, and several other Birds, will be taught to make articulate Sounds distinct enough, which yet, by no means, are capable of Language.

D

§. 2. Besides articulate Sounds therefore, it was *To make them* farther necessary, that he should be *able Signs of* Ideas. *to use these Sounds, as Signs of internal Conceptions;* and to make them stand as Marks for the *Ideas* within his own Mind, whereby they might be made known to others, and the Thoughts of Mens Minds be convey'd from one to another.

§. 3. But neither was this sufficient to make Words *To make gen-* so useful as they ought to be. It is not *eral Signs.* enough for the Perfection of Language, that Sounds can be made Signs of *Ideas,* unless those *Signs* can be so made use of, as *to comprehend several particular Things:* For the Multiplication of Words would have perplexed their Use, had every particular thing need of a distinct Name to be signified by. To remedy this Inconvenience, Language had yet a farther Improvement in the use of general Terms, whereby one Word was made to mark a Multitude of particular Existences: Which advantageous use of Sounds was obtained only by the Difference of the *Ideas* they were made Signs of. Those Names becoming general, which are made to stand for general *Ideas,* and those remaining particular, where the *Ideas* they are used for are particular.

§. 4. Besides these Names which stand for *Ideas, To make gen-* there be other Words which Men make *eral Signs.* use of, not to signify any *Idea,* but the want or absence of some *Ideas* simple or complex, or all *Ideas* together; such as are *Nihil* in Latin, and in English, *Ignorance* and *Barrenness.* All which negative or privative Words, cannot be said properly to belong to, or signify no *Ideas:* For then they would be perfectly insignificant Sounds; but they relate to positive *Ideas*, and signify their Absence.

§. 5. It may also lead us a little towards the Original of all our Notions and Knowledge, if we remark, how great a Dependance our *Words* have on common sensible *Ideas;* and how those, which are made use of to stand for Actions *Words ultimately derived from such as signify sensible Ideas.* and Notions quite remov'd from Sense, *have their rise from thence, and from obvious sensible* Ideas, *are transferred to more abstruse Significations,* and made to stand for *Ideas* that come not under the Cognizance of our Senses; *v. g.* to *Imagine, Apprehend, Comprehend, Adhere, Conceive, Instill, Disgust, Disturbance, Tranquility, &c.,* are all Words taken from the Operations of sensible Things, and applied to certain Modes of Thinking. *Spirit*, in its primary Signification, is Breath; *Angel*, a Messenger: And I doubt not, but if we could trace them to their Sources, we should find, in all Languages, the Names, which stand for Things that fall not under our Senses, to have had their first rise from sensible *Ideas.* By

which we may give some kind of guess, what kind of
Notions they were, and whence derived, which filled
their Minds, who were the first Beginners of Languages; and how Nature, even in the naming of
Things, unawares suggested to Men the Originals
and Principles of all their Knowledge: Whilst, to
give Names, that might make known to others any
Operations they felt in themselves, or any other
Ideas, that came not under their Senses, they were
fain to borrow Words from ordinary known *Ideas* of
Sensation, by that means to make others the more
easily to conceive those Operations they experimented in themselves, which made no outward
sensible Appearances; and then when they had got
known and agreed Names, to signify those internal
Operations of their own Minds, they were sufficiently
furnished to make known by Words, all their other
Ideas; since they could consist of nothing, but either
of outward sensible Perceptions, or of the inward
Operations of their Minds about them; we having,
as has been proved, no *Ideas* at all, but what originally come either from sensible Objects without, or
what we feel within ourselves, from the inward
Workings of our own Spirits, of which we are conscious to ourselves within. -

Distribution. §. 6. But to understand better the
Use and Force of Language, as subservient to In-

struction and Knowledge, it will be convenient to. consider,

First, To what it is that Names, in the use of Language, are immediately applied.

Secondly, Since all (except proper) Names are general, and so stand not particularly for this or that single Thing ; but for sorts and ranks of Things, it will be necessary to consider, in the next Place, what the Sorts and Kinds, or, if you rather like the Latin Names, *what the Species and Genera of Things* are ; wherein they consist ; and how they come to be made. These being (as they ought) well looked into, we shall the better come to find the right use of Words ; the natural Advantages and Defects of Language ; and the Remedies that ought to be used, to avoid the Inconveniencies of Obscurity or Uncertainty in the Signification of Words, without which, it is impossible to Discourse with any clearness, or order, concerning Knowledge: Which being conversant about Propositions, and those most commonly universal ones, has greater Connexion with Words, than perhaps is suspected.

These Considerations therefore, shall be the matter of the following Chapters.

CHAPTER II.

OF THE SIGNIFICATION OF WORDS.

§. 1. Man, though he has great Variety of

Words are sensible Signs necessary for Communica- tion.
Thoughts, and such, from which others, as well as himself, might receive Profit and Delight ; yet they are all within his own Breast, invisible, and hidden from others, nor can of themselves be made appear. The Comfort and Advantage of Society, not being to be had without Communication of Thoughts, it was necessary, that Man should find out some External sensible Signs, whereby those invisible *Ideas,* which his Thoughts are made up of, might be made known to others. For this purpose, nothing was so fit, either for Plenty, or Quickness, as those articulate Sounds, which with so much Ease and Variety, he found himself able to make. Thus we may conceive how *Words,* which were by Nature so well adapted to that purpose, come to be made Use of by Men, as *the Signs of* their *Ideas;* not by any natural Connexion, that there is between particular articulate Sounds and certain *Ideas,* for then there

would be but one Language amongst all Men ; but
by a voluntary Imposition, whereby such a Word is
made arbitrarily the Mark of such an *Idea*. The use
then of Words, is to be sensible Marks of *Ideas ;*
and the *Ideas* they stand for, are their proper and
immediate Signification.

§. 2. The use Men have of these Marks, being
either to record their own Thoughts for *Words are the sensible Signs of his Ideas who uses them.*
the Assistance of their own Memory;
or, as it were, to bring out their *Ideas*,
and lay them before the view of others :
*Words in their primary or immediate Signification,
stand for nothing, but the* Ideas *in the Mind of him
that uses them,* how imperfectly soever, or carelessly
those *Ideas* are collected from the Things, which they
are supposed to represent. When a Man speaks to
another, it is, that he may be understood ; and the
end of Speech is, that those Sounds, as Marks, may
make known his *Ideas* to the Hearer. That then
which Words are the Marks of, are the *Ideas* of the
Speaker : Nor can any one apply them, as Marks,
immediately to any thing else, but the *Ideas*, that he
himself hath. For this would be to make them
Signs of his own Conceptions, and yet apply them
to other *Ideas ;* which would be to make them Signs,
and not Signs of his *Ideas* at the same time ; and so
in effect, to have no Signification at all. Words

being voluntary Signs, they cannot be voluntary
Signs imposed by him on Things he knows not.
That would be to make them Signs of nothing,
Sounds without Signification. A Man cannot make
his Words the Signs either of Qualities in Things, or
of Conceptions in the Mind of another, whereof he
has none in his own. 'Till he has some *Ideas* of his
own, he cannot suppose them to correspond with the
Conceptions of another Man ; nor can he use any
Signs for them : For thus they would be the Signs of
he knows not what, which is in Truth to be the Signs
of nothing. But when he represents to himself other
Mens *Ideas*, by some of his own, if he consent to
give them the same Names, that other Men do, 'tis
still to his own *Ideas*; to *Ideas* that he has, and not
to *Ideas* that he has not.

§ 3. This is so necessary in the Use of Language,
Words are that in this respect, the knowing, and
the sensible the Ignorant; the Learned, and Un-
Signs of his learned, use the *Words* they speak (with
Ideas who any meaning) all alike. They, *in every*
uses them.
Man's Mouth, stand for the Ideas *he has*, and which
he would express by them. A Child having taken
Notice of nothing in the Metal he hears called Go'd,
but the bright shining yellow Colour, he applies the
Word Gold only to his own *Idea* of that Colour, and
nothing else ; and therefore calls the same Colour in

a Peacock's Tail, Gold. Another that has better observed, adds to shining yellow, great Weight : and then the Sound Gold, when he Uses it, stands for a complex *Idea* of a shining Yellow and very weighty Substance. Another adds to those Qualities, Fusi-bility : And then the Word Gold to him signifies a Body, bright yellow, fusible, and very heavy. Another adds Malleability. Each of these uses equally the Word Gold, when they have Occasion to express the *Idea*, which they have apply'd it to : But it is evident, that each can apply it only to his own *Idea* ; nor can he make it stand, as a Sign of such a complex *Idea*, as he has not.

§ 4. But though Words, as they are used by Men, can properly and immediately signify nothing but the *Ideas*, that are in the Mind of the Speaker; yet they in their Thoughts give them a secret Reference to two other Things. *Words often secretly re-ferred, First, to the Ideas in other Mens Minds.*

First, They suppose their Words to be marks of the Ideas *in the Minds also of other Men, with whom they communicate* : For else they should talk in vain, and could not be understood, if the Sounds they applied to one *Idea*, were such, as by the Hearer were applied to another, which is to speak two Languages. But in this, Men stand not usually to examine, whether the *Idea* they and those they Dis-

course with have in their Minds, be the same : But
think it enough, that they use the Word, as they
imagine, in the common Acceptation of that Language ; in which they suppose, that the *Idea*, they
make it a Sign of, is precisely the same, to which the
Understanding Men of that Country apply that Name.

§ 5. *Secondly*, Because *Men* would not be thought

Secondly, To the Reality of Things.
to talk *barely* of their own Imaginations, but of Things as really they
are ; therefore they *often suppose their*
Words to stand also for the Reality of Things.
But this relating more particularly to Substances,
and their Names, as perhaps the former does to
simple *Ideas* and Modes, we shall speak of these
two different ways of applying Words more at large,
when we come to treat of the Names of mixed
Modes, and Substances, in particular : Though give
me leave here to say, that it is a perverting the use
of Words, and brings unavoidable Obscurity and
Confusion into their Signification, whenever we
make them stand for any thing, but those *Ideas* we
have in our own Minds.

§ 6. Concerning Words also it is farther to be

Words by use readily excite Ideas.
considered : *First*, That they being
immediately the Signs of Mens *Ideas* ;
and, by that means, the Instruments
whereby Men communicate their Conceptions, and

express to one another those Thoughts and Imaginations they have within their own Breasts, *there comes by constant use*, to be such *a Connexion between certain Sounds, and the* Ideas *they stand for*, that the Names heard, almost as readily excite certain *Ideas*, as if the Objects themselves, which are apt to produce them, did actually affect the Senses. Which is manifestly so in all obvious sensible Qualities; and in all Substances, that frequently, and familiarly occur to us.

§ 7. *Secondly*, That though the proper and immediate Signification of Words, are *Ideas* in the Mind of the Speaker; yet because by familiar use from our Cradles, we come *Words often used without Signification.* to learn certain articulate Sounds very perfectly, and have them readily on our Tongues, and always at Hand in our Memories ; but yet are not always careful to examine, or settle their Significations perfectly, it *often* happens that *Men*, even when they would apply themselves to an attentive Consideration, do *set their Thoughts more on Words, than Things.* Nay, because Words are many of them learned before the *Ideas* are known for which they stand : Therefore some, not only Children, but Men, speak several Words, no otherwise than Parrots do, only because they have learned them, and have been accustomed to those Sounds. But so far as Words

are of Use and Signification, so far is there a constant Connexion between the Sound and the *Idea* ;
and a Designation, that the one stand for the other ;
without which Application of them, they are nothing
but so much insignificant Noise.

§ 8. *Words* by long and familiar use, as has been
said, come to excite in Men certain
Their Sig-nification per-fectly arbi-trary.
Ideas, so constantly and readily, that
they are apt to suppose a natural
Connexion between them. But that
they *signify* only Mens peculiar *Ideas,* and that *by
a perfectly arbitrary Imposition,* is evident, in that
they often fail to excite in others (even that use the
same Language) the same *Ideas,* we take them to be
the Signs of : And every Man has so inviolable a
Liberty, to make Words stand for what *Ideas* he
pleases, that no one hath the Power to make others
have the same *Ideas* in their Minds, that he has,
when they use the same Words, that he does. And
therefore the great *Augustus* himself, in the Possession of that Power which ruled the World, acknowledged, he could not make a new Latin Word : which
was as much as to say, that he could not arbitrarily
appoint, what *Idea* any Sound should be a Sign of,
in the Mouths and common Language of his Subjects. 'Tis true, common use, by a tacit Consent,
appropriates certain Sounds to certain *Ideas* in all

Languages, which so far limits the Signification of that Sound, that unless a Man applies it to the same *Idea*, he does not speak properly. And let me add, that unless a Man's Words excite the same *Ideas* in the Hearer, which he makes them stand for in speaking, he does not speak intelligibly. But whatever be the consequence of any Man's using of Words differently, either from their general Meaning, or the particular Sense of the Person to whom he Addresses them, this is certain, their Signification, in his use of them, is limited to his *Ideas*, and they can be Signs of nothing else.

CHAPTER III.

OF GENERAL TERMS.

§ 1. All Things that exist being Particulars, it
The greatest may perhaps be thought reasonable
part of Words that Words, which ought to be con-
general.
formed to Things, should be so too, I
mean in their Signification : but yet we find the quite
contrary. The far *greatest part of Words*, that make
all Languages, *are general Terms :* which has not been
the Effect of Neglect, or Chance, but of Reason, and
Necessity.

§ 2. First, *It is impossible that every particular*
Thing should have a distinct peculiar
For every *Name.* For the Signification and Use
particular
thing to have of Words, depending on that Con-
a Name is
impossible. nexion, which the Mind makes between its *Ideas*, and the Sounds it Uses
as Signs of them, it is necessary, in the Application
of Names to Things, that the Mind should have
distinct *Ideas* of the Things, and retain also the particular Name that belongs to every one, with its
peculiar Appropriation to that *Idea.* But it is

beyond the Power of Humane Capacity to frame
and retain distinct *Ideas* of all the particular Things
we meet with: Every Bird, and Beast, Men saw;
every Tree, and Plant, that affected the Senses,
could not find a Place in the most capacious Understanding. If it be looked on, as an Instance of a
prodigious Memory, That some Generals have been
able to call every Soldier in their Army, by his
proper Name: We may easily find a Reason, why
Men have never attempted to give Names to each
Sheep in their Flock, or Crow that Flies over their
Heads; much less to call every Leaf of Plants, or
Grain of Sand that came in their way, by a peculiar
Name.

§ 3. *Secondly*, If it were possible, *it would yet
be useless*; because it would not serve
to the chief end of Language. Men *And useless.*
would in vain heap up Names of particular Things,
that would not serve them to communicate their
Thoughts. Men learn Names, and use them in
Talk with others, only that they may be understood: which is then only done, when by Use or
Consent, the Sound I make by the Organs of
Speech, excites in another Man's Mind, who hears
it, the *Idea* I apply it to in mine, when I speak it.
This cannot be done by Names, apply'd to particular
Things, whereof I alone having the *Ideas* in my

Mind, the Names of them could not be significant, or intelligible to another, who was not acquainted with all those very particular Things, which had fallen under my Notice.

§ 4. *Thirdly,* But yet granting this also feasible; (which I think is not,) yet *a distinct Name for every particular Thing would not be of any great Use for the Improvement of Knowledge*: which, though founded in particular Things, enlarges itself by general Views; to which, Things reduced into Sorts under general Names, are properly subservient. These, with the Names belonging to them, come within some compass, and do not multiply every Moment, beyond what either the mind can contain, or Use requires. And therefore in these Men, have for the most part stopped; but yet not so, as to hinder themselves from distinguishing particular Things, by appropriated Names, where Convenience Demands it. And therefore in their own Species, which they have most to do with, and wherein they have often occasion to mention particular Persons, they make use of proper Names; and their distinct Individuals have distinct Denominations.

§ 5. Besides Persons, Countries also, Cities, Rivers, *What things have proper Names.* Mountains, and other the like Distinctions of Place, have usually found peculiar Names, and that for the same Reason;

they being such as Men have often an Occasion to mark particularly, and, as it were, set before others in their Discourses with them. And I doubt not, but if we had Reason to mention particular Horses, as often as we have to mention particular Men, we should have *proper Names* for the one, as familiar as for the other; and *Bucephalus* would be a Word as much in Use, as *Alexander*. And therefore we see that amongst Jockeys, Horses have their proper Names to be known and distinguished by, as commonly as their Servants: Because amongst them, there is often occasion to mention this or that particular Horse, when he is out of Sight.

§ 6. The next thing to be considered is, *how general Words come to be made.* For since all things that exist are only particulars, how come we by general Terms, or where find we those general Natures they are supposed to stand for? Words become general, by being made the Signs of general *Ideas*: And *Ideas* become general, by separating from them the Circumstances of Time, and Place, and any other *Ideas*, that may determine them to this or that particular Existence. By this way of Abstraction they are made capable of representing more Individuals than one; each of which, having in it a Con-

How general Words are made.

E

formity to that Abstract *Idea*, is (as we call it) of that
sort.

§ 7. But to deduce this a little more distinctly, it
will not perhaps be amiss to trace our Notions, and
Names, from their beginning, and observe by what
Degrees we proceed, and by what Steps we enlarge
our *Ideas* from our first Infancy. There is nothing
more evident, than that the *Ideas* of the Persons Children converse with, (to Instance in them alone) are
like the Persons themselves, only particular. The
Ideas of the Nurse, and the Mother, are well framed
in their Minds; and, like Pictures of them there,
represent only those Individuals. The Names they
first gave to them, are confined to these Individuals;
and the Names of *Nurse* and *Mamma*, the Child
Uses, determine themselves to those Persons. Afterwards, when time and a large Acquaintance has
made them observe, that there are a great many
other Things in the World, that in some common
Agreements of Shape, and several other Qualities,
resemble their Father and Mother, and those Persons
they have been used to, they frame an *Idea*, which
they find those many Particulars do partake in; and
to that they give, with others, the name *Man* for
Example. And *thus they come to have a general
Name*, and a general *Idea*. Wherein they make nothing new, but only leave out of the complex *Idea*

they had of *Peter* and *James, Mary* and *Jane,* that which is peculiar to each, and retain only what is common to them all.

§ 8. By the same way, that they come by the general Name and *Idea* of *Man*, they easily *Advance to more general Names* and Notions. For observing, that several Things that differ from their *Idea* of *Man*, and cannot therefore be comprehended under that Name, have yet certain Qualities, wherein they agree with *Man*, by retaining only those Qualities, and uniting them into one *Idea*, they have again another and a more general *Idea*; to which having given a Name, they make a Term of a more comprehensive Extension : Which new *Idea* is made, not by any new Addition, but only, as before, by leaving out the Shape, and some other Properties signified by the Name *Man*, and retaining only a Body, with Life, Sense, and Spontaneous Motion, comprehended under the Name *Animal*.

§ 9. That this is the *Way, whereby Men first formed general* Ideas, *and general Names to them,* I think, is so evident, that there needs no other Proof of it, but the considering of a Man's self, or others, and *General Natures are nothing but abstract Ideas.* the ordinary Proceedings of their Minds in Knowledge : And he that thinks general Natures or Notions, are any thing else but such abstract and

partial *Ideas* of more complex ones, taken at first
from particular Existences, will, I fear, be at a Loss
where to find them.   For let any one reflect, and
then tell me, wherein does his *Idea* of *Man* differ
from that of *Peter* and *Paul*; or his *Idea* of *Horse*
from that of *Bucephalus*, but in the leaving out something that is peculiar to each Individual ; and retaining so much of those particular complex *Ideas*, of
several particular Existences, as they are found to
agree in ?   Of the complex *Ideas*, signified by the
Names *Man*, and *Horse*, leaving out but those particulars wherein they differ, and retaining only those
wherein they agree, and of those making a new
distinct complex *Idea*, and giving the name *Animal*
to it, one has a more general Term, that Comprehends, with Man, several other Creatures.   Leave
out of the *Idea* of *Animal*, Sense and spontaneous
Motion, and the remaining complex *Idea*, made up
of the remaining simple ones of Body, Life, and
Nourishment, becomes a more general one, under the
more comprehensive Term, *Vivens*.   And not to
dwell longer upon this particular, so evident in
it self, by the same way the Mind proceeds to *Body*,
Substance, and at last to *Being*, *Thing*, and such
universal Terms, which stand for any of our *Ideas*
whatsoever.   To conclude, this whole *Mystery* of
Genera and *Species*, which make such a noise in the

Schools, and are, with Justice, so little regarded out of them, is nothing else but abstract *Ideas*, more or less comprehensive, with Names annexed to them. In all which, this is constant and unvariable, That every more general Term stands for such an *Idea*, as is but a part of any of those contained under it.

§ 10. This may shew us the Reason, *why, in the defining of Words*, which is nothing but declaring their Signification, *we make use of the Genus*, or next general Word that comprehends it. Which is not out *Why the Genus is ordinarily made use of in Definitions.* of Necessity, but only to save the Labour of enumerating the several simple *Ideas*, which the next general Word, or *Genus*, stands for ; or, perhaps, sometimes the shame of not being able to do it. But though defining by *Genus* and *Differentia*, (I crave leave to use these Terms of Art, though originally Latin, since they most properly suit those Notions they are apply'd to ;) I say, though defining by the *Genus* be the shortest way ; yet, I think, it may be doubted, whether it be the best. This I am sure, it is not the only, and so not absolutely necessary. For Definition being nothing but making another understand by Words, what *Idea* the Term defined stands for, a Definition is best made by enumerating those simple *Ideas* that are combined in the Signification of the Term defined : and if instead of such an enumeration, Men have accustomed themselves to use the next general Term, it has not been out of Necessity, or for greater clearness ; but for quickness and dispatch sake. For, I think, that to one who desired to know what *Idea* the Word *Man* stood for; if it should be said, that *Man* was a solid extended Substance, having Life, Sense, spontaneous Motion, and the Faculty of Reasoning, I doubt not but the meaning of the Term *Man*, would be as well understood, and the *Idea* it stands for, be at least as clearly made known, as when it is defined to be a *rational Animal* ; which by the several Definitions of *Animal*, *Vivens*, and *Corpus*, resolves it self into those enumerated *Ideas*. I have in explaining the Term *Man*, followed here the Ordinary Definition of the Schools : which tho', perhaps, not the most exact, yet serves well enough to my present purpose. And one may, in this Instance, see what gave Occasion to the Rule, that a Definition must consist of *Genus* and *Differentia* : and it suffices to shew us the little Necessity there is of such a Rule, or Advantage in the strict observing of it. For Definitions, as has been said, being only the explaining of one Word, by several others, so that the meaning or *Idea* it stands for, may be certainly known ; Languages are not always so made, according to the Rules of Logick, that every Term can have its Signification exactly and clearly expressed by two others. Experience sufficiently satisfies us to the contrary ; or else those who have made this Rule, have done ill that they have given us so few Definitions conformable to it. But of Definitions, more in the next Chapter.

§ 11. To return to general Words, it is plain, by what has been said, That *General and Universal,* belong not to the real existence of Things ; but *are the Inventions* and *Creatures of the Understanding,* made by it for its own use, *and concern only Signs,* whether Words, or *Ideas.* Words are general, as has been said, when used for Signs of general *Ideas* ; and so are applicable indifferently to many particular Things ; and *Ideas,* are general, when they are set up as the Representatives of many particular Things : But Universality belongs not to Things themselves, which are all of them particular in their Existence, even those Words, and *Ideas,* which in their Signification, are general. When therefore we quit Particulars, the Generals that rest, are only Creatures of our own making, their general Nature being nothing but the Capacity they are put into by the Understanding of signifying or representing many Particulars. For the Signification they have, is nothing but a Relation, that by the Mind of Man is added to them.

General and Universal are Creatures of the Understanding.

§ 12. The next thing therefore to be con-

Abstract sidered, is, *What kind of Signification*
Ideas *are the* *it is, that General Words have.* For as
Essences of
the Genera it is evident, that they do not signify
and Species. barely one particular thing; for then
they would not be general Terms, but proper Names;
so on the other side, 'tis as evident, they do not signify
a Plurality; for Man and Men would then signify
the same; and the Distinction of Numbers (as the
Grammarians call 'em) would be superfluous and
useless. That then which general Words signify, is
a sort of Things; and each of them does that, by
being a Sign of an abstract *Idea* in the Mind, to
which *Idea*, as things existing are found to agree, so
they come to be ranked under that Name; or, which
is all one, be of that sort. Whereby it is evident,
that the *Essences of the Sorts, or* (if the Latin Word
pleases better) *Species* of Things, are nothing else
but these abstract *Ideas*. For the having the Essence
of any Species, being that which makes any thing
to be of that Species, and the Conformity to the *Idea*,
to which the Name is annexed, being that which
gives a right to that Name, the having the Essence,
and the having that Conformity, must needs be the
same thing: Since to be of any Species, and to
have a right to the Name of that Species, is all one.
As for Example, to be a *Man,* or of the Species

Man, and to have right to the Name *Man*, is the same thing. Again, to be a *Man*, or of the Species *Man*, and have the Essence of a *Man*, is the same thing. Now since nothing can be a *Man*, or have a right to the Name *Man*, but what has a Conformity to the Abstract *Idea* the Name *Man* stands for ; nor any thing be a *Man*, or have a right to the Species *Man*, but what has the Essence of that Species; it follows, that the Abstract *Idea* for which the Name stands, and the Essence of the Species, is one and the same. From whence it is easy to observe, that the Essences of the sorts of things, and consequently the sorting of this, is the Workmanship of the Under-standing that Abstracts, and makes those general *Ideas.*

§ 13. I would not here be thought to forget, much less to deny, that Nature in the Production of Things, makes several of them alike : there is nothing more obvious, especially in the Races of Animals, and all things propagated by Seed. But yet, I think, we may say, *They are the Workman-ship of the Understand-ing, but have their Founda-tion in the Similitnde of things.* the *sorting* of them under Names is the *Workmanship of the Understanding, taking occasion from the Simili-tude* it observes amongst 'em, to make Abstract general *Ideas*, and set 'em up in the mind, with Names annex'd to 'em, as Patterns or Forms, (for in

that sence the word *Form* has a very proper Signification,) to which, as particular Things existing are
found to agree, so they come to be of that Species,
have that Denomination, or are put into that *Classis.*
For when we say, this is a *Man*, that a *Horse*; this
Justice, that *Cruelty*; this a *Watch*, that a *Jack*;
what do we else but rank Things under different
Specifick Names, as agreeing to those Abstract *Ideas*,
of which we have made those Names the Signs?
And what are the Essences of those Species, set out
and marked by Names, but those abstract Ideas in
the mind; which are, as it were, the Bonds between
particular Things that exist, and the Names they are
to be ranked under? And when general Names have
any Connexion with particular Beings, these Abstract
Ideas are the *Medium* that unites them: so that the
Essences of Species, as distinguished and denominated by us, neither are, nor can be any thing but
those precise Abstract *Ideas* we have in our Minds.
And therefore the supposed real Essences of Substances, if different from our Abstract *Ideas*, cannot
be the Essences of the Species we rank Things into.
For two Species may be one, as rationally, as two
different Essences be the Essence of one Species:
And I demand, what are the Alterations may, or may
not be in a *Horse* or *Lead*, without making either of
'em to be of another Species? In determining the

Species of Things by our Abstract *Ideas,* this is easy to resolve : but if any one will regulate himself herein, by supposed real Essences, he will, I suppose, be at a loss : and he will never be able to know when any thing precisely ceases to be of the Species of a *Horse,* or *Lead.*

§ 14. Nor will any one wonder, that I say these *Essences,* or abstract *Ideas,* (which are the Measures of Name, and the Boundaries of Species) are *the Workmanship of the Understanding,* who considers, that

Each distinct abstract Idea *is a distinct Essence.*

at least the complex ones are often, in several Men, different Collections of simple *Ideas* : and therefore that is *Covetousness* to one Man, which is not so to another. Nay, even in Substances, where there abstract *Ideas* seem to be taken from the Things themselves, they are not constantly the same ; no not in that Species, which is most familiar to us, and with which we have the most intimate Acquaintance : It having been more than once doubted, whether the *Fœtus* born of a Woman were a *Man,* even so far, as that it hath been debated, whether it were, or were not to be nourished and baptized : which could not be, if the abstract *Idea* or Essence, to which the Name *Man* belonged, were of Nature's making ; and were not the uncertain and various Collection of simple *Ideas*, which the Understanding puts together, and then abstracting it, affixed a Name to it. So that in truth *every distinct abstract* Idea, *is a distinct Essence*: and the Names that stand for such distinct *Ideas*, are the Names of things essentially different. Thus a Circle is as essentially different from an Oval, as a Sheep from a Goat: and Rain is as essentially different from Snow, as Water from Earth, that abstract *Idea* which is the Essence of one, being impossible to be communicated to the other. And thus any two abstract *Ideas,* that in any part vary one from another, with two distinct Names annexed to them, constitute two distinct sorts, or if you please, *Species*, as essentially different, as any two the most remote, or opposite in the World.

§ 15. But since the *Essences* of Things are thought by some, (and not without Reason,) to be wholly unknown; it may not be amiss to consider the *several Significations of the Word* Essence.

Real and nominal Essence.

First, Essence may be taken for the being of any thing, whereby it is, what it is. And thus the real internal, but generally in Substances, unknown Constitution of Things, whereon their discoverable Qualities depend, may be called their *Essence*. This is the proper original Signification of the Word, as is evident from the Formation of it ; *Essentia,* in its primary Notation, signifying properly *Being.* And in this Sense it is still used, when we speak of the *Essence* of particular things, without giving them any Name.

Secondly, The Learning and Disputes of the Schools, having been much busied about *Genus* and *Species,* the Word *Essence* has almost lost its primary Signification ; and instead of the real Constitution of things, has been almost wholly applied to the artificial Constitution of *Genus* and *Species.* 'Tis true, there is ordinarily supposed a real Constitution of the sorts of Things ; and 'tis past doubt, there must be some real Constitution, on which any Collection of simple *Ideas* co-existing, must depend. But it being evident, that Things are ranked under Names into sorts of *Species,* only as they agree to certain abstract *Ideas,* to which we have annexed those Names, the *Essence* of each *Genus,* or Sort, comes to be nothing but that abstract *Idea,* which the General, or *Sortal* (if I may have leave so to call it from *Sort,* as I do *General* from *Genus,*) Name stands for. And this we shall find to be that which the Word *Essence* imports, in its most familiar use. These two sorts of *Essences,* I suppose, may not unfitly be termed, the one the *Real,* the other the *Nominal Essence.*

§ 16. *Between the nominal Essence, and the Name,*

Constant Connection between the Name and nominal Essence.
there is so *near* a *Connection*, that the Name of any sort of Things cannot be attributed to any particular Being, but what has this *Essence*, whereby it answers that abstract *Idea*, whereof that Name is the Sign.

§ 17. Concerning the real Essences of corporeal Substances, (to mention those only,)

Supposition that Species are distinguished by their real Essences, useless.
there are, if I mistake not, two Opinions. The one is of those, who using the Word *Essence*, for they know not what, suppose a certain Number of those Essences, according to which, all natural things are made, and wherein they do exactly every one of them partake, and so become of this or that *Species*. The other, and more rational Opinion, is of those, who look on all natural things to have a real, but unknown Constitution of their insensible Parts, from which flow those sensible Qualities, which serve us to distinguish them one from another, according as we have Occasion to rank them into sorts, under common Denominations. The former of these Opinions, which supposes these *Essences*, as a certain Number of Forms or Molds, wherein all natural Things, that exist, are cast, and do equally Partake, has, I imagine, very much perplexed the Knowledge of natural Things. The frequent Productions of

Monsters, in all the Species of Animals, and of Changelings, and other strange Issues of humane Birth, carry with them Difficulties, not possible to consist with this *Hypothesis* : since it is as impossible, that two things, partaking exactly of the same real *Essence*, should have different Properties, as that two Figures partaking in the same real *Essence* of a Circle, should have different Properties. But were there no other Reason against it, yet the *Supposition of Essences, that cannot be known* ; and the making them nevertheless to be that which Distinguishes the Species of Things, *is* so *wholly useless*, and unserviceable to any part of our Knowledge, that that alone were sufficient to make us lay it by, and content our selves with such *Essences* of the Sorts or Species of Things, as come within the reach of our Knowledge ; which, when seriously considered, will be found, as I have said, to be nothing else but those abstract complex *Ideas*, to which we have annexed distinct General Names.

§ 18. *Essences* being thus distinguished into *Nominal and Real,* we may farther observe, that in the Species of *simple* Ideas *and Modes* they *are always the same :* But in *Substances, always quite different.* Thus a Figure including a Space between three Lines, is the real as well

Real and nominal Essence the same in simple Ideas and Modes, different in Substances.

as nominal *Essence* of a Triangle ; it being not only
the abstract *Idea* to which the general Name is
annexed, but the very *Essentia*, or Being, of the
thing it self, that Foundation from which all its Properties flow, and to which they are all inseparably
annexed.   But it is far otherwise concerning that
parcel of Matter, which makes the Ring on my
Finger, wherein these two *Essences* are apparently
different.   For it is the real Constitution of its insensible Parts, on which depend all those Properties of
Colour, Weight, Fusibility, Fixedness, *&c.* which
makes it to be *Gold*, or gives it a right to that Name,
which is therefore its nominal *Essence*.   Since nothing
can be called *Gold*, but what has a Conformity of
Qualities to that abstract complex *Idea*, to which that
Name is annexed.   But this Distinction of *Essences*,
belonging particularly to Substances, we shall, when
we come to consider their Names, have an occasion
to treat of more fully.

§ 19. That such *abstract* Ideas, *with Names to
them*, as we have been speaking of, *are
Essences*, may farther appear by what
we are told concerning *Essences, viz.*
that they are all ingenerable, and incorruptible.
Which cannot be true of the real Constitutions of
Things, which begin and perish with 'em.   All
things, that exist, besides their Author, are all liable

*Essences in-
generable and
incorruptible.*

to Change ; especially those Things we are acquainted with, and have ranked into Bands, under distinct Names or Ensigns. Thus that which was Grass to Day, is to Morrow the Flesh of a Sheep ; and within few Days after, becomes part of a Man : In all which, and the like Changes, 'tis evident, their real *Essence, i. e.* that Constitution, whereon the Properties of these several things depended, is destroy'd, and Perishes with them. But *Essences* being taken for *Ideas*, established in the Mind, with Names annexed to them, they are supposed to remain steddily the same, whatever Mutations the particular Substances are liable to. For whatever becomes of *Alexander* and *Bucephalus*, the *Ideas* to which *Man* and *Horse* are annexed, are supposed nevertheless to remain in the same ; and so the *Essences* of those Species are preserved whole and undestroy'd, whatever Changes happen to any, or all of the Individuals of those *Species.* By this means the *Essence* of a *Species* rests safe and entire, without the Existence of so much as one Individual of that kind. For were there now no Circle existing any where in the World, (as, perhaps, that Figure exists not any where exactly marked out,) yet the *Idea* annexed to that Name, would not cease to be what it is; nor cease to be as a Pattern, to determine which of the particular Figures we meet with, have, or have not a Right to the Name

F

Circle, and so to shew, which of them, by having that Essence, was of that *Species*. And tho' there neither were, nor had been in Nature such a Beast as an *Unicorn*, nor such a Fish as a *Mermaid*; yet supposing those Names to stand for complex abstract *Ideas*, that contained no inconsistency in them ; the *Essence* of a *Mermaid* is as intelligible, as that of a *Man* ; and the *Idea* of an *Unicorn* as certain, steddy, and permanent, as that of a Horse. From what has been said, it is evident, that the Doctrine of the Immutability of *Essences*, proves them to be only abstract *Ideas* ; and is founded on the Relation established between them, and certain Sounds as Signs. of them ; and will always be true, as long as the same Name can have the same Signification.

§ 20. To conclude, this is that which in short I *Recapitula-* would say, (*viz.*) that all the great Busi-*tion.* ness of *Genera* and *Species*, and their *Essences*, amounts to no more but this, That Men making abstract *Ideas*, and settling them in their Minds, with Names annex'd to them, do thereby enable themselves to consider Things, and Discourse of them, as it were in Bundles, for the easier and readier Improvement and Communication of their Knowledge, which would advance but slowly, were their Words and Thoughts confined only to Particulars.

CHAPTER IV.

OF THE NAMES OF SIMPLE IDEAS.

§ 1. Though all Words, as I have shewn, signify nothing immediately but the *Ideas* in the Mind of the Speaker, yet upon a nearer Survey, we shall find that the *Names of Simple* Ideas, *mixed Modes*, (under which I comprise Relations too,) *and natural Substances, have each of them something peculiar*, and different from the other. For Example.

Names of Simple Ideas, Modes, and Substances, have each something peculiar.

§ 2. *First*, The *Names of Simple* Ideas, *and Substances*, with the abstract *Ideas* in the *Mind*, which they immediately signify, *intimate* also *some real Existence*, from which was deriv'd their original Pattern. But the *Names of mixed Modes*, terminate in the Idea that is in the Mind, and lead not the Thoughts any farther, as we shall see more at large in the following Chapter.

First, Names of Simple Ideas and Substances, intimate real Existence.

§ 3. *Secondly,* The *Names of Simple* Ideas, *and Modes, signifying always the real, as well*

Secondly, Names of Simple Ideas *and Modes signify always both real and nominal Essence.*

as nominal Essence of their Species. But *the Names of natural Substances, signify* rarely, if ever, any thing but *barely the nominal Essences* of those Species, as we shall shew in the Chapter that treats of the Names of Substances in particular.

§ 4. *Thirdly,* The *Names of Simple* Ideas *are not*

Thirdly, Names of Simple Ideas *undefinable.*

capable of any Definitions; the Names of all complex *Ideas* are. It has not, that I know, hitherto been taken Notice of by any Body, what Words are, and what are not capable of being defined : the want whereof is (as I am apt to think) not seldom the occasion of great wrangling, and Obscurity in Mens Discourses, whilst some demand Definitions of Terms that cannot be defined ; and others think, they ought to rest satisfied in an Explication made by a more general Word, and its Restriction, (or to speak in Terms of Art, by a Genus and Difference,) when even after such Definition made according to Rule, those who hear it have often no more a clear Conception of the meaning of the Word, than they had before. This at least, I think, that the shewing what Words are, and what are not capable of Definitions, and wherein consists a good Definition, is not wholly besides our present purpose ; and perhaps, will afford so much Light to the Nature of these Signs, and our *Ideas*, as to deserve a more particular Consideration.

§ 5. I will not here trouble my self, to prove that all Terms are not definable from that *If all were* Progress, *in infinitum*, which it will *definable,* visibly lead us into, if we should allow, *a Process* in that all Names could be defined. For *infinitum.* if the Terms of one Definition, were still to be defined by another, Where at last should we stop ? But I shall from the Nature of our *Ideas*, and the Signification of our Words shew, *why some Names can, and others cannot be defined*, and which they are.

§ 6. I think, it is agreed, that *a Definition is* nothing else, but *the shewing the meaning of one* *What a Defi-* *Word by several other not synonymous* *nition is.* *Terms.* The meaning of Words being only the *Ideas* they are made to stand for by him that uses 'em ; the meaning of any Term is then shewed, or the Word is defined, when by other Words the *Idea* it is made the Sign of, and annexed to in the Mind of the Speaker, is as it were represented, or set before the view of another; and thus its Signification ascertained ? This is the only use and end of Definitions ; and therefore the only Measure of what is, or is not a good Definition.

§ 7. This being premised, I say, that *the Names of*
Simple Ideas, and those only, *are in-*
capable of being defined. The Reason
whereof is this, That the several Terms
of a Definition, signifying several *Ideas,* they can
altogether by no means represent an *Idea,* which has
no Composition at all : And therefore a Definition
which is properly nothing but the shewing the
meaning of one Word by several others not signifying
each the same thing, can in the Names of Simple
Ideas have no Place.

Simple Ideas
why unde-
finable.

§ 8. The not observing this difference in our *Ideas,*
and their Names, has produced that
eminent trifling in the Schools, which is
so easy to be observed in the Definitions they give
us of some few of these Simple *Ideas.* For as to
the greatest part of 'em, even those Masters of Definitions were fain to leave them untouched, meerly
by the Impossibility they found in it. What more
exquisite *Jargon* could the Wit of Man invent, than
this Definition, *The Act of a Being in Power, as far*
forth as in Power ? which would puzzle any rational
Man, to whom it was not already known by its famous
Absurdity, to guess what Word it could ever be supposed to be the Explication of. If *Tully* asking a
Dutchman what *Beweeginge* was, should have received
this Explication in his own Language, that it was

Instances;
Motion.

Actus entis in potentia quatenus in potentia ; I ask
whether any one can imagine he could thereby have
understood what the Word *Beweeginge* signified, or
have guessed what *Idea* a *Dutchman* ordinarily had
in his Mind, and would signify to another when he
used that Sound.

§ 9. Nor have the Modern Philosophers, who have
endeavoured to throw off the *Jargon* of the Schools, and
speak intelligibly, much better succeeded in defining
Simple *Ideas*, whether by explaining their Causes,
or any otherwise. The *Atomists*, who define Motion
to be a *Passage from one place to another*, What do
they more than put one synonimous Word for
another ? For what is *Passage* other than *Motion* ?
And if they were asked what Passage was, How
would they better define it than by *Motion ?* For is
it not at least as proper and significant, to say, *Passage is a Motion from one Place to another*, as to say,
Motion is a Passage, &c. This is to translate, and
not to define, when we change two Words of the
same Signification one for another ; which when one
is better understood than the other, may serve to discover what *Idea* the unknown stands for ; but is very
far from a *Definition*, unless we will say, every English
Word in the Dictionary, is the Definition of the Latin
Word it Answers, and that Motion is a Definition of
Motus. *Nor will the successive Application of the*

Parts of the Superficies *of one Body, to those of another,*
which the *Cartesians* give us, prove a much better
Definition of Motion, when well examined.

§ 10.   *The Act of Perspicuous, as far forth as per-*
Light.   *spicuous*, is another Peripatetick Definition of a Simple *Idea*; which though not more absurd
than the former of *Motion*, yet Betrays its Useless-
ness and Insignificancy more plainly, because Experience will easily convince any one, that it cannot
make the meaning of the Word *Light* (which it pretends to define) at all understood by a blind Man:
but the Definition of *Motion* appears not at first
sight so useless, because it scapes this way of Trial.
For this Simple *Idea*, entring by the Touch as well
as Sight, 'tis impossible to shew an Example of any
one, who has no other way to get the *Idea* of *Motion*,
but barely by the Definition of that Name.   Those
who tell us, that *Light* is a great Number of little
Globules, striking briskly on the Bottom of the Eye,
speak more intelligibly than the Schools: but yet
these Words ever so well understood would make the
Idea, the Word *Light* stands for, no more known to a
Man that understands it not before, than if one should
tell him, that *Light* was nothing but a Company of
little Tennis-balls, which Fairies all Day long struck
with Rackets against some Mens Foreheads, whilst
they passed by others.   For granting this Expli-

cation of the thing to be true; yet the *Idea* of the
cause of *Light*, if we had it ever so exact, would no
more give us the *Idea* of *Light* it self, as it is such a
particular Perception in us, than the *Idea* of the Figure
and Motion of a sharp piece of Steel, would give us
the *Idea* of that Pain which it is able to cause in us.
For the cause of any Sensation, and the Sensation
it self, in all the Simple *Ideas* of one Sense, are two
Ideas; and two *Ideas* so different, and distant one
from another, that, no two can be more so.   And
therefore should *Des Cartes*'s Globules strike ever so
long on the *Retina* of a Man, who was blind by a
Gutta Serena, he would thereby never have any *Idea*
of *Light*, or any thing approaching it, tho' he understood what little Globules were, and what striking on
another Body was, ever so well.   And therefore the
Cartesians very well distinguish between that Light
which is the Cause of that Sensation in us, and the
Idea which is produced in us by it, and is that which
is properly Light.

§ 11. *Simple Ideas*, as has been shewn, *are only* to
be *got by* those *Impressions*, Objects
themselves make on our Minds, by the
proper Inlets appointed to each sort. If
they are not received this way, all the

Simple Ideas
*why undefin-
able, farther
explained.*

Words in the World, *made use of to explain, or define
any of their Names, will never be able to produce in us*

the Idea *it stands for.* For Words being Sounds, can produce in us no other Simple *Ideas*, than of those very Sounds; nor excite any in us, but by that voluntary Connexion, which is known to be between 'em, and those Simple *Ideas*, which common Use has made 'em Signs of. He that thinks otherwise, let him try if any Words can give him the taste of a Pine-Apple, and make him have the true *Idea* of the Relish of that celebrated delicious Fruit. So far as he is told it has a resemblance with any Tastes, whereof he has the *Ideas* already in his Memory, imprinted there by sensible Objects, not Strangers to his Palate, so far may he approach that resemblance in his Mind. But this is not giving us that *Idea* by a *Definition*, but exciting in us other Simple *Ideas*, by their known Names; which will be still very different from the true taste of that Fruit it self. In Light and Colours, and all other Simple *Ideas*, it is the same thing : For the Signification of Sounds, is not natural, but only imposed and arbitrary. And no Definition of *Light*, or *Redness*, is more fitted, or able to produce either of those *Ideas* in us, than to Sound *Light*, or *Red*, by it self. For to hope to produce an *Idea* of Light, or Colour, by a Sound, however formed, is to expect that Sounds should be visible, or Colours audible ; and to make the Ears do the Office of all the other Senses. Which is all one as to say, that

we might Taste, Smell, and See by the Ears: a sort
of Philosophy worthy only of *Sancho Panca*, who
had the Faculty to see *Dulcinea* by Hearsay. And
therefore he that has not before received into his
Mind, by the proper Inlet, the simple *Idea* which any
word stands for, can never come to know the Signification of that Word, by any other Words, or Sounds,
whatsoever put together, according to any Rules of
Definition. The only way is, by applying to his
Senses the proper Object ; and so producing that *Idea*
in him, for which he has learned the name already.
A studious blind Man, who had mightily beat his
Head about visible Objects, and made use of the
Explication of his Books and Friends, to understand
those Names of Light and Colours, which often came
in his way; bragg'd one Day, That he now understood what *Scarlet* signify'd. Upon which his Friend
demanding, what *Scarlet* was ? The blind Man
answer'd, It was like the Sound of a Trumpet. Just
such an Understanding of the Name of any other
simple *Idea* will he have, who hopes to get it only
from a Definition, or other Words made use of to
explain it.

§ 12. The case is quite otherwise *in complex Ideas*;
which consisting of several simple ones, it is in
the Power of Words, standing for the several *Ideas*,
that makes that Composition, to imprint complex

Ideas in the Mind, which were never there before, and so make their Names be under-

The contrary shewed in complex Ideas *by Instances of a Statue and* Rain-tow.

stood. In such Collections of *Ideas*, passing under one Name, *Definition*, or the teaching the Signification of one Word, by several others, has Place, and *may make us understand the Names* of Things, which never came within the reach of our Senses; and frame *Ideas* suitable to those in other Mens Minds, when they use those Names: provided that none of the Terms of the Definition stand for any such simple *Ideas*, which he to whom the Explication is made, has never yet had in his Thought. Thus the Word *Statue* may be explain'd to a blind Man by other Words, when *Picture* cannot, his Senses having given him the *Idea* of Figure, but not of Colours, which therefore Words cannot excite in him. This gained the Prize to the Painter, against the Statuary; each of which contending for the Ex-cellency of his Art, and the Statuary bragging, that his was to be preferred, because it reached farther, and even those who had lost their Eyes, could yet perceive the excellency of it. The Painter agreed to refer himself to the Judgment of a blind Man; who being brought where there was a Statue made by the one, and a Picture drawn by the other; he was first led to the Statue, in which he traced with his

Hands, all the Lineaments of the Face and Body ; and with great Admiration, applaude'd the skill of the Workman. But being led to the Picture, and having his Hands laid upon it, was told, That now he touched the Head, and then the Forehead, Eyes, Nose, &c. as his Hand moved over the Parts of the Picture on the Cloth, without finding any the least Distinction : Whereupon, he cried out, that certainly that must needs be a very admirable and divine Piece of Workmanship, which could represent to them all those Parts, where he could neither feel nor perceive any thing.

§ 13. He that should use the Word *Rainbow*, to one who knew all those Colours, but yet had never seen that *Phænomenon*, would, by enumerating the Figure, Largeness, Position, and Order of the Colours, so well define that word, that it might be perfectly understood. But yet that *Definition*, how exact and perfect soever, would never make a blind Man understand it ; because several of the simple *Ideas* that make that complex one, being such as he never received by Sensation and Experience, no Words are able to excite them in his Mind.

§ 14. Simple *Ideas*, as has been shewed, can only be got by Experience, from those Objects, which are proper to produce in us those Perceptions. *When by this means we have our Minds stored with 'em,* and know the Names for them, then *we are in a Condition to define*, and by *Definition* to understand the Names of complex *Ideas*, that are made up of them. But when any term stands for a simple *Idea*, that a

The Names of complex Ideas when to be made intelligible by Words.

. Man has never yet had in his Mind, it is impossible, by any Words, to make known its meaning to him. When any term stands for an *Idea* a Man is acquainted with, but is ignorant, that that term is the Sign of it, there another Name, of the same *Idea* which he has been accustomed to, may make him understand its meaning. But in no case whatsoever, is any Name, of any simple *Idea*, capable of a *Definition*.

§ 15. *Fourthly*, But though the Names of *simple Ideas*, have not the help of *Definition* to determine their Signification; yet that hinders not but that they *are generally less doubtful and uncertain than those* of *mixed Modes and Substances*. Because they

Fourthly, Names of simple Ideas least doubtful.

standing only for one simple Perception, Men, for the most part, easily and perfectly agree in their Signification : And there is little room for mistake and wrangling about their meaning. He that knows once, that Whiteness is the Name of that Colour he has observed in Snow, or Milk, will not be apt to misapply that Word, as long as he retains that *Idea* ;

which when he has quite lost, he is not apt to mistake
the meaning of it, but perceives he Understands it
not. There is neither a multiplicity of simple *Ideas*
to be put together, which makes the doubtfulness in
the Names of mixed Modes : nor a supposed, but an
unknown real Essence, with Properties depending
thereon, the precise Number whereof are also unknown, which makes the Difficulty in the Names of
Substances. But on the contrary, in simple *Ideas*
the whole Signification of the Name is known at
once, and consists not of Parts, whereof more or less
being put in, the *Idea* may be varied, and so the
Signification of its Name, be obscure, or uncertain.

§ 16. *Fifthly*, This farther may be observed, concerning *simple* Ideas and their Names,
that they *have but few Ascents in linea*
Prædicamentali (as they call it,) *from*
the lowest Species, to the summum Genus.
The reason whereof is, that the lowest

Fifthly, Sim-
ple Ideas
have few As-
cents in linea
Prædicamen-
tali.

Species being but one simple *Idea*, nothing can be
left out of it, that so the difference being taken away,
it may agree with some other thing in one *Idea*
common to them both ; which having one Name, is
the *Genus* of the other two : *v. g.* There is nothing
can be left out of the *Idea* of White and Red, to
make them agree in one common Appearance, and
so have one general Name ; as *Rationality* being left

out of the complex *Idea* of *Man*, makes it agree with
Brute, in the more general *Idea* and Name of *Animal.*
And therefore when to avoid unpleasant Enumera-
tions, Men would comprehend both *White* and *Red*,
and several other such simple *Ideas*, under one general
Name ; they have been fain to do it by a Word,
which denotes only the way they get into the Mind.
For when *White*, *Red*, and *Yellow*, are all comprehended under the *Genus* or Name *Colour*, it signifies
no more, but such *Ideas*, as are produced in the
Mind only by the Sight, and have entrance only
through the Eyes.   And when they would frame yet
a more general Term, to comprehend both *Colours*
and *Sounds*, and the like simple *Ideas*, they do it by
a Word, that signifies all such as come into the Mind
only by one Sense : And so the general term *Quality*,
in its ordinary Acceptation, comprehends Colours,
Sounds, Tastes, Smells, and tangible Qualities, with
Distinction from Extension, Number, Motion, Pleasure, and Pain, which make Impressions on the Mind,
and introduce their *Ideas* by more Senses than one.

§ 17. *Sixthly*, The Names of simple *Ideas*, Substances, and mixed Modes, have also *Sixthly,*
this difference : That those *of mixed* *Names of*
simple Ideas
Modes stand for *Ideas* perfectly *Arbi-* *stand for*
Ideas *not at*
trary : Those *of Substances*, are not *all arbitrary.*
perfectly so ; but *refer to a Pattern, though with*

some Latitude : and those of simple Ideas *are* perfectly taken from the Existence of Things, and are *not arbitrary at all.* Which what difference it makes in the Significations of their Names, we shall see in the following Chapters.

The Names of simple Modes differ little from those of simple *Ideas.*

CHAPTER V.

OF THE NAMES OF MIXED MODES AND RELATIONS.

§ 1. The Names of mixed Modes being general,

They stand for abstract Ideas, as other general Names. they stand, as has been shewn, for sorts or Species of Things, each of which has its peculiar Essence. The Essences of these Species also, as has been shewed, are nothing but the abstract *Ideas* in the Mind, to which the Name is annexed. Thus far the Names and Essences of mixed Modes, have nothing but what is common to them, with other *Ideas* : But if we take a little nearer survey of them, we shall find, that they have something peculiar, which, perhaps may deserve our Attention.

§ 2. The first Particularity I shall observe in them

First, The Ideas they stand for, are made by the Understanding. is, that the abstract *Ideas*, or, if you please, the Essences of the several Species *of mixed Modes are made by the Understanding*, wherein they differ from those simple *Ideas* : in which sort, the Mind has no Power to make any one, but only receives such as are presented to it, by the real Existence of Things operating upon it.

§ 3. In the next Place, these *Essences of the Species of mixed Modes, are* not only *made* by the Mind, but made *very arbitrarily,* made without Patterns, or reference to any real Existence. Wherein they differ

Secondly, made arbitrarily, and without Patterns.

from those of Substances, which carry with them the Supposition of some real Being, from which they are taken, and to which they are conformable. But in its complex *Ideas* of mixed Modes, the Mind takes a Liberty not to follow the Existence of Things exactly. It unites and retains certain Collections, as so many distinct Specifick *Ideas*, whilst others, that as often occur in Nature, and are as plainly suggested by outward Things, pass neglected without particular Names or Specifications. Nor does the Mind, in these of mixed Modes, as in the complex *Ideas* of Substances, examine them by the real Existence of Things ; or verify them by Patterns, containing such peculiar Compositions in Nature. To know whether his *Idea* of *Adultery*, or *Incest*, be right, will a Man seek it any where amongst Things existing ? Or is it true, because any one has been Witness to such an Action ? No: but it suffices here, that Men have put together such a Collection into one complex *Idea*, that makes the *Archetype*, and Specifick *Idea*, whether ever any such Action were committed in *rerum natura*, or no.

§ 4. To understand this aright, we must consider *wherein this making of these complex* Ideas *consists*: and that is not in the making any new *Idea*, but putting together those which the Mind had before. Wherein the Mind does these three Things: First, It chuses a certain Number. Secondly, It gives them Connection, and makes them into one *Idea*. Thirdly, It ties them together by a Name. If we examine how the Mind proceeds in these, and what Liberty it takes in them, we shall easily observe, how these Essences of the Species of mixed Modes, are the Workmanship of the Mind; and consequently, that the Species themselves are of Mens making.

How this is done.

§ 5. No Body can doubt, but that these *Ideas* of mixed Modes, are made by a voluntary Collection of *Ideas* put together in the Mind, independent from any original Patterns in Nature, who will but reflect, that this sort of complex *Ideas* may be made, abstracted, and have Names given 'em, and so a Species be constituted, before any one individual of that Species ever existed. Who can doubt, but the *Ideas* of *Sacrilege*, or *Adultery*, might be framed in the Mind of Men, and have Names given them;

Evidently arbitrary, that the Idea *is often before the Existence.*

and so these Species of mixed Modes be constituted, before either of them was ever committed; and might be as well discoursed of, and reasoned about, and as certain Truths discovered of them, whilst yet they had no being but in the Understanding, as well as now, that they have but too frequently a real Existence? Whereby it is plain, how much *the sorts of mixed Modes are the Creatures of the Understanding*, where they have a being as subservient to all the ends of real Truth and Knowledge, as when they really exist: And we cannot doubt, but Lawmakers have often made Laws about Species of Actions, which were only the Creatures of their own Understanding: Beings that had no other existence, but in their own Minds. And, I think, no Body can deny, but that the *Resurrection* was a Species of mixed Modes in the Mind, before it really existed.

§ 6. To see *how arbitrarily these Essences of mixed Modes are made* by the Mind, we need but take a view of almost any of them. *Instances; Murder, Incest, Stabbing.* A little looking into them, will satisfy us, that 'tis the Mind, that combines several scattered independent *Ideas*, into one complex one; and by the common Name it gives them, makes them the Essence of a certain Species, without regulating it self by any Connection they have in Nature. For what greater Connection in Nature, has the *Idea* of a Man, than the *Idea* of a Sheep, with Killing; that this is made a particular Species of Action, signify'd by the word *Murder*; and the other not? Or what Union is there in Nature, between the *Idea* of the Relation of a Father, with Killing, than that of a Son, or Neighbour; that those are combined into one complex *Idea*, and thereby made the Essence of the distinct Species *Parricide*, whilst the other make no distinct Species at all? But though they have made killing a Man's Father, or Mother, a distinct Species from killing his Son, or Daughter; yet in some other Cases, Son and Daughter are taken in too, as well as Father and Mother; and they are all equally comprehended in the same Species, as in that of *Incest*. Thus the Mind in mixed Modes arbitrarily Unites into complex *Ideas*, such as it finds convenient; whilst others that have altogether as much Union in Nature, are left loose and never combined into one *Idea*, because they have no need of one Name. 'Tis evident then, that the Mind, by its free Choice, gives a Connection to a certain Number of *Ideas*; which in Nature have no more Union with one another, than others that it leaves out: Why else is the part of the Weapon, the beginning of the Wound is made with, taken Notice of, to make the distinct Species called *Stabbing*, and the Figure and Matter of the Weapon left out? I do not say, this is done without Reason, as we shall see more by and by; but this I say, that it is done, by the free Choice of the Mind, pursuing its own ends; and that therefore these Species of mixed Modes, are the Workmanship of the Understanding: And there is nothing more evident, than that for the most part, in the framing these *Ideas*, the Mind searches not its Patterns in Nature, nor refers the *Ideas* it makes to the real Existence of Things; but puts such together, as may best serve its own Purposes, without tying it self to a precise Imitation of any thing that really exists.

§ 7. But though these complex *Ideas*, or *Essences of mixed Modes*, depend on the Mind, and are made by it with great Liberty; yet they *are not made at Random*, and jumbled together without any reason at *But still subservient to the end of Language.* all. Though these complex *Ideas* be not always copied from Nature, yet they are always suited to the end for which abstract *Ideas* are made: And though they be Combinations made of *Ideas*, that are loose enough, and have as little Union in themselves, as several other, to which the Mind never gives a Connection that combines them into one *Idea*; yet they are always made for the convenience of Communication, which is the chief end of Language. The use of Language is, by short Sounds to

signify with ease and dispatch general Conceptions ;
wherein not only abundance of particulars may be
contained, but also a great Variety of independent
Ideas collected into one complex one.   In the making
therefore of the Species of mixed Modes, Men have
had regard only to such Combinations, as they had
occasion to mention one to another.   Those they
have combined into distinct complex *Ideas*, and given
Names to ; whilst others that in Nature have as near
an Union, are left loose and unregarded.   For to go
no farther than humane Actions themselves, if they
would make distinct abstract *Ideas* of all the Varieties
might be observed in them, the Number must be
infinite, and the Memory confounded with the Plenty,
as well as overcharged to little Purpose.   It suffices,
that Men make and Name so many complex *Ideas*
of these mixed Modes, as they find they have occasion to have Names for, in the ordinary occurrence of
their Affairs.   If they join to the *Idea* of Killing,
the *Idea* of Father, or Mother, and so make a distinct
Species from Killing a Man's Son, or Neighbour, it is
because of the different Heinousness of the Crime,
and the distinct Punishment is due to the murdering
a Man's Father and Mother, different from what
ought to be inflicted on the Murder of a Son or
Neighbour ; and therefore they find it necessary to
mention it by a distinct Name, which is the end of

making that distinct Combination. But though the *Ideas* of Mother and Daughter, are so differently treated, in reference to the *Idea* of Killing, that the one is joined with it to make a distinct abstract *Idea* with a Name, and so a distinct Species, and the other not ; yet in respect of carnal Knowledge, they are both taken in under *Incest*; and that still for the same convenience of expressing under one Name, and reckoning of one Species, such unclean Mixtures, as have a peculiar turpitude beyond others ; and this to avoid Circumlocutions, and tedious Descriptions.

§ 8. A moderate skill *in different Languages*, will easily satisfy one of the Truth of this, it being so obvious to observe great store of *Words in one* Language, *which have not any that answer them in another*. *Whereof the intranslatable Words of divers Languages are a Proof.* Which plainly shews, that those of one Country, by their Customs and Manner of Life, have found occasion to make several complex *Ideas*, and give Names to them, which others never collected into specifick *Ideas*. This could not have happened, if these Species were the steddy Workmanship of Nature ; and not Collections made and abstracted by the Mind, in order to Naming, and for the convenience of Communication. The Terms of our Law, which are not empty Sounds, will hardly find Words that answer them in the *Spanish* or *Italian*, no

scanty Languages; much less, I think, could any one
translate them into the *Caribbee*, or *Westoe* Tongues :
And the *Versura* of the *Romans* or *Corban* of the
Jews, have no Words in other Languages to answer
them : The Reason whereof is plain, from what has
been said. Nay, if we will look a little more nearly
into this matter, and exactly compare different Languages, we shall find, that though they have Words,
which in Translations and Dictionaries, are supposed
to answer one another; yet there is scarce one of
ten, amongst the Names of complex *Ideas*, especially of mixed Modes, that stands for the same
precise *Idea*, which the Word does that in Dictionaries it is rendred by. There are no *Ideas* more
common, and less compounded, than the Measures of
Time, Extension, and Weight, and the Latin Names
Hora, *Pes*, *Libra*, are without Difficulty rendred by
the *English* Names, *Hour*, *Foot*, and *Pound* : But yet
there is nothing more evident, than that the *Ideas* a
Roman annexed to these Latin Names, were very
far different from those which an *Englishman* ex-
presses by those *English* ones. And if either of
these should make use of the Measures that those of
the other Language designed by their Names, he
would be quite out in his account. These are too
sensible Proofs to be doubted ; and we shall find this
much more so, in the Names of more abstract and

compounded *Ideas* ; such as are the greatest part of those which make up Moral Discourses : Whose Names, when Men come curiously to compare with those they are translated into, in other Languages, they will find very few of them exactly to correspond in the whole extent of their Significations.

§ 9. The Reason why I take so particular Notice of this, is, that we may not be mistaken about *Genera*, and *Species*, and their *Essences*, as if they were Things regularly and constantly *This shews Species to be made for Communication.* made by Nature, and had a real Existence in Things ; when they appear, upon a more wary survey, to be nothing else but an Artifice of the Understanding, for the easier signifying such Collections of *Ideas*, as it should often have occasion to communicate by one general Term ; under which divers particulars, as far forth as they agreed to that abstract *Idea*, might be comprehended. And if the doubtful Signification of the word *Species*, may make it sound harsh to some, that I say, that the Species of mixed Modes are made by the Understanding ; yet, I think, it can by no Body be denied, that 'tis the Mind makes those abstract complex *Ideas*, to which specifick Names are given. And if it be true, as it is, that the Mind makes the Patterns, for sorting and naming of Things, I leave it to be considered,

who makes the Boundaries of the Sort, or *Species*;
since with me, *Species* and *Sort* have no other difference, than that of a Latin and English *Idiom*.

§ 10. *The near Relation* that there is *between*
Species, Essences, and their *general*
Name, at least in *mixed Modes,* will
farther appear, when we consider, that
it is the Name that seems to preserve those *Essences,* and give them
their lasting Duration. For the Connection between the loose parts of those complex
Ideas, being made by the Mind, this Union, which
has no particular Foundation in Nature, would cease
again, were there not something that did, as it were,
hold it together, and keep the Parts from scattering.
Though therefore it be the Mind that makes the
Collection, 'tis the Name which is, as it were, the
Knot, that ties them fast together. What a vast
Variety of different *Ideas,* does the word *Triumphus*
hold together, and deliver to us as one *Species!*
Had this Name been never made, or quite lost, we
might no doubt, have had Descriptions of what
passed in that Solemnity: But yet, I think, that
which holds those different Parts together, in the
Unity of one complex *Idea,* is that very Word
annexed to it; without which, the several Parts of
that would no more be thought to make one thing,

In Mixed Modes, 'tis the Name that ties the Combination together, and makes it a Species.

than any other shew, which having never been made
but once, had never been united into one complex
Idea, under one Denomination. How much therefore, in mixed Modes, the Unity necessary to any
Essence depends on the Mind ; and how much the
Continuation and fixing of that Unity depends on
the Name in common Use annexed to it, I leave to
be considered by those, who look upon *Essences* and
Species, as real established Things in Nature.

§ 11. Suitable to this, we find, that *Men speaking
of mixed Modes, seldom* imagine or *take any other for
Species of them, but such as are set out by Name*:
Because they being of Man's making only, in order
to naming, no such *Species* are taken Notice of, or
supposed to be, unless a *Name* be joined to it, as
the Sign of Man's having combined into one *Idea*
several loose ones ; and by that *Name*, giving a lasting Union to the Parts, which would otherwise cease
to have any, as soon as the Mind laid by that
abstract *Idea*, and ceased actually to think on it.
But when a Name is once annexed to it, wherein the
Parts of that complex *Idea* have a settled and permanent Union ; then is the *Essence*, as it were
established, and the *Species* looked on as compleat.
For to what purpose should the Memory charge
it self with such Compositions, unless it were by
Abstraction to make them general ? And to what

purpose make them general, unless it were, that they might have general *Names*, for the convenience of Discourse, and Communication? Thus we see, that Killing a Man with a Sword, or a Hatchet, are looked on as no distinct Species of Action: But if the point of the Sword first enter the Body, it passes for a distinct *Species*, where it has a distinct *Name*, as in *England*, in whose Language it is called *Stabbing*: But in another Country, where it has not happened to be specified under a peculiar *Name*, it passes not for a distinct *Species*. But in the *Species* of corporeal Substances, though it be the Mind that makes the nominal Essence: yet since those *Ideas*, which are combined in it, are supposed to have an Union in Nature, whether the Mind joins them or no, therefore those are looked on as distinct *Species*, without any Operation of the Mind, either abstracting, or, giving a *Name* to that complex *Idea*.

For the Originals of mixed Modes, we look no farther than the Mind, which also shews them to be the Workmanship of Understanding.

§ 12. Conformable also to what has been said concerning the *Essences* of the *Species* of *mixed Modes*, that they are the Creatures of the Understanding, rather than the Works of Nature: Conformable, I say, to this, we find, that *their Names lead our Thoughts to the Mind, and no farther.* When we speak

of *Justice,* or *Gratitude,* we frame to our selves no
Imagination of any thing existing, which we would
conceive ; but our Thoughts terminate in the
abstract *Ideas* of those Vertues, and look not farther ; as they do, when we speak of a *Horse,* or *Iron,*
whose Specifick *Ideas* we consider not, as barely in the
Mind, but as in things themselves, which afford the
original Patterns of those *Ideas.* But in mixed Modes,
at least the most considerable Parts of them, which
are moral Beings, we consider the original Patterns,
as being in the Mind ; and to those we refer for the
distinguishing of particular Beings under Names.
And hence I think it is, That these *Essences* of the
Species of mixed Modes, are by a more particular
Name called *Notions* : as by a peculiar Right apper-
taining to the Understanding.

§ 13. Hence likewise we may learn, *Why the complex* Ideas *of mixed Modes are commonly
more compounded and decompounded, than
those of natural Substances.* Because
they being the Workmanship of the
Understanding, pursuing only its own
ends, and the conveniency of expressing
in short those *Ideas* it would make
*Their being
made by the
Understand-
ing without
Patterns,
shews the rea-
son why they
are so com-
pounded.*
known to another, does with great Liberty unite often
into one abstract *Idea* Things that in their Nature
have no coherence ; and so under one Term, bundle

together a great Variety of compounded, and decompounded *Ideas.* Thus the Name of *Procession,* what
a great mixture of independent *Ideas* of Persons,
Habits, Tapers, Orders, Motions, Sounds, does it
contain in that complex one, which the Mind of
Man has arbitrarily put together, to express by that
one Name ? Whereas the complex *Ideas* of the sorts
of Substances are usually made up of only a small
Number of simple ones ; and in the *Species* of
Animals, these two, *viz.* Shape and Voice, commonly
make the whole nominal Essence.

§ 14. Another thing we may observe from what
Names of has been said, is, That *the Names of*
mixed Modes *mixed Modes always signify* (when they
stand always
for their real have any determined Signification) *the*
Essences. *real Essences of their Species.* For these
abstract *Ideas*, being the Workmanship of the Mind,
and not referred to the real Existence of Things,
there is no Supposition of any thing more signified
by that Name, but barely that complex *Idea*, the
Mind it self has formed, which is all it would have
expressed by it ; and is that on which all the Properties of the *Species* depend, and from which alone
they all flow : and so in these the *real* and *nominal*
Essence is the same ; which of what Concernment it
is to the certain Knowledg of general Truth, we shall
see hereafter.

§ 15. This also may shew us the Reason, *Why for the most part the Names of mixed Modes are got, before the* Ideas *they stand for are perfectly known.* Because there being no *Species*, of these ordinarily taken *Why their Names are usually got before their Ideas.* Notice of, but what have Names; and those *Species*, or rather their Essences, being abstract complex *Ideas* made arbitrarily by the Mind, it is convenient, if not necessary, to know the Names, before one endeavour to frame these complex *Ideas* : unless a Man will fill his Head with a Company of abstract complex *Ideas*, which others having no Names for, he has nothing to do with, but to lay by, and forget again. I confess, that in the Beginning of Languages, it was necessary to have the *Idea*, before one gave it the Name : And so it is still, where making a new complex *Idea*, one also, by giving it a new Name, makes a new Word. But this concerns not Languages made, which have generally pretty well provided for *Ideas*, which Men have frequent Occasion to have, and communicate : And in such, I ask, whether it be not the ordinary Method, that Children learn the Names of mixed Modes, before they have their *Ideas?* What one of a Thousand ever frames the abstract *Idea* of *Glory* and *Ambition* before he has heard the Names of them. In simple *Ideas* and Substances, I grant it is otherwise ; which being such *Ideas*, as

H

have a real Existence and Union in Nature, the *Ideas*, or Names, are got one before the other, as it happens.

§ 16. What has been said here of mix'd Modes, is
with very little difference applicable

Reason of my being so large on this Subject.
also to Relations; which since every Man himself may observe, I may spare

my self the Pains to enlarge on : especially, since what I have here said concerning Words
in this Third Book, will possibly be thought by some
to be much more than what so slight a Subject
required. I allow, it might be brought into a nar-
rower Compass : But I was willing to stay my Reader
on an Argument, that appears to me new, and a little
out of the Way, (I am sure 'tis one, I thought not of,
when I began to write,) That by searching it to the
Bottom, and turning it on every side, some part or
other might meet with every one's Thoughts, and give
occasion to the most averse, or negligent, to reflect on
a general Miscarriage; which, though of great consequence, is little taken Notice of. When it is considered, what a pudder is made about *Essences,* and
how much all sorts of Knowledge, Discourse, and
Conversation, are pestered and disordered by the
careless, and confused Use and Application of Words,
it will, perhaps, be thought worth while throughly
to lay it open. And I shall be pardoned if I have

dwelt long on an Argument which I think therefore needs to be inculcated ; because the Faults, Men are usually guilty of in this kind, are not only the greatest Hindrances of true Knowledge ; but are so well thought of, as to pass for it. Men would often see what a small pittance of Reason and Truth, or possibly none at all, is mixed with those huffing Opinions they are swelled with ; if they would but look beyond fashionable Sounds, and observe what *Ideas* are, or are not comprehended under those Words, with which they are so armed at all Points, and with which they so confidently lay about them. I shall imagine I have done some Service to Truth, Peace, and Learning, if, by an enlargement on this Subject, I can make Men reflect on their own Use of Language ; and give them Reason to suspect, that since it is frequent for others, it may also be possible for them, to have sometimes very good and approved Words in their Mouths, and Writings, with very uncertain, little, or no Signification. And therefore it is not unreasonable for them to be wary herein themselves, and not to be unwilling to have them examined by others. With this Design therefore, I shall go on with what I have farther to say, concerning this matter.

CHAPTER VI.

OF THE NAMES OF SUBSTANCES.

§ 1. *The common Names of Substances* as well as other General Terms, *stand for Sorts*;

The common Names of Substances stand for Sorts.

which is nothing else but the being made Signs of such complex *Ideas*, wherein several particular Substances do, or might agree, by virtue of which they are capable of being comprehended in one common Conception, and signify'd by one Name. I say, do or might agree: for though there be but one Sun existing in the World, yet the *Idea* of it being abstracted, so that more Substances (if there were several) might each agree in it; it is as much a Sort, as if there were as many Suns as there are Stars. They want not their Reasons, who think there are, and that each fixed Star, would answer the *Idea* the Name *Sun* stands for, to one who were placed in a due Distance ; which, by the way, may shew us how much the Sorts, or, if you please, *Genera* and *Species*

of Things (for those Latin Terms signify to me no
more than the English word *Sort*) depend on such
Collections of *Ideas*, as Men have made ; and not
on the real Nature of Things : since 'tis not impossible, but that in Propriety of Speech, that might be
a Sun to one which is a Star to another.

§ 2. The measure and boundary of each Sort, or
Species, whereby it is constituted that
particular Sort, and distinguished from *The Essence of each sort is the abstract Ideas.*
others, is that we call its *Essence*, which
is nothing but that *abstract* Idea *to which*
the Name is annexed : So that every thing contained
in that *Idea*, is essential to that Sort. This, though
it be all the *Essence* of natural Substances that we
know, or by which we distinguish them into Sorts ;
yet I call it by a peculiar Name, the *nominal
Essence*, to distinguish it from that real Constitution
of Substances, upon which depends this *nominal
Essence*, and all the Properties of that sort, which
therefore, as has been said, may be called the *real
Essence*, *v. g.* the *nominal Essence* of. *Gold*, is that
complex *Idea* the word *Gold* stands for, let it be,
for instance, a Body yellow, of a certain weight,
malleable, fusible, and fixed. But the *real Essence* is
the Constitution of the insensible Parts of that Body,
on which those Qualities, and all the other Properties
of *Gold* depend. How far these two are different,

though they are both called *Essence*, is obvious, at first sight, to discover.

§ 3. For though, perhaps, voluntary Motion, with Sense and Reason, join'd to a Body of a certain Shape, be the complex *Idea*, to which I, and others, annex the Name *Man* ; and so be the *nominal Essence* of the *Species* so called ; yet no Body will say, that that complex *Idea* is the *real Essence* and Source of all those Operations, which are to be found in any Individual of that sort.   The Foundation of all those Qualities, which are the Ingredients of our complex *Idea*, is something quite different : And had we such a Knowledg of that Constitution of *Man*, from which his Faculties of Moving, Sensation, and Reasoning, and other Powers flow, and on which his so regular shape depends, as 'tis possible Angels have, and 'tis certain his Maker has, we should have a quite other *Idea* of his *Essence*, than what now is contained in our Definition of that *Species*, be it what it will : And our *Idea* of any individual *Man* would be as far different from what it now is, as is his who knows all the Springs and Wheels, and other Contrivances within, of the famous Clock at *Strasburg*, from that which a gazing Countryman has of it, who barely sees the Motion of the Hand, and hears the Clock strike, and observes only some of the outward Appearances.

The nominal and real Essence different.

§ 4. That *Essence*, in the ordinary Use of the Word, relates to *Sorts*, and that it is considered in particular Beings, no farther than as they are ranked into *Sorts*, appears from

hence: That but take away the abstract *Ideas*, by which we sort Individuals, and rank them under common Names, and then the thought of any thing *essential* to any of them, instantly vanishes: we have no Notion of the one, without the other: which plainly shews their Relation. 'Tis necessary for me to be as I am; GOD and Nature has made me so: But there is nothing I have is essential to me. An Accident, or Disease, may very much alter my Colour, or Shape; a Fever, or Fall, may take away my Reason or Memory, or both; and an Apoplexy leave neither Sense, nor Understanding, no, nor Life. Other Creatures of my shape may be made with more, and better, or fewer, and worse Faculties than I have: and others may have Reason and Sense in a shape and body very different from mine. None of these are essential to the one, or the other, or to any Individual whatsoever, till the Mind refers it to some Sort or *Species* of Things; and then presently, according to the abstract *Idea* of that sort, something is found *essential*. Let any one examine his own Thoughts, and he will find, that as soon as he supposes or speaks of *Essential*, the Consideration of some *Species*, or the complex *Idea*, signified by some general Name, comes into his Mind: And 'tis in reference to that, that this or that Quality is said to be *essential*. So that if it be asked, whether it be *essential* to me, or any other particular corporeal Being to have Reason? I say no; no more than it is *essential* to this white thing I write on, to have Words in it. But if that particular Being be to be counted of the Sort *Man*, and to have the Name *Man* given it, then Reason is *essential* to it, supposing Reason to be a part of the complex *Idea*, the Name *Man* stands for: as it is *essential* to this thing I write on to contain Words, if I will give it the Name *Treatise*, and rank it under that *Species*. So that *essential, and not essential, relate only to our abstract Ideas, and the Names annexed to them,* which Amounts to no more but this, That whatever particular Thing has not in it those Qualities, which are contained in the abstract *Idea*, which any general Term stands for, cannot be ranked under that *Species*, nor be called by that Name, since that abstract *Idea* is the very *Essence* of that *Species*.

§ 5. Thus if the *Idea* of *Body*, with some People, be bare Extension or Space, then Solidity is not *essential* to Body: If others make the *Idea*, to which they give the Name *Body*, to be Solidity and Extension, then Solidity is essential to *Body*. That therefore, and *that alone is* considered as *essential, which makes a part of the complex* Idea *the Name of a Sort stands for*, without which no particular thing can be reckoned of that Sort, nor be intituled to that Name. Should there be found a parcel of Matter, that had all the other Qualities that are in *Iron*, but wanted Obedience to the Load-stone; and would neither be drawn by it, nor receive Direction from it, would any one Question, whether it wanted any thing *essential?* It would be absurd to ask, Whether a thing really existing wanted any thing *essential* to it. Or could it be demanded, Whether this made an *essential* or *specifick* difference, or no; since we have no other measure of *essential* or *specifick*, but our abstract *Ideas?* And to talk of specifick Differences in Nature, without reference to general *Ideas* and Names, is to talk unintelligibly. For I would ask any one, What is sufficient to make an *essential* difference in Nature, between any two particular Beings, without any regard had to some abstract *Idea*, which is looked upon as the Essence and Standard of a *Species?* All such Patterns and Standards, being quite laid aside, particular Beings, considered barely in themselves, will be found to have all their Qualities equally *essential*; and every thing, in each Individual, will be *essential* to it, or, which is more, nothing at all. For though it may be reasonable to ask, Whether obeying the

Magnet, be *essential* to *Iron* ? yet, I think, it is very improper and insignificant to ask, Whether it be *essential* to the particular parcel of Matter I cut my Pen with, without considering it under the Name *Iron*, or as being of a certain *Species?* And if, as has been said, our abstract *Ideas*, which have Names annexed to them, are the Boundaries of *Species*, nothing can be *essential* but what is contained in those *Ideas*.

§ 6. 'Tis true, I have often mention'd a *real Essence*, distinct in Substances, from those abstract *Ideas* of them, which I call their *nominal Essence*. By this *real Essence*, I mean, that real constitution of any thing, which is the Foundation of all those Properties, that are combined in, and are constantly found to co-exist with the *nominal Essence*; that particular Constitution which every Thing has within it self, without any Relation to any thing without it. But *Essence*, even in this Sense, *relates to a sort*, and supposes a *Species*: For being that real Constitution, on which the Properties depend, it necessarily supposes a sort of Things, Properties belonging only to Species, and not to Individuals; *v. g.* Supposing the nominal Essence of *Gold*, to be Body of such a peculiar Colour and Weight, with Malleability and Fusibility, the *real Essence* is that Constitution of the Parts of Matter, on which these Qualities, and their Union,

depend ; and is also the Foundation of its Solubility
in *Aq. Regia*, and other Properties accompanying
that complex *Idea*. Here are *Essences* and *Properties*, but all upon Supposition of a sort, or general
abstract *Idea*, which is considered as immutable: but
there is no Individual parcel of Matter, to which any
of these Qualities are so annexed, as to be *essential*
to it, or inseparable from it. That which is *essential*,
belongs to it as a Condition, whereby it is of this or
that sort: But take away the Consideration of its
being ranked under the Name of some abstract *Idea*,
and then there is nothing necessary to it, nothing
inseparable from it. Indeed, as to the *real Essences*
of Substances, we only suppose their Being, without
precisely knowing what they are: But that which
annexes 'em still to the *Species*, is the nominal
Essence, of which they are the supposed Foundation
and Cause.

§ 7. The next thing to be consider'd is, by which
of those *Essences* it is, that *Substances*
are *determined into* Sorts, *or Species*; and
that, 'tis evident, is *by the nominal*
Essence. For 'tis that alone, that the Name, which
is the mark of the sort, signifies. 'Tis impossible
therefore, that any thing should determine the sorts
of Things, which we rank under general Names, but
that *Idea*, which that Name is designed as a mark

*The nominal
essence bounds
the Species.*

for ; which is that, as has been shewn, which we call
the *Nominal Essence.* Why do we say, This is a
Horse, and that a *Mule* ; this is an *Animal*, that an
Herb? How comes any particular thing to be of this
or that Sort, but because it has that *nominal Essence*,
or, which is all one, agrees to that abstract *Idea*, that
Name is annexed to? And I desire any one but to
reflect on his own Thoughts, when he hears or speaks
any of those, or other Names of Substances, to know
what sort of *Essences* they stand for.

§ 8. And that the Species *of Things to us, are
nothing but the ranking them under distinct Names,
according to the complex* Ideas *in us*; and not according
to precise, distinct, real *Essences* in them, is plain
from hence, That we find many of the Individuals
that are rank'd into one sort, call'd by one common
Name, and so receiv'd as being of one *Species*, have
yet Qualities depending on their real Constitutions,
as far different one from another, as from others, from
which they are accounted to differ *specifically.* This,
as it is easy to be observed by all, who have to do
with natural Bodies; so Chymists especially are often,
by sad Experience, convinced of it, when they, sometimes in vain, seek for the same Qualities in one
parcel of Sulphur, Antimony, or Vitriol, which they
have found in others. For though they are Bodies
of the same *Species*, having the same nominal *Essence*,

under the same Name; yet do they often, upon
severe ways of Examination, betray Quâlities so
different one from another, as to frustrate the Ex-
pectation and Labour of very wary Chymists. But
if Things were distinguished into *Species*, according
to their real Essences, it would be as impossible to
find different Properties in any two individual Substances of the same *Species*, as it is to find different
Properties in two Circles, or two equilateral Triangles.
That is properly the *Essence* to us, which determines
every particular to this or that *Classis*; or, which is
the same Thing, to this or that general Name: And
what can that be else, but that abstract *Idea*, to
which that Name is annexed? And so has, in truth,
a Reference, not so much to the Being of particular
Things, as to their general Denominations.

§ 9. Nor indeed *can we* rank, and *sort Things*, and
consequently (which is the end of sort- *Not the real*
ing) denominate them *by their real Essence which*
Essences, because we know them not. *we know not.*
Our Faculties carry us no farther towards the Knowledg and Distinction of Substances, than a Collection
of those sensible *Ideas*, which we observe in them;
which however made with the greatest diligence and
exactness, we are capable of, yet is more remote from
the true internal Constitution, from which those
Qualities flow, than, as I said, a Countryman's *Idea*

is from the inward contrivance of that famous Clock at *Strasburg*, whereof he only sees the outward Figure and Motions. There is not so contemptible a Plant or Animal, that does not confound the most inlarged Understanding. Though the familiar use of things about us, take off our Wonder; yet it cures not our Ignorance. When we come to examine the Stones, we tread on; or the Iron, we daily handle, we presently find, we know not their Make; and can give no Reason of the different Qualities we find in them. 'Tis evident the internal Constitution, whereon their Properties depend, is unknown to us. For to go no farther than the grossest and most obvious we can imagine amongst them, What is that Texture of Parts, that real *Essence*, that makes Lead and Antimony fusible; Wood and Stones not? What makes Lead and Iron malleable; Antimony and Stones not? And yet how infinitely these come short of the fine Contrivances, and unconceivable *real Essences* of Plants or Animals, every one knows. The Workmanship of the All-wise, and Powerful God, in the great Fabrick, of the Universe, and every part thereof, farther exceeds the Capacity and Comprehension of the most inquisitive and intelligent Man, than the best contrivance of the most ingenious Man, doth the Conceptions of the most ignorant of rational Creatures. Therefore we in vain pretend to range

Things into Sorts, and dispose them into certain Classes, under Names, by their *real Essences*, that are so far from our Discovery or Comprehension. A blind Man may as soon sort Things by their Colours, and he that has lost his Smell, as well distinguish a Lilly and a Rose by their Odors, as by those internal Constitutions which he knows not. He that thinks he can distinguish Sheep and Goats by their real *Essences,* that are unknown to him, may be pleased to try his Skill in those *Species,* called *Cassiowary,* and *Querechinchio* ; and by their internal real *Essences* determine the Boundaries of those *Species,* without knowing the complex *Idea* of sensible Qualities, that each of·those Names stand for, in the Countries where those Animals are to be found.

§ 10. Those therefore who have been taught, that the several Species of Substances had their distinct *internal substantial Forms* ; and that it was those *Forms,* which made the Distinction of Substances into their *Not substantial Forms which we know less.* true *Species* and *Genera,* were led yet farther out of the Way, by having their Minds set upon fruitless Enquiries after *substantial Forms,* wholly unintelligible, and whereof we have scarce so much as any obscure, or confused Conception in general.

§ 11. That our *ranking,* and *distinguishing* natural *Substances into* Species, *consists in the nominal Es-*

sences the mind makes, and not in the *real Essences*

That the no-
minalEssence
is that where-
by we distin-
guish Species
farther evi-
dent from
Spirits.

to be found in the Things themselves, is farther evident from our *Ideas* of Spirits. For the Mind getting, only by reflecting on its own Operations, those simple *Ideas* which it attributes to Spirits, it hath, or can have no other Notion of Spirit, but by attributing all those Operations, it finds in itself, to a sort of Beings, without Consideration of Matter. And even the most advanced Notion we have of God, is but attributing the same simple *Ideas* which we have got from Reflection on what we find in our selves, and which we conceive to have more Perfection in them, than would be in their absence, attributing, I say, those simple *Ideas* to him in an unlimited Degree. Thus having got from reflecting on our selves, the *Idea* of *Existence*, Knowledg, Power, and Pleasure, each of which we find it better to have than to want ; and the more we have of each, the better ; joyning all these together, with Infinity to each of them, we have the complex *Idea* of an Eternal, Omniscient, Omnipotent, infinitely Wise, and happy Being. And though we are told, that there are different Species *of Angels* ; yet we know not how to frame distinct specifick *Ideas* of them ; not out of any Conceit, that the Existence of more Species than one of Spirits, is impossible : But

because having no more simple *Ideas* (nor being able
to frame more) applicable to such Beings, but only
those few taken from our selves, and from the Actions
of our own Minds in thinking, and being delighted,
and moving several Parts of our Bodies, we can no
otherwise distinguish in our Conceptions the several
Species of Spirits, one from another, but by attributing those Operations and Powers, we find in our
selves, to them in a higher or lower Degree ; and so
have no very distinct specifick *Ideas* of Spirits, except
only of GOD, to whom we attribute both Duration,
and all those other *Ideas* with Infinity ; to the other
Spirits, with Limitation : Nor as I humbly conceive
do we, between GOD and them in our *Ideas*, put any
difference by any Number of simple *Ideas*, which we
have of one, and not of the other, but only that of
Infinity. All the particular *Ideas* of Existence,
Knowledg, Will, Power, and Motion, *&c.* being *Ideas*
derived from the Operations of our Minds, we attribute all of them to all sorts of Spirits, with the
difference only of Degrees, to the utmost we can
imagine, even Infinity, when we would frame, as well
as we can, an *Idea* of the first Being ; who yet, 'tis
certain, is infinitely more remote in the real Excellency of his Nature, from the highest and perfectest
of all created Beings, than the greatest Man, nay,
purest Seraphim, is from the most contemptible part

I

of Matter ; and consequently must infinitely exceed what our narrow Understanding can conceive of him.

§ 12. It is not impossible to conceive, nor repugnant to Reason, that there may be many *Species of Spirits,* as much separated and diversified one from another,

Whereof there are probably numberless Species.

by distinct Properties, whereof we have no *Ideas,* as the Species of sensible Things are distinguished one from another, by Qualities, which we know, and observe in them. That there should be more *Species* of intelligent Creatures above us, than there are of sensible and material below us, is probable to me from hence ; That in all the visible corporeal World, we see no Chasms or Gaps. All quite down from us, the Descent is by easy Steps, and a continued series of Things, that in each remove differ very little one from the other. There are Fishes that have Wings, and are not Strangers to the airy Region : and there are some Birds, that are Inhabitants of the Water ; whose Blood is cold as Fishes, and their Flesh so like in taste, that the scrupulous are allowed them on Fish days. There are Animals so near of kin both to Birds and Beasts, that they are in the middle between both : Amphibious Animals link the Terrestrial and Aquatick together ; Seals live at Land and at Sea, and Porpoises have the warm Blood and Entrails of a Hog, not to mention what is confidently reported of Mermaids, or Seamen. There are some Brutes, that seem to have as much Knowledg and Reason, as some that are called Men: and the Animal and Vegetable Kingdoms are so nearly joined, that if you will take the lowest of one, and the highest of the other, there will scarce be perceived any great difference between them; and so on till we come to the lowest and the most inorganical Parts of Matter, we shall find everywhere, that the several Species are linked together, and differ but in almost insensible Degrees. And when we consider the infinite Power and Wisdom of the Maker, we have Reason to think, that it is suitable to the magnificent Harmony of the Universe, and the great Design and infinite Goodness of the Architect, that the Species of Creatures should also, by gentle Degrees, ascend upward from us toward his infinite Perfection, as we see they gradually descend from us downwards: Which if it be probable, we have Reason then to be perswaded, that there are far more *Species* of Creatures above us, than there are beneath; we being in Degrees of Perfection, much more remote from the infinite Being of GOD, than we are from the lowest State of Being, and that which approaches nearest to nothing. And yet of all those distinct Species, for the Reasons above-said, we have no clear distinct *Ideas.*

§ 13. But to return to the Species of corporeal

The nominal Substances. If I should ask any one
Essence that whether *Ice* and *Water* were two distinct
of the Species,
proved from Species of Things, I doubt not but I
Water & Ice. should be answered in the affirmative:
And it cannot be denied, but he that says, they are
two distinct *Species,* is in the right. But if an
Englishman, bred in *Jamaica,* who, perhaps, had
never seen nor heard of *Ice,* coming into *England* in
the Winter, find the Water he put in his Bason at
Night, in a great part frozen in the Morning, and not
knowing any peculiar Name it had, should call it
hardened Water; I ask, Whether this would be a
new *Species* to him, different from Water? And, I
think, it would be answered here, It would not be
to him a new *Species,* no more than congealed Gelly,
when it is cold, is a distinct *Species,* from the same
Gelly fluid and warm ; or than liquid Gold, in the
Furnace, is a distinct *Species* from hard Gold in the
Hands of a Workman. And if this be so, 'tis plain,
that our *distinct Species are nothing but distinct com-*
plex Ideas, *with distinct Names annexed to them.* 'Tis
true, every Substance that exists, has its peculiar
Constitution, whereon depend those sensible Qualities, and Powers, we observe in it : But the ranking
of Things into *Species,* which is nothing but sorting
them under several Titles, is done by us, according to

the *Ideas* that we have of them : Which though sufficient to distinguish them by Names ; so that we may be able to Discourse of them, when we have them not present before us ; yet if we suppose it to be done by their real internal Constitutions, and that Things existing are distinguished by Nature into Species, by *real Essences*, according as we distinguish them into Species by Names, we shall be liable to great Mistakes.

§ 14. To distinguish substantial Beings into Species, according to the usual Supposition, that there are certain precise *Essences* or *Forms* of things, whereby all the Individuals existing, are, by Nature distinguish'd into Species, these Things are necessary.

Difficulties against a certain Number of real Essences.

§ 15. *First*, To be assured, that Nature, in the Production of Things, always Designs them to partake of certain regulated established *Essences*, which are to be the Models of all Things to be produced. This, in that crude Sense, it is usually proposed, would need some better Explication, before it can fully be assented to.

§ 16. *Secondly*, It would be necessary to know, whether Nature always attains that *Essence* it Designs in the Production of Things. The irregular and monstrous Births, that in divers sorts of Animals

have been observed, will always give us Reason to
doubt of one, or both of these.

§ 17. *Thirdly*, It ought to be determined, whether
those we call *Monsters*, be really a distinct Species,
according to the scholastick Notion of the Word
Species; since it is certain, that every thing that exists,
has its particular Constitution: And yet we find, that
some of these monstrous Productions, have few or
none of those Qualities, which are supposed to result
from, and Accompany the Essence of that Species,
from whence they derive their Originals, and to
which, by their Descent, they seem to belong.

§ 18. *Fourthly*, The *real Essences* of those Things,
which we distinguish into Species, and
as so distinguished we Name, ought to   *Our nominal
be known; i.e.* we ought to have *Ideas*   *Essences of
Substances,*
of them. But since we are ignorant in   *not perfect
Collections of
Properties.*
these four Points, *the supposed real Es-*
sences of Things stand us not in stead for the distin-
guishing Substances into Species.

§ 19. *Fifthly*, The only imaginable help in this
case would be, that having framed perfect complex
Ideas of the *Properties* of things, flowing from their
different real Essences, we should thereby distinguish
them into Species. But neither can this be done:
for being ignorant of the real Essence it self, it is
impossible to know all those Properties that flow

from it, and are so annexed to it, that any one of them being away, we may certainly conclude, that that Essence is not there, and so the thing is not of that Species. We can never know what are the precise Number of Properties depending on the real Essence of *Gold,* any one of which failing, the real Essence of Gold, and consequently Gold, would not be there, unless we knew the real Essence of Gold it self, and by that determined that Species. By the Word *Gold* here, I must be understood to design a particular piece of Matter; *v. g.* the last Guinea that was coined. For if it should stand here in its ordinary Signification for that complex *Idea* which I or any one else calls Gold; *i. e.* for the nominal Essence of Gold, it would be *Jargon*: so hard is it to shew the various Meaning and Imperfection of Words, when we have nothing else but Words to do it by.

§ 20. By all which it is clear, That our *distinguishing Substances into* Species by Names, *is not* at all *founded on their real Essences*; nor can we pretend to range, and determine 'em exactly into Species, according to internal essential Differences.

§ 21. But since, as has been remarked, we have need of general Words, though we know not the real Essences of Things; all we can do, is to collect such a Number *But such a Collection as our Name stands for.* of simple *Ideas*, as by Examination, we find to be

united together in Things existing, and thereof to
make one complex *Idea.* Which though it be not
the real Essence of any Substance that exists, is yet
the specifick Essence, to which our Name belongs, and
is convertible with it ; by which we may at least try
the Truth of these *nominal Essences.* For Example,
there be that say, that the *Essence* of *Body* is Extension : If it be so, we can never mistake in putting the
Essence of any thing for the Thing it self. Let us
then in Discourse, put *Extension* for *Body* ; and when
we would say, that Body moves, let us say that
Extension moves, and see how it will look. He that
should say, that one *Extension* by impulse moves
another *Extension,* would, by the bare *Expression,*
sufficiently shew the Absurdity of such a Notion.
The *Essence* of any thing, in respect of us, is the
whole complex *Idea,* comprehended and marked by
that Name ; and in Substances, besides the several
distinct simple *Ideas* that make them up, the confused one of Substance, or of an unknown support
and cause of their Union, is always a part : and
therefore the *Essence* of Body is not bare *Extension,*
but an extended solid thing ; and so to say, an
extended solid thing moves, or impels another, is all
one, and as intelligible, as to say, *Body* moves, or
impels. Likewise, to say, that a rational Animal is
capable of Conversation, is all one, as to say, a *Man.*

But no one will say, That Rationality is capable of Conversation, because it makes not the whole *Essence* to which we give the Name *Man*.

§ 22. There are Creatures in the World that have Shapes like ours, but are hairy, and want Language, and Reason. There are Naturals amongst us, that have perfectly our Shape, but want Reason, and some of them Language too. There *Our abstract Ideas are to us the Measures of Species; instance, in that of Man.* are Creatures, as 'tis said, (*sit fides penes Authorem*, but there appears no Contradiction that there should be such) that with Language, and Reason, and a shape in other Things agreeing with ours, have hairy Tails ; others where the Males have no Beards, and others where the Females have. If it be asked, whether these be all *Men*, or no, all of humane Species ; 'tis plain, the Question refers only to the nominal Essence : For those of them to whom the Definition of the Word *Man*, or the complex *Idea* signify'd by that Name, agrees, are *Men*, and the other not. But if the enquiry be made concerning the supposed *real Essence* ; and whether the internal Constitution and Frame of these several Creatures be specifically different, it is wholly impossible for us to answer, no part of that going into our specifick *Ideas* ; only we have Reason to think, that where the Faculties, or outward Frame so much differs, the

internal Constitution is not exactly the same: But
what Difference in the internal real Constitution
makes a specifick Difference, it is in vain to enquire;
whilst *our Measures of Species* be, as they *are, only
our abstract Ideas*, which we know; and not that
internal Constitution, which makes no part of them.
Shall the Difference of Hair only on the Skin, be a
mark of a different internal specifick Constitution
between a Changeling and a Drill, when they agree
in Shape, and want of Reason and Speech? And
shall not the want of Reason and Speech be a sign
to us of different real Constitutions and Species
between a Changeling and a reasonable Man? And
so of the rest, if we pretend that the Distinction of
Species or Sorts is fixedly establish'd by the real
Frame, and secret Constitutions of Things.

§ 23. Nor let any one say, that the Power of Propagation in Animals by the mixture of
Species not distinguished by Genera-tion. Male and Female, and in Plants by
Seeds, keeps the supposed real *Species*
distinct and entire. For granting this
to be true, it would help us in the Distinction of the
Species of Things no farther than the Tribes of
Animals and Vegetables. What must we do for the
rest? But in those too it is not sufficient: for if
History lye not, Women have conceived by Drills,
and what real Species, by that measure, such a Pro-

duction will be in Nature, will be a new Question: and we have Reason to think this is not impossible, since Mules and Jumarts, the one from the Mixture of an Ass and a Mare, the other from the Mixture of a Bull and a Mare, are so frequent in the World. I once saw a Creature that was the Issue of a Cat and a Rat, and had the plain Marks of both about it; wherein Nature appeared to have followed the Pattern of neither sort alone, but to have jumbled them both together. To which, he that shall add the monstrous Productions, that are so frequently to be met with in Nature, will find it hard, even in the race of Animals, to determine by the Pedigree of what *Species* every Animal's Issue is; and be at a loss about the *real Essence*, which he thinks certainly convey'd by Generation, and has alone a right to the specifick Name. But farther, if the *Species* of Animals and Plants are to be distinguished only by Propagation, must I go to the *Indies* to see the Sire and Dam of the one, and the Plant from which the Seed was gather'd, that produced the other, to know whether this be a Tyger or that Tea?

§ 24. Upon the whole matter, 'tis evident, that 'tis their own Collections of sensible Qua- *Not by sub-* lities, that Men make the Essences of *stantial Forms.* their several sorts of Substances; and that their real internal Structures are not considered by the greatest part of Men, in the sorting them. Much less were any *substantial Forms* ever thought on by any, but those who have in this one part of the World learned the Language of the Schools; and yet those ignorant Men, who pretend not any insight into the real Essences, nor trouble themselves about substantial Forms, but are content with knowing Things one from another, by their sensible Qualities, are often better acquainted with their Differences, can more nicely distinguish them from their Uses, and better know what they may expect from each, than those learned quick-sighted Men, who look so deep into them, and talk so confidently of something more hidden and essential.

§ 25. But supposing that the *real Essences* of Substances were discoverable by those that

The specifick Essences are made by the Mind.

would severely apply themselves to that Enquiry; yet we could not reasonably think, that the *ranking of things under general Names, was regulated by* those internal real Constitutions, or any thing else but *their obvious Appearances*: since Languages, in all Countries, have been established long before Sciences. So that they have not been Philosophers, or Logicians, or such who have troubled themselves about *Forms* and *Essences*, that have made the general Names, that are in use amongst the several Nations of Men: But those, more or less comprehensive Terms, have for the most part, in all Languages, received their Birth and Signification, from ignorant and illiterate People, who sorted and denominated Things, by those sensible Qualities they found in them, thereby to signify them, when absent, to others, whether they had an Occasion to mention a Sort, or a particular Thing.

§ 26. Since then it is evident, that we sort and name Substances by their *nominal,* and not by their real *Essences*; the next thing to be considered is, how, and by whom these *Essences* come to be made. *Therefore very various and uncertain.* As to the latter, 'tis evident they *are made by the Mind*, and not by Nature: For were they Nature's Workmanship, they could not be so various and different in several Men, as experience tells us they are. For if we will examine it, we shall not find the nominal Essence of any one *Species* of Substances, in all Men the same; no not of that, which of all others we are the most intimately acquainted with. It could not possibly be, that the abstract *Idea*, to which the Name *Man* is given, should be different in several Men, if it were of Nature's making; and that to one it should be *Animal rationale*, and to another, *Animal implume bipes latis unguibus.* He that annexes the Name *Man*, to a complex *Idea*, made up of Sense and spontaneous Motion, joined

to a Body of such a Shape, has thereby one Essence
of the *Species Man*: And he that, upon farther
Examination, adds Rationality, has another Essence
of the *Species* he calls *Man* : By which means, the
same individual will be a true *Man* to the one, which
is not so to the other. I think, there is scarce any
one will allow this upright Figure, so well known, to
be the essential difference of the *Species Man* ; and
yet how far Men determine of the sorts of Animals,
rather by their Shape, than Descent, is very visible ;
since it has been more than once debated, whether
several humane *Fœtus*'s should be preserved, or received to Baptism, or no, only because of the difference of their outward Configuration, from the
ordinary Make of Children, without knowing whether
they were not as capable of Reason, as Infants cast
in another Mould : Some whereof, though of an
approved shape, are never capable of as much appearance of Reason, all their Lives, as is to be
found in an Ape, or an Elephant ; and never give any
Signs of being acted by a rational Soul. Whereby
it is evident, that the outward Figure, which only
was found wanting, and not the Faculty of Reason,
which no Body could know would be wanting in its
due Season, was made essential to the Humane
Species. The learned Divine and Lawyer, must, on
such Occasions, renounce his sacred Definition of

Animal Rationale, and substitute some other Essence of the humane Species. Monsieur *Menage* furnishes us with an Example worth the taking Notice of on this occasion. *When the Abbot of St.* Martin, says he, *was born, he had so little of the Figure of a Man, that he bespake him rather a Monster. 'Twas for some time under Deliberation, whether he should be baptized or no. However, he was baptized and declared a Man provisionally* [till time should shew what he would prove] *Nature had moulded him so untowardly, that he was called all his Life the Abbot* Malotru, i. e. Ill-shaped. *He was of* Caen, Menagiana ₁₃₈. This Child we see was very near being excluded out of the Species of *Man,* barely by his Shape. He escaped very narrowly as he was, and 'tis certain a Figure a little more odly turned had cast him, and he had been executed as a thing not to be allowed to pass for a Man. And yet there can be no Reason given, why if the Lineaments of his Face had been a little altered, a rational Soul could not have been lodged in him, why a Visage somewhat longer, or a Nose flatter, or a wider Mouth could not have consisted, as well as the rest of his ill Figure, with such a Soul, such Parts, as made him, disfigured as he was, capable to be a Dignitary in the Church.

§ 27. Wherein then, would I gladly know, consists

the precise and *unmoveable Boundaries of that Species?*
'Tis plain, if we examine, there is *no* such Thing
made by Nature, and established by her amongst
Men. The real Essence of that, or any other sort
of Substances, 'tis evident we know not ; and therefore are so undetermined in our nominal Essences,
which we make our selves, that if several Men were
to be asked, concerning some odly shaped *Fœtus*,
as soon as born, whether it were a *Man*, or no, 'tis
past doubt, one should meet with different Answers.
Which could not happen, if the nominal Essences,
whereby we limit and distinguish the Species of
Substances, were not made by Man, with some
Liberty ; but were exactly copied from precise
Boundaries set by Nature, whereby it distinguished
all Substances into certain Species. Who would
undertake to resolve, what *Species* that Monster was
of, which is mentioned by *Licetus, lib.* I. *c.* 3. with a
Man's Head and Hog's Body ? Or those other, which
to the Bodies of Men had the Heads of Beasts, as
Dogs, Horses, *&c.* If any of these Creatures had
lived, and could have spoke, it would have increased
the Difficulty. Had the upper part, to the middle,
been of Humane Shape, and all below Swine ; Had
it been Murder to destroy it ? Or must the Bishop
have been consulted, whether it were Man enough
to be admitted to the Font, or no ? As I have

been told, it happened in *France* some Years since, in somewhat a like Case. So uncertain are the Boundaries of Species of Animals to us, who have no other Measures, than the complex *Ideas* of our own collecting : And so far are we from certainly knowing what a *Man* is ; though, perhaps, it will be judged great Ignorance to make any doubt about it. And yet, I think, I may say, that the certain Boundaries of that *Species*, are so far from being determined, and the precise number of simple *Ideas*, which make the nominal Essence, so far from being settled, and perfectly known, that very material Doubts may still arise about it : And I imagine, none of the Definitions of the Word *Man*, which we yet have, nor Descriptions of that sort of Animal, are so perfect and exact, as to satisfy a considerate inquisitive Person ; much less to obtain a general Consent, and to be that which Men would every where stick by, in the Decision of Cases, and determining of Life and Death, Baptism or no Baptism, in Productions that might happen.

§ 28. But though these *nominal Essences of Substances* are made by the Mind, they are *not yet made so arbitrarily, as those of mixed Modes.* To the making of any nominal Essence, it is necessary, *First,* That the *Ideas* whereof it consists, have such an Union as

But not so arbitrary as mixed Modes.

K

to make but one *Idea*, how compounded soever.
Secondly, That the particular *Ideas* so united, be
exactly the same, neither more nor less.   For if two
abstract complex *Ideas*, differ either in Number or
Sorts, of their component Parts, they make two
different, and not one and the same Essence.   In
the first of these, the Mind, in making its complex
Ideas of Substances, only follows Nature ; and puts
none together, which are not supposed to have an
Union in Nature.   No Body joins the Voice of a
Sheep, with the Shape of a Horse ; nor the Colour
of Lead, with the Weight and Fixedness of Gold, to
be the complex *Ideas* of any real Substances ; unless
he has a Mind to fill his Head with *Chimera*'s, and
his Discourse with unintelligible Words.   Men observing certain Qualities always joined and existing
together, therein copied Nature ; and of *Ideas* so
united, made their complex ones of Substances.
For though Men may make what complex *Ideas* they
please, and give what Names to them they will ; yet
if they will be understood, when they speak of
Things really existing, they must in some degree
conform their *Ideas* to the Things they would speak
of : Or else Mens Language will be like that of
Babel ; and every Man's Words being intelligible
only to himself, would no longer serve to Conversation, and the ordinary Affairs of Life, if the *Ideas*

they stand for be not some way answering the common appearances and agreement of Substances, as they really exist.

§ 29. *Secondly*, Though the Mind of Men, *in making* its *complex Ideas of Substances,* never puts any together that do not *Tho' very imperfect.* really, or are not suppos'd to co-exist ; and so it truly borrows that Union from Nature : Yet *the Number* it combines, *depends upon the various Care, Industry, or Fancy of him that makes it.* Men generally content themselves with some few sensible obvious Qualities ; and often, if not always, leave out others as material, and as firmly united, as those that they take. Of sensible Substances there are two sorts ; one of organized Bodies, which are propagated by Seed ; and in these, the Shape is that, which to us is the leading Quality, and most characteristical Part, that determines the *Species* : And therefore in Vegetables and Animals, an extended solid Substance of such a certain Figure usually serves the turn. For however some Men seem to prize their Definition of *Animal Rationale,* yet should there a Creature be found, that had Language and Reason, but partook not of the usual shape of a Man, I believe it would hardly pass for a *Man,* how much soever it were *Animal Rationale.* And if *Balaam's* Ass had, all his Life, discoursed as rationally as he

did once with his Master, I doubt yet, whether any
one would have thought him worthy the Name *Man*,
or allowed him to be of the same Species with
himself. As in Vegetables and Animals, 'tis the
Shape, so in most other Bodies, not propagated by
Seed, 'tis the Colour we most fix on, and are most
led by. Thus where we find the Colour of Gold, we
are apt to imagine all the other Qualities, comprehended in our complex *Idea*, to be there also : and
we commonly take these two obvious Qualities, *viz.*
Shape and Colour, for so presumptive *Ideas* of several
Species, that in a good Picture, we readily say, this
is a Lion, and that a Rose ; this is a Gold, and that
a Silver Goblet, only by the different Figures and
Colours, represented to the Eye by the Pencil.

§ 30. But though this serves well enough for gross

Which yet serve for common Converse. and confused Conceptions, and unac-
curate ways of Talking and Thinking ;
yet *Men are far enough from having
agreed on the precise number of simple* Ideas, *cr*
Qualities *belonging to any sort of Things, signified
by its Name.* Nor is it a wonder, since it requires
much Time, Pains and Skill, strict Enquiry, and
long Examination, to find out what, and how many
those simple *Ideas* are, which are constantly and
inseparably united in Nature, and are always to be
found together in the same Subject. Most Men

wanting either Time, Inclination, or Industry enough
for this, even to some tolerable degree, content
themselves with some few obvious, and outward
Appearances of Things, thereby readily to distinguish and sort them for the common Affairs of Life.
And so, without farther Examination, give them
Names, or take up the Names already in use.
Which, though in common Conversation they pass
well enough for the Signs of some few obvious
Qualities co-existing, are yet far enough from comprehending, in a settled Signification, a precise
Number of simple *Ideas* ; much less all those, which
are united in Nature. He that shall consider, after
so much stir, about *Genus* and *Species*, and such a
deal of Talk of specifick Differences, how few Words
we have yet settled Definitions of, may, with Reason,
imagine, that those *Forms*, which there hath been so
much noise made about, are only *Chimæras*, which
give us no light into the specifick Natures of Things.
And he that shall consider, how far the Names of
Substances are from having Significations, wherein
all who use them do agree, will have Reason to
conclude, that though the nominal Essences of Substances are all supposed to be copied from Nature,
yet they are all, or most of them, very imperfect.
Since the Composition of those complex *Ideas*, are,
in several Men, very different: and therefore, that

these Boundaries of *Species*, are as Men, and not as
Nature makes them, if at least there are in Nature
any such prefixed Bounds. 'Tis true, that many
particular Substances are so made by Nature, that
they have agreement and likeness one with another,
and so afford a Foundation of being ranked into
sorts. But the sorting of Things by us, or the
making of determinate *Species*, being in order to
naming and comprehending them under general
Terms, I cannot see how it can be properly said,
that Nature sets the Boundaries of the Species of
Things : Or if it be so, our Boundaries of Species
are not exactly conformable to those in Nature. For
we having need of general Names for present use,
stay not for a perfect Discovery of all those Qualities,
which would best shew us their most material Differences and Agreements ; but we our selves divide
them, by certain obvious Appearances, into *Species*,
that we may the easier, under general Names, communicate our Thoughts about them. . For having no
other Knowledg of any Substance, but of the simple
Ideas, that are united in it ; and observing several
particular Things to agree with others, in several of
those simple *Ideas*, we make that Collection our
specifick *Idea*, and give it a general Name ; that in
recording our own Thoughts, and in our Discourse
with others, we may in one short Word design all

the Individuals that agree in that complex *Idea,*
without enumerating the simple *Ideas,* that make it
up; and so not waste our Time and Breath in
tedious Descriptions: which we see they are fain to
do, who would Discourse of any new sort of Things,
they have not yet a Name for.

§ 31. But however, these *Species* of Substances
pass well enough in ordinary Conversa-
tion, it is plain, that this complex *Idea,* *Species under*
wherein they observe several Individuals *Name very*
to agree, is, by different Men, made *different.*
very differently; by some more, and others less
accurately. In some, this complex *Idea* contains a
greater, and in others a smaller Number of Qualities;
and so is apparently such as the Mind makes it.
The yellow shining Colour makes *Gold* to Children;
others add Weight, Malleableness, and Fusibility;
and others yet other Qualities, which they find joined
with that yellow Colour, as constantly as its Weight
and Fusibility :. For in all these, and the like Qualities, one has as good a Right to be put into the
complex *Idea* of that Substance, wherein they are
all joined, as another. And therefore *different Men*
leaving out, or putting in several simple *Ideas,*
which others do not, according to their various
Examination; Skill, or Observation of that Subject, *have different Essences of Gold*; which must

therefore be of their own, and not of Nature's making.

§ 32. If the *Number of simple* Ideas, *that make the nominal Essence* of the lowest *Species,* or

The more general our Ideas are, the more incomplete and partial they are. first sorting of Individuals, *depends on the Mind* of Man, variously collecting them, it is much more evident that they do so, in the more comprehensive *Classis,* which, by the Masters of Logick are called *Genera.* These are complex *Ideas* designedly imperfect: And 'tis visible at first sight, that several of those Qualities, that are to be found in the Things themselves, are purposely left out of *generical Ideas.* For as the Mind, to make general *Ideas,* comprehending several particulars, leaves out those of Time, and Place, and such other that make them incommunicable to more than one Individual ; so to make other yet more general *Ideas,* that may comprehend different sorts, it leaves out those Qualities that distinguish them, and puts into its new Collection, only such *Ideas,* as are common to several sorts. The same Convenience that made Men express several Parcels of yellow Matter coming from *Guinea* and *Peru,* under one Name, sets them also upon making of one Name, that may comprehend both Gold, and Silver, and some other Bodies of different sorts. This is done by leaving out those Qualities, which are peculiar to each sort; and retaining a complex *Idea* made up of those that are common to them all. To which the Name *Metal* being annexed, there is a *Genus* constituted; the *Essence* whereof being that abstract *Idea*, containing only Malleableness and Fusibility, with certain Degrees of Weight and Fixedness, wherein some Bodies of several Kinds agree, leaves out the Colour, and other Qualities peculiar to Gold and Silver, and the other sorts comprehended under the Name *Metal*. Whereby it is plain, that Men follow not exactly the Patterns set them by Nature, when they make their general *Ideas* of Substances; since there is no Body to be found, which has barely Malleableness and Fusibility in it, without other Qualities as inseparable as those. But Men, in making their general *Ideas*, seeing more the convenience of Language and quick dispatch, by short and comprehensive Signs, than the true and precise Nature of Things, as they exist, have, in the framing their abstract *Ideas*, chiefly pursued that end, which was to be furnished with store of general and variously comprehensive Names. So that in this whole business of *Genera* and *Species*, the *Genus*, or more comprehensive, is but a partial Conception of what is in the *Species*, and the *Species*, but a partial *Idea* of what is to be found in each Individual. If therefore any one will think, that a *Man*, and a

Horse, and an *Animal,* and a *Plant, &c.* are distinguished by real Essences made by Nature, he must think Nature to be very liberal of these real Essences, making one for Body, another for an Animal, and another for a Horse, and all these *Essences* liberally bestowed upon *Bucephalus.* But if we would rightly consider what is done, in all these *Genera* and *Species,* or *Sorts,* we should find, that there is no new Thing made, but only more or less comprehensive Signs whereby we may be enabled to express, in a few Syllables, great Numbers of particular Things, as they agree in more or less general Conceptions, which we have framed to that purpose. In all which, we may observe, that the more general Term, is always the Name of a less complex *Idea*; and that each *Genus* is but a partial Conception of the Species comprehended under it. So that if these abstract general *Ideas* be thought to be complete, it can only be in respect of a certain established Relation between them and certain Names, which are made use of to signify them; and not in respect of any thing existing, as made by Nature.

This all accommodated to the end of Speech. § 33. *This* is *adjusted to the true end of Speech,* which is to be the easiest and shortest way of communicating our Notions. For thus he, that would discourse of Things, as they agreed in the complex

Idea of Extension and Solidity, needed but use the Word *Body* to denote all such. He that to these would join others, signified by the Words Life, Sense, and spontaneous Motion, needed but use the word *Animal*, to signify all which partook of those *Ideas*: and he that had made a complex *Idea* of a Body, with Life, Sense, and Motion, with the Faculty of Reasoning, and a certain Shape joined to it, needed but use the short Monosyllable *Man* to express all particulars that correspond to that complex *Idea*. This is the proper business of *Genus* and *Species*: And this Men do, without any Consideration of *real Essences* or *substantial Forms*, which come not within the reach of our Knowledg, when we think of those things; nor within the Signification of our Words, when we Discourse with others.

§ 34. Were I to talk with any one of a sort of Birds, I lately saw in St. *James's* Park, about Three or Four Foot High, with a *Instance in Cassuaries.* Covering of something between Feathers and Hair, of a dark brown Colour, without Wings, but in the Place thereof, two or three little Branches, coming down like Sprigs of *Spanish* Broom: long great Legs, with Feet only of Three Claws, and without a Tail; I must make this Description of it, and so may make others understand me: But when I am told, that the Name of it is *Cassuaris*, I may then use that Word

to stand in Discourse for all my complex *Idea* mentioned in that Description ; though by that Word,
which is now become a specifick Name, I know no
more of the real Essence, or Constitution of that
sort of Animals, than I did before ; and knew probably as much of the Nature of that *Species* of Birds,
before I learned the Name, as many *Englishmen* do
of Swans, or Herons, which are specifick Names, very
well known of sorts of Birds common in *England*.

§ 35. From what has been said, 'tis evident, that

Men deter- *Men make sorts of Things.* For it being
mine the sorts. different *Essences* alone that make different *Species*, 'tis plain, that they who make those
abstract *Ideas*, which are the *nominal Essences*, do
thereby make the *Species*, or Sort. Should there be
a Body found, having all the other Qualities of Gold,
except Malleableness, 'twould, no doubt, be made a
Question whether it were Gold or no ; *i. e.* whether
it were of that *Species*. This could be determined
only by that abstract *Idea*, to which every one
annexed the Name *Gold* : so that it would be true
Gold to him, and belong to that *Species* who included
not Malleableness in his *nominal Essence*, signified
by the Sound *Gold* ; and on the other side, it would
not be true Gold, or of that *Species* to him, who
included Malleableness in his specifick *Idea*. And
who, I pray, is it, that makes these diverse *Species*,

even under one and the same Name, but Men that make two different abstract *Ideas*, consisting not exactly of the same Collection of Qualities? ·Nor is it a mere Supposition to imagine, that a Body may exist, wherein the other obvious Qualities of Gold may be without Malleableness; since it is certain, that Gold it self will be sometimes so eager, (as Artists call it) that it will as little endure the Hammer, as Glass it self. .What we have said, of the putting in, or leaving Malleableness out of the complex *Idea*, the Name *Gold* is by any one annexed to, may be said of its peculiar Weight, Fixedness, and several other the like Qualities: For whatsoever is left out, or put in, 'tis still the complex *Idea*, to which that Name is annexed, that makes the *Species*: and as any particular parcel of matter answers that *Idea*, so the Name of the sort belongs truly to it; and it is of that *Species*. And thus any thing is true *Gold*, perfect *Metal*. All which Determination of the Species, 'tis plain, depends on the Understanding of Man, making this or that complex *Idea*.

§ 36. This then, in short, is the Case: *Nature makes many particular Things which do agree one with another, in many sensible Qualities*, and probably too, in their internal Frame and Constitution: but 'tis not this *real Essence* that distinguishes them into *Species*; 'tis *Men*, who, taking

Nature makes the Simili-tude.

occasion from the Qualities they find united in them, and wherein they observe often several Individuals to agree, *range them into Sorts, in order to their Naming*, for the convenience of comprehensive Signs; under which Individuals according to their Conformity to this or that abstract *Idea*, come to be ranked as under Ensigns ; so that this is of the Blue, that the Red Regiment ; this is a Man, that a Drill : And in this, I think, consists the whole business of *Genus* and *Species*.

§ 37. I do not deny, but Nature, in the constant Production of particular Beings, makes them not always new and various, but very much alike, and of kin one to another : But I think it nevertheless true, that *the Boundaries of the* Species, *whereby Men sort them, are made by Men* ; since the Essences of the Species, distinguished by different Names, are, as has been proved, of Man's making, and seldom adequate to the internal Nature of the Things they are taken from.   So that we may truly say, such a manner of sorting of Things, is the Workmanship of Men.

§ 38. One thing I doubt not, but will seem very strange in this Doctrine ; which is, that from what has been said, it will follow, that *each abstract* Idea, *with a Name to it, makes a distinct Species*.   But who can help it, if Truth will have it so ?   For so it must remain till

Each abstract Idea is an Essence.

some body can shew us the *Species* of Things, limited and distinguished by something else : and let us see, that general Terms signify not our abstract *Ideas*, but something different from them. I would fain know, why a Shock and a Hound, are not as distinct Species, as a Spaniel and an Elephant. We have no other *Idea* of the different Essence of an Elephant and a Spaniel, than we have of the different Essence of a Shock and a Hound ; all the essential difference, whereby we know and distinguish them one from another, consisting only in the different Collection of simple *Ideas*, to which we have given those different Names.

§ 39. How much *the making of* Species *and* Genera *is in order to general Names*, and how much general Names are necessary, if not to the Being, yet at least to the completing of a Species, and making it

> Genera *and* Species *are in order to naming.*

pass for such, will appear, besides what has been said above concerning Ice and Water, in a very familiar Example. A silent and a striking *Watch*, are but one *Species*, to those who have but one Name for 'em : but he that has the Name *Watch* for one, and *Clock* for the other, and distinct complex *Ideas*, to which those Names belong, to him they are different Species. It will be said, perhaps, that the inward Contrivance and Constitution is different between these two, which the Watch-maker has a clear *Idea* of. And yet, 'tis plain, they are but one Species to him, when he has but one Name for them. For what is sufficient in the inward Contrivance, to make a new *Species?* There are some *Watches,* that are made with four Wheels, others with five: Is this a specifick difference to the Workman? Some have Strings and Physies, and others none; some have the Balance loose, and others regulated by a spiral Spring, and others by Hogs Bristles: Are any, or all of these enough to make a specifick Difference to the Workman, that knows each of these, and several other different Contrivances, in the internal Constitutions of *Watches?* 'Tis certain, each of these hath a real Difference from the rest: But whether it be an essential, a specifick difference or no, relates only to the complex *Idea,* to which the Name *Watch* is given: as long as they all agree in the *Idea* which that Name stands for, and that Name does not as a generical Name comprehend different *Species* under it, they are not essentially nor specifically different. But if any one will make minuter Divisions from Differences that he knows in the internal Frame of Watches, and to such precise complex *Ideas,* give Names that shall prevail, they will then be new *Species* to them, who have those *Ideas* with Names to them; and can, by those Differences, distinguish

Watches into these several sorts, and then *Watch*
will be a generical Name. But yet they would be
no distinct *Species* to Men, ignorant of Clock-work,
and the inward Contrivances of Watches, who had no
other *Idea*, but the outward Shape and Bulk, with
the marking of the Hours by the Hand. For to
them all those other Names would be but synonymous Terms for the same *Idea*, and signify no more,
nor no other thing but a *Watch*. Just thus, I think,
it is in natural Things. No Body will doubt, that
the Wheels, or Springs (if I may so say) within, are
different in a *rational Man*, and a *Changeling*, no
more than that there is a Difference in the Frame
between a *Drill*, and a *Changeling*. But whether one
or both these Differences be essential, or specifical,
is only to be known to us, by their Agreement, or
Disagreement with the complex *Idea* that the Name
Man stands for : For by that alone can it be determined, whether one, or both, or neither of those be
a Man, or no.

§ 40. From what has been before said, we may
see the Reason *why, in the Species of
artificial Things, there is generally less*   *Species of ar-*
Confusion and Uncertainty, than in   *tificial things*
Natural. Because an *artificial* thing   *less confused*
than natural.
being a Production of Man, which the Artificer
design'd, and therefore well knows the *Idea* of, the

L

Name of it is supposed to stand for no other *Idea*, nor to import any other Essence, than what is certainly to be known, and easy enough to be apprehended. For the *Idea*, or *Essence*, of the several sorts of *artificial* Things, consisting, for the most part, in nothing but the determinate Figure of sensible Parts ; and sometimes Motion depending thereon, which the Artificer fashions in Matter, such as he finds for his Turn, it is not beyond the reach of our Faculties to attain a certain *Idea* thereof ; and so settle the Signification of the Names whereby the Species of *artificial* Things are distinguished, with less Doubt, Obscurity, and Equivocation, than we can in Things natural, whose Differences and Operations depend upon Contrivances, beyond the reach of our Discoveries.

§ 41. I must be excused here, if I think, *artificial*

Artificial things of distinct Species. *Things are of distinct Species*, as well as natural : Since I find they are as plainly and orderly ranked into sorts, by different abstract *Ideas*, with general Names annexed to them, as distinct one from another as those of natural Substances. For why should we not think a Watch, and Pistol, as distinct Species one from another, as a *Horse*, and a *Dog*, they being expressed in our Minds by distinct *Ideas*, and to others, by distinct Appellations ?

§ 42. This is farther to be observed concerning *Substances*, that they *alone* of all our several sorts of *Ideas, have* particular, or *proper Names*, whereby one only par- *Substances a- lone have pro- per Names.* ticular thing is signify'd. Because in simple *Ideas*, Modes, and Relations, it seldom happens that Men have occasion to mention often this, or that particular, when it is absent. Besides, the greatest part of mixed Modes, being Actions which perish in their Birth, are not capable of a lasting Duration, as Sub- stances, which are the Actors ; and wherein the simple *Ideas* that make up the complex *Ideas* designed by the Name, have a lasting Union.

§ 43. I must beg pardon of my Reader, for having dwelt so long upon this Sub- ject, and perhaps, with some Ob- *Difficulty to treat of Words.* scurity. But I desire it may be con- sidered, how *difficult* it is, *to lead another by Words into the Thoughts of Things, strip'd of those speci- fical Differēnces* we give 'em : Which things, if I name not, I say nothing ; and if I do name them, I thereby rank them into some sort, or other, and suggest to the mind the usual abstract *Idea* of that Species ; and so cross my purpose. For to talk of a *Man*, and to lay by, at the same time, the ordinary Signification of the Name *Man*, which is our complex *Idea*, usually annexed to it ; and bid

the Reader consider *Man*, as he is in himself, and as
he is really distinguished from others, in his internal
Constitution, or real Essence, that is, by something,
he knows not what, looks like trifling : and yet thus
one must do, who would speak of the supposed real
Essences and Species of Things, as thought to be
made by Nature, if it be but only to make it understood, that there is no such thing signified by the
general Names, which Substances are called by. But
because it is difficult by known familiar Names to do
this, give me leave to endeavour by an Example, to
make the different Consideration, the Mind has of
specifick Names and *Ideas,* a little more clear ; and to
shew how the complex *Ideas* of Modes are referred
sometimes to Archetypes in the Minds of other intelligent Beings ; or, which is the same, to the Signification annexed by others to their received Names ;
and sometimes to no Archetypes at all. Give me
leave also to shew how the Mind always refers its
Ideas of Substances, either to the Substances themselves, or to the Signification of their Names, as to
the *Archetypes* ; and also to make plain the Nature
of Species, or sorting of Things, as apprehended,
and made use of by us ; and of the Essences belonging to those Species, which is, perhaps, of more
Moment, to discover the Extent and Certainty of
our Knowledg, than we at first imagine.

§ 44. Let us suppose *Adam* in the State of a grown Man, with a good Understanding, but in a strange Country, with all Things new, and unknown about him ; and no other Faculties, to attain the Knowledg *Instances of mixed Modes in Kinneah and Niouph.* of them, but what one of this Age has now. He observes *Lamech* more Melancholy than usual, and imagines it to be from a Suspicion he has of his Wife *Adah* (whom he most ardently loved) that she had too much kindness for another Man. *Adam* Discourses these his Thoughts to *Eve*, and desires her to take care that *Adah* commit not Folly : And in these Discourses with *Eve*, he makes use of these two new Words, *Kinneah* and *Niouph*. In time, *Adam*'s Mistake appears, for he finds *Lamech*'s Trouble proceeded from having killed a Man : But yet the two Names, *Kinneah* and *Niouph* ; the one standing for Suspicion, in a Husband, of his Wife's Disloyalty to him, and the other, for the Act of committing Disloyalty, lost not their distinct Significations. It is plain then, that here were two distinct complex *Ideas* of mixed Modes, with Names to them, two distinct Species of Actions essentially different ; I ask wherein consisted the Essences of these two distinct *Species* of Actions ? And 'tis plain, it consisted in a precise Combination of simple *Ideas*, different in one from the other. I ask, whether the complex *Idea* in *Adam's* Mind, which he called *Kinneah,* were adequate or no ? And it is plain it was ; for it being a · Combination of simple *Ideas,* which he without any regard to any Archetype, without respect to any thing as a Pattern, voluntarily put together, abstracted and gave the Name *Kinneah* to, to express in short to others, by that one sound, all the simple *Ideas* contained · and united in that complex one ; it must necessarily follow, that it was an adequate *Idea*. His own Choice having made that Combination, it had all in it he intended it should, and so could not but be perfect, could not but be adequate, it being referred to no other Archetype, which it was supposed to represent.

§ 45. These Words, *Kinneah* and *Niouph,* by Degrees grew into common Use ; and then the Case was somewhat altered. *Adam's* Children had the same Faculties, and thereby the same Power that he had, to make what complex *Ideas* of mixed Modes they pleased in their own Minds ; to abstract them, and make what Sounds, they pleased, the Signs of them : But the use of Names being to make our *Ideas* within us known to others, that cannot be done, but when the same Sign stands for the same *Idea* in two who would communicate their Thoughts, and Discourse together. Those therefore of *Adam's* Children, that found these two Words, *Kinneah* and

Niouph, in familiar use, could not take them for insignificant Sounds ; but must needs conclude, they stood for something, for certain *Ideas,* abstract *Ideas,* they being general Names, which abstract *Ideas* were the Essences of the Species distinguished by those Names. If therefore they would use these Words, as Names of Species already established and agreed on, they were obliged to Conform the *Ideas,* in their Minds, signify'd by these Names, to the *Ideas,* that they stood for in other Mens Minds, as to their Patterns and *Archetypes* ; and then indeed their *Ideas* of these complex Modes were liable to be inadequate, as being very apt (especially those that consisted of Combinations of many simple *Ideas*) not to be exactly conformable to the *Ideas* in other Mens Minds, using the same Names ; though for this, there be usually a Remedy at Hand, which is, to ask the meaning of any Word, we understand not, of him that Uses it : it being as impossible to know certainly, what the Words Jealousy and Adultery (which I think answer קנאה and נאוף) stand for in another Man's Mind, with whom I would discourse about them ; as it was impossible, in the beginning of Language, to know what *Kinneah* and *Niouph* stood for in another Man's Mind, without Explication, they being voluntary Signs in every one.

§ 46. Let us now also consider after the same

Manner, the Names of Substances, in their first

Instance of Application. One of *Adam*'s Children,
Substances in roving in the Mountains, lights on a
Zahab.
glittering Substance, which pleases his
Eye, home he carries it to *Adam*, who, upon Consideration of it, finds it to be hard, to have a bright yellow
Colour, and an exceeding great Weight. These,
perhaps at first, are all the Qualities he takes Notice
of in it, and abstracting this complex *Idea*, consisting
of a Substance having that peculiar bright Yellowness, and a Weight very great in Proportion to its
Bulk, he gives it the Name *Zahab*, to denominate
and mark all Substances that have these sensible
Qualities in them. 'Tis evident now that, in this
Case, *Adam* acts quite differently, from what he did
before in forming those *Ideas* of mixed Modes, to
which he gave the Name *Kinneah* and *Niouph*. For
there he puts *Ideas* together, only by his own Imagination, not taken from the Existence of any thing ;
and to them he gave Names to denominate all
Things, that should happen to agree to those his
abstract *Ideas*, without considering whether any such
thing did exist, or no ; the Standard there was of
his own making. But in the forming his *Idea* of
this new Substance he takes the quite contrary
Course ; here he has a Standard made by Nature ;
and therefore being to represent that to himself,

by the *Idea* he has of it, even when it is absent, he puts in no simple *Idea* into his complex one, but what he has the Perception of from the thing it self. He takes care that his *Idea* be conformable to this *Archetype*, and intends the Name should stand for an *Idea* so conformable.

§ 47. This piece of Matter, thus denominated *Zahab* by *Adam*, being quite different from any he had seen before, no Body, I think, will deny to be a distinct Species, and to have its peculiar Essence ; and that the Name *Zahab* is the mark of the Species, and a Name belonging to all Things partaking in that Essence. But here it is plain, the Essence *Adam* made the Name *Zahab* stand for, was nothing but a Body hard, shining, yellow, and very heavy. But the inquisitive Mind of Man, not content with the Knowledg of these, as I may say, superficial Qualities, puts *Adam* on farther Examination of this Matter. He therefore knocks, and beats it with Flints, to see what was discoverable in the Inside : He finds it yield to Blows, but not easily separate into Pieces : he finds it will bend without breaking. Is not now Ductility to be added to his former *Idea*, and made part of the *Essence* of the *Species* that Name *Zahab* stands for ? Farther Trials discover Fusibility, and Fixedness. Are not they also, by the same Reason, that any of the others were, to be put into the com-

plex *Idea*, signified by the Name *Zahab*? If not,
What Reason will there be shewn more for the one
than the other? If these must, then all the other
Properties, which any farther Trials shall discover in this Matter, ought by the same Reason
to make a part of the Ingredients of the complex *Idea*, which the Name *Zahab* stands for,
and so be the *Essence* of the *Species*, marked by
that Name. Which Properties, because they are
endless, it is plain, that the *Idea* made after this
Fashion by this *Archetype*, will be always inadequate.

§ 48. But this is not all, it would also follow, that
the *Names of Substances* would not
Their Ideas
imperfect, only have, (as in Truth they have) but
and therefore would also be supposed to *have different*
various.
Significations, as us'd by different Men,
which would very much cumber the Use of Language. For if every distinct Quality, that were discovered in any Matter by any one, were supposed to
make a necessary part of the complex *Idea*, signified
by the common Name given it, it must follow, that
Men must suppose the same Word to signify different
Things in different Men: since they cannot doubt,
but different Men may have discovered several Qualities in Substances of the same Denomination, which
others know nothing of.

§ 49. To avoid this therefore, they have *supposed a real Essence belonging to every Species*, from which these Properties all flow, and would have their Name of the Species stand for that. But they not having any *Idea* of that *real Essence* in Substances, and their Words signifying nothing but the *Ideas* they have, that which is done by this Attempt, is only to put the Name or Sound, in the Place and Stead of the thing having that real Essence, without knowing what the *real Essence* is ; and this is that which Men do, when they speak of Species of Things, as supposing them made by Nature, and distinguished by real Essences.

Therefore to fix their Species, a real Essence is supposed.

§ 50. For let us consider, when we affirm, that all *Gold* is fixed, either it means that Fixedness is a part of the Definition, part of the nominal Essence the Word *Gold* stands for ; and so this Affirmation, *all Gold is fixed*, contains nothing but the Signification of the Term *Gold.* Or else it means, that Fixedness not being a part of the Definition in the Word *Gold*, is a Property of that Substance it self : in which Case, it is plain, that the Word *Gold* stands in the Place of a Substance, having the real Essence of a Species of Things, made by Nature. In which way of Substitution, it has so confused and uncertain a Significa-

Which Supposition is of no use.

tion, that though this Proposition, *Gold is fixed*, be in that Sense an Affirmation of something real ; yet 'tis a Truth will always fail us in its particular Application, and so is of no real Use nor Certainty.   For let it be ever so true, that all *Gold*, *i. e.* all that has the real Essence of *Gold*, is fixed, What serves this for, whilst we know not in this Sense, what is, or is not *Gold*?   For if we know not the real Essence of Gold, 'tis impossible we should know what parcel of Matter has that Essence, and so whether it be true *Gold* or no.

§ 51. To conclude ; What liberty *Adam* had at
Conclusion.   first to make any complex *Ideas* of mix'd Modes, by no other Pattern, but by his own Thoughts, the same have all Men ever since had.   And the same Necessity of conforming his *Ideas* of Substances to Things without him, as to *Archetypes* made by Nature, that *Adam* was under, if he would not wilfully impose upon himself, the same are all Men ever since under too.   The same Liberty also, that *Adam* had of affixing any new Name to any *Idea*, the same has any one still, (especially the beginners of Languages, if we can imagine any such,) but only with this Difference, that in Places, where Men in Society have already established a Language amongst them, the Signification of Words are very warily and sparingly to be

altered. Because Men being furnished already with Names for their *Ideas*, and common Use having appropriated known Names to certain *Ideas*, an affected Misapplication of them cannot but be very ridiculous. He that hath new Notions, will, perhaps, venture sometimes on the coining new Terms to express them : But Men think it a Boldness, and 'tis uncertain, whether common Use will ever make them pass for currant. But in Communication with others, it is necessary, that we conform the *Ideas* we make the Vulgar Words of any Language stand for, to their known proper Significations, (which I have explained at large already,) or else to make known that new Signification we apply them to.

CHAPTER VII.

OF PARTICLES.

§ 1. Besides Words, which are Names of *Ideas* in
the Mind, there are a great many others
Particles con-
nect Parts, or that are made use of, to signify the
whole Senten-
ces together. *Connection* that the Mind gives to *Ideas*,
or Propositions, one with another. The
Mind in communicating its Thought to others, does
not only need Signs of the *Ideas* it has then before
it, but others also, to shew or intimate some particular Action of its own, at that time, relating to
those *Ideas.* This it does several ways ; as, *Is*, and
Is not, are the general Marks of the Mind affirming
or denying. But besides Affirmation, or Negation,
without which there is in Words no Truth or Falshood, the Mind does, in declaring its Sentiments to
others, connect not only the Parts of Propositions,
but whole Sentences one to another, with their
several Relations and Dependencies, to make a
coherent Discourse.

§ 2. The Words, whereby it signifies what Con-

nection it gives to the several Affirmations. and Negations, that it Unites in one con-
tinu'd Reasoning or Narration, are gene- *In them consists the Art of well speaking.* rally called *Particles*; and 'tis in the right Use of these, that more particularly consists the clearness and beauty of a good Stile. To think well, it is not enough, that a Man has his *Ideas* clear and distinct in his Thoughts, nor that he observes the Agreement, or Disagreement, of some of them ; but he must think in train, and observe the dependence of his Thoughts and Reasonings, one upon another : And to express well such methodical and rational Thoughts, he must have Words to *shew* what *Connection, Restriction, Distinction, Opposition, Emphasis,* &c. he gives to each respective *part of his Discourse.* To mistake in any of these, is to puzzle, instead of informing his Hearer : and therefore it is, that those Words, which are not truly, by themselves, the Names of any *Ideas*, are of such constant and indispensible use in Language, and do much to contribute to Mens well expressing themselves.

§ 3. This part of Grammar has been, perhaps, as much neglected, as some others over-diligently cultivated. 'Tis easy for Men to write, one after another, *They shew what Relation the Mind gives to its own Thoughts.* of *Cases* and *Genders, Moods* and *Tenses, Gerunds* and *Supines*: In these and the like, there has been great Diligence used; and Particles themselves, in some Languages, have been with great shew of exactness, ranked into their several Orders. But though *Prepositions* and *Conjunctions*, &c. are Names well known in Grammar, and the Particles contained under them carefully ranked into their distinct Subdivisions; yet he who would shew the right use of Particles, and what Significancy and Force they have, must take a little more Pains, enter into his own Thoughts, and observe nicely the several Postures of his Mind in discoursing.

§ 4. Neither is it enough, for the explaining of these Words, to render them, as is usually in Dictionaries, by Words of another Tongue which came nearest to their Signification: For what is meant by them, is commonly as hard to be understood in one, as another Language. They are all *marks of some Action or Intimation of the Mind*; and therefore to understand them rightly, the several Views, Postures, Stands, Turns, Limitations, and Exceptions, and several other Thoughts of the Mind, for which we have either none, or very deficient Names, are diligently to be studied. Of these, there are a great Variety, much exceeding the number of Particles, that most Languages have to express them

They shew what Relation the Mind gives to its own Thoughts.

by ; and therefore it is not to be wondred, that most of these Particles have divers, and sometimes almost opposite Significations. In the Hebrew Tongue, there is a particle consisting but of one single Letter, of which there are reckoned up, as I remember, Seventy, I am sure above Fifty several Significations.

§ 5. *BUT* is a Particle, none more familiar in our Language : and he that says it is a dis- *Instance in* cretive Conjunction, and that it answers *But.* *Sed* in Latin, or *Mais* in *French*, thinks he has sufficiently explained it. But it seems to me to intimate several Relations, the Mind gives to the several Propositions or Parts of them, which it joins by this Monosyllable.

First, *BUT to say no more* : Here it intimates a Stop of the Mind, in the Course it was going, before it came to the end of it.

Secondly, *I saw BUT two Plants* : Here it shews, that the Mind limits the Sense to what is expressed, with a Negation of all other.

Thirdly, *You Pray* ; *BUT it is not that GOD would bring you to the true Religion.*

Fourthly, *BUT that he would confirm you in your own* : The first of these *BUTS* intimates a Supposition in the Mind of something otherwise than it should be ; the latter shews, that the Mind makes a

M

direct Opposition between that, and what goes before it.

Fifthly, *All Animals have Sense* ; *BUT a Dog is an Animal* : Here it signifies little more, but that the latter Proposition is joined to the former, as the *Minor* of a Syllogism.

§ 6. To these, I doubt not, might be added a great many other Significations of this Particle, if it were my business to examine it in its full Latitude, and consider it in all the Places it is to be found : which if one should do, I doubt, whether in all those Manners it is made Use of, it would deserve the Title of *Discretive*, which Grammarians give to it. But I intend not here a full Explication of this sort of Signs. The Instances I have given in this one, may give occasion to reflect upon their Use and Force in Language, and lead us into the Contemplation of several Actions of our Minds in discoursing, which it has found a way to intimate to others by these Particles, some whereof constantly, and others in certain Constructions, have the Sense of a whole Sentence contained in them.

CHAPTER VIII.

OF ABSTRACT AND CONCRETE TERMS.

§ 1. The ordinary Words of Language, and our common use of 'em, would have given us light into the Nature of our *Ideas*, if they had been but considered with Attention. The Mind, as has been *Abstract Terms not predicable one of another, and why.* shewn, has a Power to abstract its *Ideas*, and so they become Essences, general Essences, whereby the sorts of Things are distinguished. Now each abstract *Idea* being distinct, so that of any two the one can never be the other, the Mind will, by its intuitive Knowledg, perceive their difference ; and therefore in Propositions, no two whole *Ideas* can ever be affirmed one of another. This we see in the common use of Language, which permits *not any two Abstract Words, or Names of abstract Ideas*, to be *affirmed one of another.* For how near of kin soever they may seem to be, and how certain soever it is, that Man is an Animal, or Rational, or White, yet every one, at first hearing, perceives the Falshood of these

Propositions ; *Humanity is Animality,* or *Rationality,* or *Whiteness* : And this is as evident, as any of the most allowed Maxims. All our Affirmations then are only inconcrete, which is the affirming, not one abstract *Idea* to be another, but one abstract *Idea* to be joined to another ; which abstract *Ideas,* in Substances, may be of any sort ; in all the rest, are little else but of Relations ; and in Substances, the most frequent are of Powers ; *v. g. a Man is White,* signifies, that the Thing that has the Essence of a Man, has also in it the Essence of Whiteness, which is nothing but a Power to produce the *Idea* of Whiteness in one, whose Eyes can discover ordinary Objects ; or *a Man is rational,* signifies, that the same Thing, that hath the Essence of a Man, hath also in it the Essence of Rationality, *i. e.* a Power of Reasoning.

§ 2. This Distinction of Names, shews us also the

They shew the difference of our Ideas.

difference of our *Ideas* : For if we observe them, we shall find, that our *Simple Ideas have all Abstract, as well as Concrete Names* : The one whereof is (to speak the Language of Grammarians) a Substantive, the other an Adjective ; as Whiteness, White, Sweetness, Sweet. The like also holds in our *Ideas* of Modes and Relations ; as Justice, Just ; Equality, Equal ; only with this difference, That some of the Concrete

Names of Relations, amongst Men chiefly, are Sub-
stantives; as *Paternitas, Pater*; whereof it were
easy to render a Reason. But as to our *Ideas* of
Substances, we have very few or *no Abstract Names*
at all. For though the Schools have introduced
Animalitas, Humanitas, Corporietas, and some others;
yet they hold no Proportion with that infinite
Number of Names of Substances, to which they
never were ridiculous enough to attempt the coining
of abstract ones: and those few that the Schools
forged, and put into the Mouths of their Scholars,
could never yet get Admittance into common Use,
or obtain the License of publick Approbation.
Which seems to me at least to intimate the Con-
fession of all Mankind, that they have no *Ideas* of
the real Essences of Substances, since they have not
Names for such *Ideas*: Which no doubt they would
have had, had not their consciousness to themselves
of their Ignorance of them, kept them from so idle
an attempt. And therefore though they had *Ideas*
enough to distinguish Gold from a Stone, and Metal
from Wood; yet they but timorously ventured on
such Terms, as *Aurietas* and *Saxietas*, *Metallietas*
and *Lignietas*, or the like Names, which should
pretend to signify the real Essences of those Substances, whereof they knew they had no *Ideas*. And
indeed, it was only the Doctrine of *substantial Forms*,

and the Confidence of mistaking Pretenders to a Knowledg that they had not, which first coined, and then introduced *Animalitas*, and *Humanitas*, and the like; which yet went very little farther than their own Schools, and could never get to be current amongst Understanding Men. Indeed, *Humanitas* was a Word familiar amongst the *Romans*; but in a far different Sence, and stood not for the abstract Essence of any Substance; but was the abstract Name of a Mode, and its concrete *Humanus*, not *Homo.*

CHAPTER IX.

OF THE IMPERFECTION OF WORDS.

§ 1. From what has been said in the foregoing Chapters, it is easy to perceive, what Imperfection there is in Language, and how the very Nature of Words makes it almost unavoidable, for many of them *Words are us'd for recording and communicating our Thoughts.* to be doubtful and uncertain in their Significations. To examine the Perfection, or Imperfection of Words it is necessary first to consider their use and end: For as they are more or less fitted to attain that, so are they more or less perfect. We have, in the former part of this Discourse, often, upon occasion, mentioned *a double use of Words.*

First, One for the recording of our own Thoughts.

Secondly, The other for the communicating of our Thoughts to others.

§ 2. As to the first of these, *for the recording our own Thoughts* for the help of our own Memories, whereby, as it were, we talk to our selves, any Words will serve the *Any Words will serve for recording.* turn. For since Sounds are voluntary and indifferent

Signs of any *Ideas*, a Man may use what Words he pleases, to signify his own *Ideas* to himself: and there will be no Imperfection in them, if he constantly use the same Sign for the same *Idea*, for then he cannot fail of having his meaning understood, wherein consists the Right Use and Perfection of Language.

§ 3. *Secondly*, As to *Communication of Words*, that too *has a double Use.*

Communica-
tion by Words   I. *Civil.*
Civil or Philo-
sophical.   II. *Philosophical.*

First, By their *Civil Use*, I mean such a Communication of Thoughts and *Ideas* by Words, as may serve for the upholding common Conversation and Commerce about the ordinary Affairs and Conveniences of Civil Life, in the Societies of Men one amongst another.

Secondly, By the *Philosophical Use* of Words, I mean such an use of them, as may serve to convey the precise Notions of Things, and to express, in general Propositions, certain and undoubted Truths, which the Mind may rest upon and be satisfied with, in its search after true Knowledg. These two Uses are very distinct; and a great deal less exactness will serve in the one, than in the other, as we shall see in what follows.

§ 4. The chief End of Language in Communication being to be understood, Words serve not well for that end, neither in Civil, nor Philosophical Discourse, when any Word does not excite in the Hearer the same *Idea* which it stands for in the Mind of the Speaker. Now since Sounds have no natural Connection with our *Ideas* but have all their Signification from the arbitrary Imposition of Men, the *doubtfulness* and uncertainty *of their Signification*, which is *the Imperfection* we here are speaking of, has its cause more in the *Ideas* they stand for, than in any Incapacity there is in one Sound more than in another, to signify any *Idea*: For in that regard they are all equally perfect.

The Imperfection of Words is the doubtfulness of their Signification.

That then which makes doubtfulness and uncertainty in the Signification of some more than other Words, is the difference of *Ideas* they stand for.

§ 5. Words having naturally no Signification, the *Idea* which each stands for must be learned and retained by those who would exchange Thoughts, and hold intelligible Discourse with others, in any Language. But this is hardest to be done, where,

Causes of their Imperfection.

First, The *Ideas* they stand for are very complex, and made up of a great Number of *Ideas* put together.

Secondly, Where the *Ideas* they stand for have no certain Connection in Nature ; and so no settled Standard any where in Nature existing, to rectify and adjust them by.

Thirdly, Where the Signification of the Word is refered to a Standard, which Standard is not easy to be known.

Fourthly, Where the Signification of the Word and the real Essence of the Thing, are not exactly the same.

These are Difficulties that attend the Signification of several Words that are intelligible. Those which are not intelligible at all, such as Names standing for any simple *Ideas*, which another has not Organs or Faculties to attain : as the Names of Colours to a blind Man, or Sounds to a deaf Man, need not here be mentioned.

In all these Cases we shall find an Imperfection in Words, which I shall more at large explain, in their particular Application to our several sorts of *Ideas* : For if we examine them, we shall find, that the *Names of mixed Modes are most liable to Doubtfulness and Imperfection, for the two first of Reasons ; and the Names of Substances chiefly for the two latter.*

§ 6. *First*, The Names of *mixed Modes*, are many of them liable to great Uncertainty, and Obscurity in their Signification.

I. *Because of* that *great Composition* these complex *Ideas* are often made up of. To make Words serviceable to the End of Communication, it is necessary, (as has been said) that they excite, in the Hearer, exactly the same *Idea* they stand for in the Mind of the Speaker. Without this, Men fill one another's Heads with Noise and Sounds ; but convey not thereby their Thoughts, and lay not before one another their *Ideas*, which is the end of Discourse and Language. But when a Word stands for a very complex *Idea*, that is compounded and decompounded, it is not easy for Men to form and retain that *Idea* so exactly, as to make the Name in common use stand for the same precise *Idea*, without any the least Variation. Hence it comes to pass, that Mens Names of very compound *Ideas*, such as for the most part are moral Words, have seldom, in two different Men, the same precise Signification, since one Man's complex *Idea* seldom agrees with anothers, and often differs from his own, from that which he had Yesterday, or will have to Morrow.

The Names of mixed Modes doubtful. First, Because the Ideas *they stand for, are so complex.*

§ 7. II. *Because the Names of mixed Modes*, for the most part, *want Standards* in Nature, whereby Men may rectify and adjust their Significations ; therefore

Secondly, Because they have no Standards.

they are very various and doubtful. They are Assemblages of *Ideas* put together at the Pleasure of the Mind, pursuing its own Ends of Discourse and suited to its own Notions, whereby it designs not to Copy any thing really existing, but to denominate and rank Things as they come to agree, with those *Archetypes* or *Forms* it has made. He that first brought the Word *Sham*, *Wheedle*, or *Banter* in use, put together, as he thought fit, those *Ideas* he made it stand for: And as it is with any new Names of Modes, that are now brought into any Language; so was it with the old ones, when they were first made use of. Names therefore that stand for Collections of *Ideas*, which the Mind makes at pleasure, must needs be of doubtful Signification, when such Collections are no where to be found constantly united in Nature, nor any Patterns to be shewn whereby Men may adjust them. What the word *Murther*, or *Sacriledge*, *&c.* signifies, can never be known from Things themselves: There be many of the Parts of those complex *Ideas*, which are not visible in the Action it self, the Intention of the Mind, or the Relation of holy Things, which make a part of *Murder*, or *Sacriledge*, have no necessary Connection with the outward and visible Action of him that commits either: and the pulling the Trigger of the Gun, with which the Murther is committed, and is all the Action, that, perhaps, is visible, has no natural Connection with those other *Ideas*, that make up the complex one, named *Murder*. They have their Union and Combination only from the Understanding which unites them under one Name: But uniting them without any Rule, or Pattern, it cannot be but that the Signification of the Name, that stands for such voluntary Collections, should be often various in the Minds of different Men, who have scarce any standing Rule to regulate themselves, and their Notions by, in such arbitrary *Ideas.* ·

§ 8. 'Tis true, *common Use*, that is the Rule of Propriety,· may be supposed here to afford some aid, to settle the Significa- *Propriety not* tion of Language; and it cannot be *a sufficient Remedy.* denied, but that in some Measure it does. Common use *regulates the meaning of Words* pretty well for common Conversation; but no Body having an Authority to establish the precise Signification of Words, nor determine to what *Ideas* any one shall annex them, common Use is not sufficient to adjust them to Philosophical Discourses; there being scarce any Name, of any very complex *Idea* (to say nothing of others,) which, in common Use, has not a great Latitude, and which keeping within the Bounds of Propriety, may not be made the Sign of far different *Ideas*. Besides, the Rule and Measure of Propriety

it self being no where established, it is often matter
of Dispute, whether this or that way of using a
Word, be Propriety of Speech, or no. From all
which, it is evident, that the Names of such kind of
very complex *Ideas,* are naturally liable to this Imperfection, to be of doubtful and uncertain Signification ;
and even in Men, that have a Mind to understand
one another, do not always stand for the same *Idea*
in Speaker and Hearer. Tho' the Names *Glory* and
Gratitude be the same in every Man's Mouth thro' a
whole Country, yet the complex collective *Idea,*
which every one thinks on, or intends by that Name,
is apparently very different in Men using the same
Language.

§ 9. *The way* also *wherein the Names of mixed
Modes are ordinarily learned, does* not a

*The way of
learning these
Names con-
tributes also
to their Doubt-
fulness.* little *contribute to the Doubtfulness of
their Signification.* For if we will observe how Children learn Languages,
we shall find, that to make them under-
stand what the Names of simple *Ideas,* or Substances,
stand for, People ordinarily shew them the thing
whereof they would have them have the *Idea,* and
then repeat to them the Name that stands for it, as
White, Sweet, Milk, Sugar, Cat, Dog. But as for
mixed Modes, especially the most material of them,
moral Words, the Sounds are usually learned first,

and then to know what complex *Ideas* they stand
for, they are either beholden to the Explication of
others, or (which happens for the most part) are left
to their own Observation and Industry ; which being
little laid out in the search of the true and precise
meaning of Names, these moral Words are, in most
Mens Mouths, little more than bare Sounds ; or when
they have any, 'tis for the most part but a very loose
and undetermined, and consequently obscure and
confused Signification.   And even those themselves,
who have with more Attention settled their Notions,
do yet hardly avoid the Inconvenience, to have them
stand for complex *Ideas*, different from those which
other, even intelligent and studious Men, make them
the Signs of.   Where shall one find any, either *con-
troversial Debate*, or *familiar Discourse*, concerning
Honour, Faith, Grace, Religion, Church, &c. wherein
it is not easy to observe the different Notions Men
have of them ; which is nothing but this, that they
are not agreed in the Signification of those Words ;
nor have in their Minds the same complex *Ideas*
which they make them stand for : and so all the
Contests that follow thereupon, are only about the
meaning of a Sound.   And hence we see, that in the
Interpretation of Laws, whether Divine, or Humane,
there is no end ; Comments beget Comments, and
Explications make new Matter for Explications :

And of limiting, distinguishing, varying the Signification of these moral Words, there is no end.   These
Ideas of Mens making, are, by Men still having the
same Power, multiplied *in infinitum*.   Many a Man,
who was pretty well satisfy'd of the meaning of a
Text of Scripture, or Clause in the Code, at first
reading, has by consulting Commentators, quite lost
the sense of it, and by those Elucidations, given rise
or increase to his Doubts, and drawn Obscurity upon
the Place.   I say not this, that I think Commentaries needless ; but to shew how uncertain the
Names of mixed Modes naturally are, even in the
Mouths of those who had both the Intension and
the Faculty of speaking as clearly as Language was
capable to express their Thoughts.

§ 10. What Obscurity this has unavoidably brought
upon the Writings of Men, who have
Hence una-
voidable Ob- lived in remote Ages, and different
scurity in an- Countries, it will be needless to take
tient Authors.
Notice ; since the numerous Volumes of
learned Men, employing their Thoughts that way,
are Proofs more than enough to shew what Attention,
Study, Sagacity, and Reasoning are required, to find
out the true meaning *of Antient Authors*.   But there
being no Writings we have any great concernment
to be very sollicitous about the meaning of, but those
that contain either Truths we are required to believe,

or Laws we are to obey, and draw Inconveniences on us when we mistake or transgress, we may be less anxious about the Sense of other Authors, who Writing but their own Opinions, we are under no greater necessity to know them, than they to know ours. Our good or evil depending not on their Decrees, we may safely be ignorant of their Notions: And therefore in the reading of them, if they do not use their Words with a due clearness and perspicuity, we may lay them aside, and without any injury done them, resolve thus with our selves,

Si non vis intelligi, debes negligi.

§ 11. If the Signification of the Names of mixed Modes are uncertain, because there be no real Standards existing in Nature, to which those *Ideas* are refered, and by which they may be adjusted, the *Names of Substances are of a doubtful Signification*, for a contrary Reason, *viz. because* the *Ideas* they stand for are supposed conformable to the Reality of Things, and are *refered to Standards* made by Nature. In our *Ideas* of Substances we have not the Liberty as in mixed Modes, to frame what Combinations we think fit, to be the characteristical Notes, to rank and denominate Things by. In these we must follow Nature, suit our complex *Ideas* to real Existences, and regulate the Signification of their Names by the Things themselves, if we will

N

have our Names to be the Signs of them, and stand
for them.   Here, 'tis true, we have Patterns to follow ; but Patterns that will make the Signification of
their Names very uncertain : For Names must be of
a very unsteady and various meaning, if the *Ideas*
they stand-for be refered to Standards without us,
*that either cannot be known at all, or can be known but
imperfectly and uncertainly.*

§ 12. The *Names of Substances have,* as has been
shewed, a double *Reference* in their
ordinary Use.

*Names of Substances re-
fer'd, First,
To real Es-
sences that
cannot be
known.*

First, Sometimes they are made to
stand for, and so their Signification is
supposed to agree to, *The real Constitution of Things,* from which all their Properties
flow, and in which they all centre.   But this real
Constitution, or (as it is apt to be call'd) Essence,
being utterly unknown to us, any Sound that is put
to stand for it, must be very uncertain in its Application ;   and it will be impossible to know, what
Things are, or ought to be called an *Horse,* or *Antimony,* when those Words are put for real Essences,
that we have no *Ideas* of at all.   And therefore in
this Supposition, the Names of Substances being
refered to Standards that cannot be known, their
Significations can never be adjusted and established
by those Standards.

§ 13. *Secondly*, The *simple Ideas* that are found to co-exist *in Substances*, being that which their Names immediately signify, these, as united in the several Sorts of Things, *are* the proper *Standards* to which their Names are refered, and by which their

Secondly, To co - existing Qualities, which are known but imperfectly.

Significations may be best rectify'd. But neither will these *Archetypes* so well serve to this purpose, as to leave these Names, without very various and uncertain Significations. Because these simple *Ideas* that co-exist, and are united in the same Subject, being very numerous, and having all an equal Right to go into the complex *specifick Idea*, which the specifick Name is to stand for, Men, though they propose to themselves the very same Subject to consider, yet frame very different *Ideas* about it ; and so the Name they use for it, unavoidably comes to have, in several Men, very different Significations. The simple Qualities which make up the complex *Ideas*, being most of them Powers, in Relation to Changes, which they are apt to make in, or receive from other Bodies, are almost infinite. He that shall but observe, what a great Variety of Alterations any one of the baser Metals is apt to receive, from the different Application only of Fire ; and how much a greater Number of Changes any of them will receive in the Hands of a Chymist, by the Application of other Bodies, will not think it strange, that I count the Properties of any sort of Bodies not easy to be collected, and completely known by the ways of enquiry, which our Faculties are capable of. They being therefore at least so many, that no Man can know the precise and definite Number, they are differently discovered by different Men, according to their various Skill, Attention, and Ways of handling ; who therefore cannot chuse but have different *Ideas* of the same Substance, and therefore make the Signification of its common Name very various and uncertain. For the complex *Ideas* of Substances, being made of such simple ones as are supposed to co-exist in Nature, every one has a Right to put into his complex *Idea*, those Qualities he has found to be united together. For though in the Substance *Gold*, one satisfies himself with Colour and Weight, yet another thinks Solubility in *Aq. Regia*, as necessary to be joined with that Colour in his *Idea* of Gold, as any one does its Fusibility : Solubility in *Aq. Regia*, being a Quality as constantly joined with its Colour and Weight, as Fusibility, or any other ; others put in its Ductility or Fixedness, *&c.* as they have been taught by Tradition, or Experience. Who of all these has established the right Signification of the Word *Gold*? Or who shall be the Judge to determine ? Each has his Standard in Nature, which he appeals to, and with Reason thinks he has the same right to put into his complex *Idea*, signify'd by the Word *Gold*, those Qualities, which upon Trial he has found united ; as another, who has not so well examined, has to leave 'em out ; or a third, who has made other Trials, has to put in others. For the Union in Nature of these Qualities, being the true Ground of their Union in one complex *Idea*, who can say, one of them has more Reason to be put in, or left out, than another ? From whence it will always unavoidably follow, that the complex *Ideas* of Substances in Men using the same Name for them, will be very various ; and so the Significátions of those Names, very uncertain.

§ 14. Besides, there is scarce any particular thing existing, which, in some of its simple *Ideas*, does not communicate with a greater, and in others a less Number of particular Beings : Who shall determine in this Case, which are those that are to *Thirdly, To co-existing Qualities which are known but imperfectly.* make up the precise Collection, that is to be signified by the specifick Name ; or can with any just Authority prescribe, which obvious or common Qualities are to be left out ; or which more secret, or more particular, are to be put into the Signification of the Name of any Substance ? All *which* together, seldom or never fail to *produce* that various and *doubtful*

Signification in the Names of Substances, which causes
such Uncertainty, Disputes, or Mistakes, when we
come to a Philosophical Use of them.

§ 15. 'Tis true, as *to civil and common Conversation*,
the general *Names of Substances*, regu-
With this Imperfection they may serve for Civil but not well for Philosophical Use. lated in their ordinary Signification by
some obvious Qualities, (as by the Shape
and Figure in Things of known seminal
Propagation, and in other Substances,
for the most part by Colour, joined
with some other sensible Qualities,) *do well enough*
to design the Things Men would be understood to
speak of : And so they usually conceive well enough
the Substances meant by the word *Gold*, or *Apple*, to
distinguish the one from the other. *But in Philosophical Enquiries and Debates*, where general Truths
are to be established, and Consequences drawn from
Positions laid down, there the precise Signification of
the Names of Substances will be found, not only *not*
to be *well established*, but also very hard to be so.
For Example, he that shall make Malleableness, or a
certain Degree of Fixedness, a part of his complex
Idea of *Gold*, may make Propositions concerning
Gold, and draw Consequences from them, that will
truly and clearly follow from *Gold*, taken in such a
Signification : But yet such as another Man can never
be forced to admit, nor be convinced of their Truth,

who makes not Malleableness, or the same Degree of Fixedness, part of that complex *Idea*, that the Name *Gold*, in his use of it, stands for.

§ 16. This is a natural, and almost unavoidable Imperfection in almost all the Names of Substances, in all Languages whatsoever, *Instance, Liquor.* which Men will easily find, when once passing from confused or loose Notions, they come to more strict and close Enquiries. For then they will be convinced how doubtful and obscure those Words are in their Signification, which in ordinary use appeared very clear and determined. I was once in a Meeting of very learned and ingenious Physicians, where by chance there arose a Question, whether any Liquor passed through the Filaments of the Nerves. The debate having been managed a good while, by Variety of Arguments on both sides, I (who had been used to suspect, that the greatest part of Disputes were more about the Signification of Words, than a real Difference in the Conception of Things) desired, That before they went any farther on in this Dispute, they would first examine, and establish amongst them, what the Word *Liquor* signify'd. They at first were a little surprized at the Proposal; and had they been Persons less ingenious, they might perhaps have taken it for a very frivolous or extravagant one : Since there was no one there that thought not himself to understand very perfectly, what the word Liquor stood for; which I think too none of the most perplexed Names of Substances. However, they were pleased to comply with my Motion, and upon Examination found, that the Signification of that Word was not so settled and certain, as they had all imagined; but that each of them made it a Sign of a different complex *Idea.* This made them perceive, that the main of their Dispute was about the Signification of that Term; and that they differed very little in their Opinions, concerning some fluid and subtile Matter, passing through the Conduits of the Nerves; tho' it was not so easy to agree whether it was to be called *Liquor* or no, a thing which when considered, they thought it not worth the contending about.

§ 17. How much this is the Case in the greatest *Instance,* part of Disputes, that Men are engag'd *Gold.* so hotly in, I shall, perhaps, have an Occasion in another place to take Notice. Let us only here consider a little more exactly the forementioned instance of the Word *Gold,* and we shall see how hard it is precisely to determine its Signification. I think all agree, to make it stand for a Body of a certain yellow shining Colour; which being the *Idea* to which Children have annexed that Name, the shining yellow part of a Peacock's Tail is

properly to them Gold. Others finding Fusibility
joined with that yellow Colour in certain parcels of
Matter, make of that Combination a complex *Idea*
to which they give the Name *Gold* to denote a sort
of Substances ; and so exclude from being *Gold* all
such yellow shining Bodies, as by Fire will be reduced to Ashes, and admit to be of that *Species*, or
to be comprehended under that Name *Gold*, only
such Substances as having that shining yellow Colour
will by Fire be reduced to Fusion, and not to Ashes.
Another by the same Reason adds the Weight,
which being a Quality, as straitly joined with that
Colour, as its Fusibility, he thinks has the same
Reason to be joined in its *Idea*, and to be signify'd
by its Name : And therefore the other made up of
Body, of such a Colour and Fusibility, to be imperfect ; and so on of all the rest : Wherein no one
can shew a Reason, why some of the inseparable
Qualities, that are always united in Nature, should
be put into the nominal Essence, and others left out :
Or why the Word *Gold*, signifying that sort of Body
the Ring on his Finger is made of, should determine
that sort, rather by its Colour, Weight, and Fusibility ; than by its Colour, Weight, and Solubility in
Aq. Regia : Since the dissolving it by that Liquor, is
as inseparable from it, as the Fusion by Fire ; and
they are both of them nothing, but the Relation

which that Substance has to two other Bodies, which
have a Power to operate differently upon it. For by
what right is it, that Fusibility comes to be a part
of the Essence, signify'd by the Word *Gold*, and
Solubility but a Property of it? Or what is its
Colour part of the Essence, and its Malleableness
but a Property? That which I mean, is this, That
these being all but Properties, depending on its real
Constitution; and nothing but Powers, either active
or passive, in Reference to other Bodies, no one has
Authority to determine the Signification of the
Word *Gold*, (as refered to such a Body existing in
Nature) more to one Collection of *Ideas* to be found
in that Body, than to another: Whereby the Signification of that Name must unavoidably be very
uncertain. Since, as has been said, several People
observe several Properties in the same Substance;
and, I think, I may say no Body all. And therefore we have but very imperfect Descriptions of
Things, and Words have very uncertain Significations.

§ 18. From what has been said, it is easy to

The Names observe, what has been before remarked,
of simple viz. That the *Names of simple* Ideas
Ideas the
least doubt- are, of all others, the *least liable to Mis-*
ful.
takes, and that for these Reasons. *First*,
because the *Ideas* they stand for, being each but one

single Perception, are much easier got, and more clearly retained, than the more complex ones, and therefore are not liable to the uncertainty, which usually attends those compounded ones of *Substances and mixed Modes*, in which the precise Number of simple *Ideas*, that make them up, are not easily agreed, and so readily kept in the Mind. And *Secondly*, Because they are never refered to any other Essence, but barely that Perception they immediately signify : Which Reference is that which renders the Signification of the Names of Substances naturally so perplexed, and gives occasion to so many Disputes. Men that do not perversly use their Words, or on purpose set themselves to cavil, seldom mistake in any Language, which they are acquainted with, the Use and Signification of the Names of simple *Ideas* : *White*, and *Sweet*, *Yellow*, and *Bitter*, carry a very obvious meaning with them, which every one precisely comprehends, or easily perceives he is Ignorant of, and seeks to be informed. But what precise Collection of simple *Ideas*, *Modesty*, or *Frugality* stand for in another's Use, is not so certainly known. And however we are apt to think, we well enough know, what is meant by *Gold* or *Iron* ; yet the precise complex *Idea*, others make them the Signs of, is not so certain : And I believe it is very seldom that in Speaker and Hearer, they

stand for exactly the same Collection. Which must
needs produce Mistakes and Disputes, when they are
made use of in Discourses, wherein Men have to do
with universal Propositions, and would settle in their
Minds universal Truths, and consider the Consequences that follow from them.

§ 19. By the same Rule, the *Names of simple*

And next to them simple Modes.

Modes are next to those of simple Ideas,
least liable to Doubt and Uncertainty,
especially those of Figure and Number,
of which Men have so clear and distinct *Ideas.*
Whoever, that had a Mind to understand them,
mistook the ordinary meaning of *Seven,* or
a Triangle? And in general the least compounded *Ideas* in every kind have the least dubious
Names.

§ 20. Mixed Modes therefore, that are made up

The most doubtful are the Names of very com-pounded mixed Modes and Sub-stances.

but of a few and obvious simple *Ideas,*
have usually Names of no very uncertain Signification. But the Names of
mixed Modes, which comprehend a great
Number of simple *Ideas,* are commonly
of a very doubtful, and undetermined
meaning, as has been shewn. The Names of Substances, being annexed to *Ideas,* that are neither the
real Essences, nor exact Representations of the
Patterns they are refer'd to, are liable yet to greater

Imperfection and Uncertainty, especially when we come to a Philosophical use of them.

§ 21. The great disorder that happens in our Names of Substances, proceeding for the most part from our want of Knowledg, and Inability to penetrate into their real Constitutions, it may probably *Why this Imperfection charged upon Words.* be wondered, *Why I charge this as an Imperfection,* rather *upon our Words* than Understandings. This Exception has so much appearance of Justice, that I think my self obliged to give a Reason, why I have followed this Method. I must confess then, that when I first began this Discourse of the Understanding, and a good while after, I had not the least Thought that any Consideration of Words was at all necessary to it. But when having passed over the Original and Composition of our *Ideas,* I began to examine the Extent and Certainty of our Knowledg, I found it had so near a Connection with Words, that unless their Force and Manner of Signification were first well observed, there could be very little said clearly and pertinently concerning Knowledg: which being conversant about Truth, had constantly to do with Propositions. And though it terminated in Things, yet it was for the most part so much by the intervention of Words, that they seemed scarce separable from our general Knowledg. At

least they interpose themselves so much between
our Understandings, and the Truth, which it would
contemplate and apprehend, that like the *Medium*
through which visible Objects pass, their Obscurity
and Disorder does not seldom cast a Mist before our
Eyes, and impose upon our Understandings. If we
consider, in the Fallacies Men put upon themselves,
as well as others, and the Mistakes in Mens Disputes
and Notions, how great a part is owing to Words,
and their uncertain or mistaken Significations, we
shall have Reason to think this no small obstacle
in the way to Knowledg, which, I conclude, we are
the more carefully to be warned of, because it has
been so far from being taken Notice of as an Inconvenience, that the Arts of improving it have been
made the business of Mens Study; and obtained the
Reputation of Learning and Subtilty, as we shall see
in the following Chapter. But I am apt to imagine,
that were the Imperfections of Language, as the
Instrument of Knowledg, more throughly weighed,
a great many of the Controversies that make such a
Noïse in the World, would of themselves cease; and
the way to Knowledg, and, perhaps, Peace too, lie a
great deal opener than it does.

§ 22. Sure I am, that the Signification of Words,
in all Languages, depending very much on the
Thoughts, Notions, and *Ideas* of him that uses

them, must unavoidably be of great uncertainty to Men of the same Language and Country. This is so evident in the *Greek* Authors, that he that shall peruse their Writings, will find in almost every one of them a distinct Language, though the same Words. But when to this natural *This should teach us Moderation, in imposing our own Sense of old Authors.* Difficulty in every Country, there shall be added different Countries, and remote Ages, wherein the Speakers and Writers had very different Notions, Tempers, Customs, Ornaments, and Figures of Speech, *&c.* every one of which influenced the Signification of their Words then, though to us now they are lost and unknown, *it would become us to be charitable one to another in our Interpretations or Misunderstanding of those antient Writings,* which though of great Concernment to be understood, are liable to the unavoidable Difficulties of Speech, which, (if we except the Names of simple *Ideas,* and some very obvious Things) is not capable without a constant defining the Terms of conveying the Sense and Intention of the Speaker, without any manner of doubt and uncertainty to the Hearer. And in Discourses of Religion, Law, and Morality, as they are Matters of the highest Concernment, so there will be the greatest Difficulty.

§ 23. The Volumes of Interpreters, and Commentators on the Old and New Testament, are but too manifest Proofs of this. Tho' every thing said in the Text be infallibly true, yet the Reader may be, nay cannot chuse 'but be very fallible in the understanding of it. Nor is it to be wondred, that the Will of GOD, when clothed in Words, should be liable to that doubt and uncertainty, which unavoidably attends that sort of Conveyance ; when even his Son, whilst clothed in Flesh, was subject to all the Frailties and Inconveniences of humane Nature, Sin excepted. And we ought to magnify his Goodness, that he hath spread before all the World, such legible Characters of his Works and Providence, and given all Mankind so sufficient a light of Reason, that they, to whom this written Word never came, could not (whenever they set themselves to search) either doubt of the Being of a GOD, or of the Obedience due to Him. Since then the Precepts of natural Religion are plain, and very intelligible to all Mankind, and seldom come to be controverted ; and other revealed Truths, which are conveyed to us by Books and Languages, are liable to the common and natural Obscurities and Difficulties incident to Words, methinks it would become us to be more careful and diligent in observing the former, and less magisterial, positive, and imperious, in imposing our own Sense and Interpretations of the latter.

CHAPTER X.

OF THE ABUSE OF WORDS.

§ 1. Besides the Imperfection that is naturally in Language, and the Obscurity and Con- *Abuse of* fusion that is so hard to be avoided in *Words.* the Use of Words, there are several *wilful Faults and Neglects*, which Men are guilty of, in this way of Communication, whereby they render these Signs less clear and distinct in their Signification, than naturally they need to be.

§ 2. *First,* In this kind, the first and most palpable abuse is, the using of Words, without clear and distinct *Ideas*; or, which is *First, Words without any,* worse, Signs without any thing signify'd. *or without clear Ideas.* Of these there are two Sorts:

1. One may observe, in all Languages, certain Words, that if they be examined, will be found, in the first Original, and their appropriated Use, not to stand for any clear and distinct *Ideas.* These, for the most part, the several *Sects* of Philosophy and Religion have introduced. For their Authors, or Promoters, either affecting something singular, and

O

out of the way of common Apprehensions, or to
support some strange Opinions, or cover some Weakness of their Hypothesis, seldom fail to *Coin* new
Words, and such as, when they come to be examined,
may justly be called *Insignificant Terms.* For having
either had no determinate Collection of *Ideas* annexed
to them, when they were first invented; or at least
such as, if well examined, will be found inconsistent,
'tis no wonder if afterwards, in the vulgar use of the
same Party, they remain empty Sounds, with little
or no Signification, amongst those who think it
enough to have them often in their Mouths, as the
distinguishing Characters of their Church, or School,
without much troubling their Heads to examine what
are the precise *Ideas* they stand for. I shall not need
here to heap up Instances, every one's Reading and
Conversation will sufficiently furnish him: Or if he
wants to be better stored, the great Mint-Masters of
these kind of Terms, I mean the School-men and
Metaphysicians, (under which, I think, the disputing
Natural and Moral Philosophers of these latter Ages
may be comprehended,) have where-withal abundantly to content him.

§ 3. II. Others there be, who extend this abuse
yet farther, who take so little care to lay by Words,
which in their primary Notation have scarce any
clear and distinct *Ideas* which they are annexed to,

that by an unpardonable Negligence, they familiarly *use Words*, which the Propriety of Language has affixed to very important *Ideas, without any distinct meaning* at all. *Wisdom, Glory, Grace, &c.* are Words frequent enough in every Man's Mouth ; but if a great many of those who use them, should be asked, what they mean by them ? they would be at a stand, and not know what to answer : A plain Proof, that though they have learned those Sounds, and have them ready at their Tongue's-end, yet there are no determined *Ideas* laid up in their Minds, which are to be expressed to others by them.

§ 4. *Men* having been *accustomed* from their Cradles *to learn Words*, which are easily got and retained, *before they knew*, or had framed *the complex Ideas*, to which they were annexed, or which were to be found in *Occasioned by learning Names before the* Ideas *they belong to.* the Things *they* were thought to *stand* for, they *usually continue to do so* all their Lives, and without taking the Pains necessary to settle in their Minds determined *Ideas*, they use their Words for such un-steady and confused Notions as they have, contenting themselves with the same Words other People use ; as if their very Sound necessarily carried with it constantly the same meaning. This, though Men make a shift with in the ordinary Occurrences of Life, where they find it necessary to be understood, and therefore they make Signs till they are so : Yet this Insignificancy in their Words, when they come to Reason concerning either their Tenets or Interest, manifestly fills their Discourse with abundance of empty unintelligible Noise and Jargon, especially in Moral Matters, where the Words, for the most part, standing for arbitrary and numerous Collections of *Ideas*, not regularly and permanently united in Nature, their bare Sounds are often only thought on, or at least very obscure and uncertain Notions annexed to them. Men take the Words they find in use amongst their Neighbours ; and that they may not seem ignorant what they stand for, use them confidently, without much troubling their Heads about a certain fixed meaning ; whereby, besides the ease of it, they obtain this Advantage, That as in such Discourses they seldom are in the Right, so they are as seldom to be convinced that they are in the wrong ; it being all one to go about to draw those Men out of their Mistakes, who have no settled Notions, as to dispossess a Vagrant of his Habitation, who has no settled abode. This I guess to be so ; and every one may observe in himself and others, whether it be or no.

§ 5. *Secondly,* Another great abuse of Words is, *Inconstancy* in the use of them. It is hard to find a Discourse written of any Subject, especially of

Controversy, wherein one shall not observe, if he read with Attention, the same Words (and those commonly the most material in the Discourse, and upon which the Argument turns) used sometimes for one *Secondly, Unsteady Application of them.* Collection of simple *Ideas*, and sometimes for another, which is a perfect Abuse of Language. Words being intended for Signs of my *Ideas*, to make them known to others, not by any natural Signification, but by a voluntary Imposition, 'tis plain cheat and Abuse, when I make them stand sometimes for one thing, and sometimes for another; the wilful doing whereof, can be imputed to nothing but great Folly, or greater Dishonesty. And a Man, in his Accompts with another, may, with as much fairness, make the Characters of Numbers stand sometimes for one, and sometimes for another Collection of Units (*v. g.* this Character 3 stand sometimes for three, sometimes for four, and sometimes for eight) as in his Discourse, or Reasoning, make the same Words stand for different Collections of simple *Ideas*. If Men should do so in their Reckonings, I wonder who would have to do with them? One who would speak thus, in the Affairs and Business of the World, and call 8 sometimes 7, and sometimes nine, as best served his Advantage, would presently have clap'd upon him one of the two Names Men are constantly disgusted with. And yet in Arguings, and learned Contests, the same sort of proceeding passes commonly for Wit and Learning ; but to me it appears a greater dishonesty, than the misplacing of Counters, in the casting up a Debt ; and the Cheat the greater, by how much Truth is of greater Concernment and Value than Money.

§ 6. *Thirdly,* Another abuse of Language is, an

Thirdly, Affected Obscurity by wrong Application.
affected *Obscurity,* by either applying old Words to new and unusual Significations, or introducing new and ambiguous Terms, without defining either ; or else putting them so together, as may confound their ordinary meaning. Though the Peripatetick Philosophy has been most eminent in this way, yet other Sects have not been wholly clear of it. There is scarce any of them that are not cumber'd with some Difficulties, (such is the Imperfection of Humane Knowledg,) which they have been fain to cover with Obscurity of Terms, and to confound the Signification of Words, which, like a Mist before Peoples Eyes, might hinder their weak Parts from being discovered. That *Body* and *Extension,* in common use, stand for two distinct *Ideas,* is plain to any one that will but reflect a little. For were their Signification precisely the same, it would be proper, and as intelligible to say, the *Body of an Extension,*

as *the Extension of a Body* ; and yet there are those
who find it necessary to confound their Signification.
To this Abuse, and the Mischiefs of confounding
the Signification of Words, Logick and the liberal
Sciences, as they have been handled in the Schools,
have given Reputation ; and the admired Art of
Disputing hath added much to the natural Imperfection of Languages, whilst it has been made use of
and fitted to perplex the Signification of Words,
more than to discover the Knowledg and Truth of
Things : And he that will look into that sort of
learned Writings, will find the Words there much
more obscure, uncertain, and undetermined in their
Meaning, than they are in ordinary Conversation.

§ 7. This is unavoidably to be so, where Mens
Parts and Learning, are estimated by
their Skill in *Disputing.* And if Repu-   *Logick and
Dispute has
much contri-
buted to this.*
tation and Reward shall attend these
Conquests, which depend mostly on the
Fineness and Niceties of Words, 'tis no Wonder if
the Wit of Man so employ'd, should perplex, involve, and subtilize the Signification of Sounds, so
as never to want something to say, in opposing or
defending any Question ; the Victory being adjudged
not to him who had Truth on his side, but the last
Word in the Dispute.

§ 8. This, though a very useless skill, and that

which I think the direct opposite to the ways of

Calling it Subtilty. Knowledg, hath yet passed hitherto under the laudable and esteemed Names of *Subtilty* and *Acuteness* ; and has had the applause of the Schools, and Encouragement of one part of the learned Men of the World. And no wonder, since the Philosophers of old, (the disputing and wrangling Philosophers I mean, such as *Lucian* wittily and with Reason taxes,) and the Schoolmen since, aiming at Glory and Esteem, for their great and universal Knowledg, easier a great deal to be pretended to, than really acquired, found this a good Expedient to cover their Ignorance, with a curious and unexplicable Web of perplexed Words, and procure to themselves the Admiration of others, by unintelligible Terms, the apter to produce Wonder, because they could not be understood : whilst it appears in all History, that these profound Doctors were no wiser, nor more useful than their Neighbours ; and brought but small Advantage to humane Life, or the Societies wherein they lived : Unless the coining of new Words, where they produced no new Things to apply them to, or the perplexing or obscuring the Signification of old ones, and so bringing all things into Question and dispute, were a thing profitable to the Life of Man, or worthy Commendation and Reward.

§ 9. For notwithstanding these learned Disputants, these all-knowing Doctors, it was to the unscholastick Statesman, that the Governments of the World owed their Peace, Defence, and Liberties ; and from *This Learning very little benefits Society.* the illiterate and contemned Mechanick, (a Name of Disgrace) that they received the Improvements of useful Arts. Nevertheless, this artificial Ignorance, and *learned Gibberish*, prevailed mightily in these last Ages, by the Interest and Artifice of those, who found no easier way to that pitch of Authority and Dominion they have attained, than by amusing the Men of Business and Ignorant with hard Words, or imploying the Ingenious and Idle in intricate Disputes, about unintelligible Terms, and holding them perpetually entangled in that endless Labyrinth. Besides, there is no such way to gain Admittance, or give Defence to strange and absurd Doctrines, as to guard them round about with Legions of obscure, doubtful, and undefined Words : which yet make these Retreats, more like the Dens of Robbers, or Holes of Foxes, than the Fortresses of fair Warriours ; which if it be hard to get them out of, it is not for the Strength that is in them, but the Briars and Thorns, and the Obscurity of the Thickets they are beset with. For Untruth being unacceptable to the Mind of Man, there is no other defence left for Absurdity, but Obscurity.

§ 10. Thus learned Ignorance, and this Art of keeping, even inquisitive Men, from true Knowledg, hath been propagated in the World, and hath much perplexed, whilst it pretended to inform the Understanding. For we see, that other well-meaning and wise Men, whose Education and Parts had not acquir'd that *acuteness*, could intelligibly express themselves to one another; and in its plain use, make a benefit of Language. But though unlearned Men well enough understood the Words *White* and *Black*, &c. and had constant Notions of the *Ideas* signified by those Words; yet there were Philosophers found, who had learning and *subtilty* enough to prove, that *Snow was black*, *i. e.* to prove, that *White* was *Black*. Whereby they had the Advantage to destroy the Instruments and Means of Discourse, Conversation, Instruction, and Society; whilst with great Art and *Subtilty* they did no more but perplex and confound the Signification of Words, and thereby render Language less useful, than the real Defects of it had made it a Gift, which the illiterate had not attained to.

But destroys the Instruments of Knowledg and Communication.

§ 11. These learned Men did equally instruct Mens Understandings, and profit their Lives, as he who should alter the Signification of known Characters, and, by a subtle Device of Learning, far surpass-

As useful as to confound the Sound of the Letters.

ing the Capacity of the Illiterate, Dull, and Vulgar, should, in his Writing, shew, that he could put *A* for *B*, and *D* for *E*, *&c.* to the no small Admiration and Benefit of his Reader. It being as sensless to put *Black*, which is a word agreed on to stand for one sensible *Idea*, to put it, I say, for another, or the contrary *Idea*, *i. e.* to call *Snow Black*, as to put this mark *A*, which is a Character agreed on to stand for one Modification of Sound, made by a certain Motion of the Organs of Speech, for *B* which is agreed on to stand for another Modification of Sound, made by another certain Motion of the Organs of Speech.

§ 12. Nor hath this Mischief stopp'd in logical Niceties, or curious empty Speculations; it hath invaded the great Concernments of humane Life and Society; obscured and perplexed the material Truths of *This Art has perplexed Religion and Justice.* Law and Divinity; brought Confusion, Disorder and Uncertainty into the Affairs of Mankind; and if not destroy'd, yet in great Measure render'd useless, those two great Rules, Religion and Justice. What have the greatest part of the Comments and Disputes, upon the Laws of GOD and Man served for, but to make the meaning more doubtful, and perplex the Sense? What have been the Effect of those multiplied curious Distinctions, and acute Niceties, but Obscurity and Uncertainty, leaving the Words more unintelligible, and the Reader more at a loss? How else comes it to pass, that Princes, speaking or writing to their Servants, in their ordinary Commands, are easily understood; speaking to their People, in their Laws, are not so? And, as I remarked before, doth it not often happen, that a Man of an ordinary Capacity, very well understands a Text, or a Law, that he reads, till he consults an Expositor, or goes to Council; who by that time he hath done explaining them, makes the Words signify either nothing at all, or what he pleases.

§ 13. Whether any By-Interests of these Professions have occasion'd this, I will not *And ought* here examine; but I leave it to be con- *not to pass for* sidered, whether it would not be well *Learning.* for Mankind, whose concernment it is to know Things as they are, and to do what they ought, and not to spend their Lives in talking about them, or tossing Words to and fro; whether it would not be well, I say, that the Use of Words were made plain and direct; and that Language, which was given us for the Improvement of Knowledg, and bond of Society, should not be employ'd to darken Truth, and unsettle Peoples Rights; to raise Mists, and render unintelligible both Morality and Religion? Or that at least, if this will happen, it should not be thought Learning or Knowledg to do so?

§ 14 *Fourthly,* Another great *Abuse of Words is, the taking them for Things.* This though it in some degree concerns all Names in general, yet more particularly *Fourthly, taking them for Things.* affects those of Substances. To this Abuse those Men are most subject, who confine their Thoughts to any one System, and give themselves up into a firm belief of the Perfection of any received Hypothesis; whereby they come to be perswaded, that the Terms of that Sect, are so suited to the Nature of Things, that they perfectly correspond with their real Existence. Who is there, that has been bred up in the Peripatetick Philosophy, who does not think the ten Names, under which are ranked the ten Predicaments, to be exactly conformable to the Nature of Things? who is there of that School, that is not perswaded, that *substantial Forms, vegetative Souls, abhorrence of a* Vacuum, *intentional Species,* &c. are something real? These Words Men have learned from their very entrance upon Knowledg, and have found their Masters and Systems lay great Stress upon them; and therefore they cannot quit the Opinion, that they are conformable to Nature, and are the Representations of something that really exists. The *Platonists* have their *Soul of the World,* and the *Epicureans* their *endeavour towards Motion* in their Atoms, when at rest. There is scarce any Sect in Philosophy has not a distinct set of Terms, that others understand not. But yet this Gibberish, which in the Weakness of Humane Understanding, serves so well to palliate Mens Ignorance, and cover their Errors, comes by familiar use amongst those of the same Tribe, to seem the most important part of Language, and of all other the Terms the most significant : And should *Aerial* and *Ætherial Vehicles* come once, by the prevalency of that Doctrine, to be generally received any where, no doubt those Terms would make Impressions on Mens Minds, so as to establish them in the Persuasion of the Reality of such Things, as much as *Peripatetick Forms* and *intentional Species* have heretofore done.

§ 15. How much *Names taken for Things* are apt *Instance, in Matter.* to *mislead the Understanding*, the attentive reading of Philosophical Writers would abundantly discover ; and that, perhaps, in Words little suspected of any such Misuse. I shall instance in one only, and that a very familiar one. How many intricate Disputes have there been about *Matter*, as if there were some such thing really in Nature, distinct from *Body* ; as 'tis evident, the Word *Matter* stands for an *Idea* distinct from the *Idea* of Body ? For if the *Ideas* these two Terms stood for were precisely the same, they might indifferently in all Places be put one for another. But we see, that though it be proper to say, There is *one Matter of all Bodies*, one cannot say, There is *one Body of all Matters*: We familiarly say, one *Body* is bigger than another; but it Sounds harsh (and I think is never used) to say, one *Matter* is bigger than another. Whence comes this then? *Viz.* from hence, that though *Matter* and *Body* be not really distinct, but wherever there is the one, there is the other; Yet *Matter* and *Body* stand for two different Conceptions, whereof the one is incomplete, and but a part of the other. For *Body* stands for a solid extended figured Substance, whereof *Matter* is but a partial and more confused Conception, it seeming to me to be used for the Substance and Solidity of Body, without taking in its Extension and Figure: And therefore it is that speaking of *Matter*, we speak of it always as one, because in truth, it expressly contains nothing but the *Idea* of a solid Substance, which is every where the same, every where uniform. This being our *Idea* of *Matter*, we no more conceive, or speak of different *Matters* in the World, than we do of different Solidities; though we both conceive, and speak of different Bodies, because Extension and Figure are capable of Variation. But since Solidity cannot exist without Extension and Figure, the taking *Matter* to be the

Name of something really existing under that Precision, has no doubt produced those obscure and unintelligible Discourses and Disputes, which have filled
the Heads and Books of Philosophers concerning
Materia prima ; which Imperfection or Abuse, how
far it may concern a great many other general Terms,
I leave to be consider'd. This, I think, I may at
least say, that we should have a great many fewer
Disputes in the World, if Words were taken for what
they are, the Signs of our *Ideas* only, and not for
Things themselves. For when we argue about *Matter*, or any the like Term, we truly argue only about
the *Idea* we express by that Sound, whether that
precise *Idea* agree to any thing really existing in
Nature, or no. And if Men would tell, what *Ideas*
they make their Words stand for, there could not be
half that Obscurity or Wrangling, in the search or
support of Truth, that there is.

§ 16. But whatever Inconvenience follows from
This makes this mistake of Words, this I am sure,
Errors last- that by constant and familiar use, they
ing. charm Men into Notions far remote from
the Truth of Things. 'Twould be a hard Matter to
persuade any one that the Words which his Father or
School-master, the Parson of the Parish, or such a
Reverend Doctor us'd, signify'd nothing that really
existed in Nature : Which, perhaps, is *none of the least*

Causes, that Men are so hardly drawn to quit their Mistakes, even in Opinions purely Philosophical, and where they have no other Interest but Truth. For the Words, they have a long time been used to, remaining firm in their Minds, 'tis no wonder, that the wrong Notions annexed to them should not be removed.

§ 17. *Fifthly,* Another *Abuse of Words, is the setting them in the place of Things, which they do or can by no means signify.* We may observe, that in the general Names of Substances, whereof the nominal

Fifthly, setting them for what they cannot signify.

Essences are only known to us, when we put them into Propositions, and affirm or deny any thing about them, we do most commonly tacitly suppose, or intend they should stand for the real Essence of a certain sort of Substances. For when a Man says *Gold is Malleable,* he means and would insinuate something more than this, for *what I call Gold is Malleable,* (though truly it amounts to no more) but would have this understood, *viz.* that *Gold,* i.e. *what has the real Essence of Gold is Malleable,* which amounts to thus much, that *Malleableness depends on, and is inseparable from the real Essence of Gold.* But a Man not knowing wherein that real Essence consists, the Connection in his Mind of Malleableness is not truly with an Essence he knows not, but only with the Sound Gold he puts for it. Thus

P

when we say, that *Animal rationale* is, and. *Animal implume bipes latis unguibus*, is not a good Definition of a Man; 'tis plain, we suppose the Name *Man* in this case to stand for the real Essence of a Species, and would signify, that a *rational Animal* better described that real Essence than a *two leg'd Animal with broad Nails, and without Feathers.* For else, why might not *Plato* as properly make the Word ἄνθρωπος or *Man*, stand for his complex *Idea*, made up of the *Ideas* of a Body, distinguished from others by a certain Shape, and other outward Appearances, as *Aristotle*, make the complex *Idea*, to which he gave the Name ἄνθρωπος or *Man*, of Body, and the Faculty of Reasoning joined together; unless the Name ἄνθρωπος or *Man*, were supposed to stand for something else, than what it signifies; and to be put in the place of some other thing than the *Idea* a Man professes he would express by it?

§ 18. 'Tis true, the Names of Substances would be much more useful, and Propositions *V. g. Putting 'em for the real Essences of Substances.* made in them much more certain, were the real Essences of Substances the *Ideas* in our Minds, which those Words signified. And 'tis for want of those real Essences, that our Words convey so little Knowledg or Certainty in our Discourses about them: And therefore the Mind, to remove that Imperfection as much as it can, makes them, by a secret Supposition, to stand for a Thing having that real Essence, as if thereby it made some nearer approaches to it. For though the Word *Man* or *Gold*, signifying nothing truly but a complex *Idea* of Properties, united together in one sort of Substances : Yet there is scarce any Body in the use of these Words, but often supposes each of those Names to stand for a thing having the real Essence, on which those Properties depend. Which is so far from diminishing the Imperfection of our Words, that by a plain Abuse it adds to it, when we would make them stand for something, which not being in our complex *Idea*, the Name we use can no ways be the sign of.

§ 19. This shews us the Reason why in *mixed Modes* any of the *Ideas* that make the Composition of the complex one, being left out or changed, it is allowed to be another thing, *i. e.* to be of another Species, as is plain in *Chance-medly, Man-slaughter, Murder, Parricide,* &c.

Hence we think every change of our Idea in Substances not to change the Species.

The Reason whereof is, because the complex *Idea* signified by that Name is the real as well as nominal Essence ; and there is no secret Reference of that Name to any other Essence but that. But in *Substances* it is not so. For though in that called *Gold* one puts into his complex *Idea* what another leaves

out, and *Vice Versa*; yet Men do not usually think
that therefore the Species is changed : Because they
secretly in their Minds refer that Name, and suppose
it annexed to a real immutable Essence of a thing
existing, on which those Properties depend. He
that adds to his complex *Idea* of *Gold*, that of
Fixedness and Solubility in *Aq. Regia*, which he put
not in it before, is not thought to have changed the
Species ; but only to have a more perfect *Idea*, by
adding another simple *Idea*, which is always in fact
joined with those other, of which his former complex
Idea consisted.   But this reference of the Name to a
thing, whereof we have not the *Idea*, is so far from
helping at all, that it only serves the more to involve
us in Difficulties.   For by this tacit reference to the
real Essence of that Species of Bodies, the Word
Gold (which by standing for a more or less perfect
Collection of simple *Ideas*, serves to design that sort
of Body well enough in civil Discourse) comes to
have no Signification at all, being put for somewhat,
whereof we have no *Idea* at all, and so can signify
nothing at all, when the Body it self is away.   For
however it may be thought all one; yet, if well
considered, it will be found a quite different
thing, to argue about *Gold* in Name, and about
a parcel of the Body it self, *v. g.* a piece of
Leaf Gold laid before us ; though in Discourse

we are fain to substitute the Name for the thing.

§ 20. That which I think very much disposes Men to substitute their Names for the real Essences of *Species*, is the Supposition before mentioned, that Nature works regularly in the Production of Things, and sets the Boundaries to each of those Species, by giving exactly the same real

The Cause of the Abuse, a Supposition of Nature's working always regularly.

internal Constitution to each Individual, which we rank under one general Name. Whereas any one who observes their different Qualities can hardly doubt, that many of the Individuals, called by the same Name, are, in their internal Constitution, as different one from another, as several of those which are ranked under different specifick Names. *This Supposition,* however *that the same precise internal Constitution goes always with the same specifick Name, makes Men forward to take* those *Names for the Representatives* of those real *Essences,* though indeed they signify nothing but the complex *Ideas* they have in their Minds when they use them. So that, if I may so say, signifying one thing, and being supposed for or put in the place of another, they cannot but, in such a kind of use, cause a great deal of Uncertainty in Mens Discourses ; especially in those who have thoroughly imbibed the Doctrine of *substantial Forms*, whereby they firmly imagine the several Species of Things to be determined and distinguished.

§ 21. But however preposterous and absurd it be,
to make our Names stand for *Ideas* we
have not, or (which is all one) Essences
that we know not, it being in effect to
make our Words the signs of nothing ;

This Abuse contains two false Suppositions.

yet 'tis evident to any one, who reflects ever so little on the use Men make of their Words, that there is nothing more familiar. When a Man asks whether this or that thing he sees, let it be a Drill, or a monstrous *Fœtus*, be a *Man*, or no ; 'tis evident, the Question is not, Whether that particular thing agree to his complex *Idea*, expressed by the Name *Man* : But whether it has in it the real Essence of a Species of Things, which he supposes his Name *Man* to stand for. In which way of using the Names of Substances, there are these false Suppositions contained.

First, That there are certain precise Essences, according to which Nature makes all particular Things, and by which they are distinguished into *Species*. That every thing has a real Constitution, whereby it is what it is, and on which its sensible Qualities depend, is past Doubt : But I think it has been proved, that this makes not the Distinction of

Species, as we rank them ; nor the Boundaries of their Names.

Secondly, This tacitly also insinuates, as if we had *Ideas* of these proposed Essences. For to what purpose else is it, to enquire whether this or that thing have the real Essence of the Species *Man*, if we did not suppose that there were such a specifick Essence known ? Which yet is utterly false : And therefore such Application of Names, as would make them stand for *Ideas* which we have not, must needs cause great Disorder in Discourses and Reasonings about them, and be a great Inconvenience in our Communication by Words.

§ 22. *Sixthly*, There remains yet another more general, though perhaps less observed *Abuse of Words* ; and that is, that Men having by a long and familiar use annexed to them certain *Ideas*, they are apt *to imagine so near and necessary a Connection between the Names and the Signification* they use 'em in, that they forwardly *Sixthly, A Supposition that Words have a certain and evident Signification.* suppose one cannot but understand what their meaning is ; and therefore one ought to acquiesce in the Words delivered, as if it were past doubt, that in the use of those common received Sounds, the Speaker and Hearer had necessarily the same precise *Ideas.* Whence presuming, that when they have in

Discourse used any Term, they have thereby, as it were, set before others the very thing they talk of. And so likewise taking the Words of others, as naturally standing for just what they themselves have been accustomed to apply thém to, they never trouble themselves to explain their own, or understand clearly others meaning. From whence commonly proceeds Noise, and Wrangling, without Improvement or Information ; whilst Men take Words to be the constant regular marks of agreed Notions, which in truth are no more but the voluntary and unsteddy Signs of their own *Ideas.* And yet Men think it strange, if in Discourse, or (where it is often absolutely necessary) in Dispute, one sometimes asks the meaning of their Terms : Though the Arguings one may every Day observe in Conversation, make it evident, that there are few Names of complex *Ideas,* which any two Men use for the same just precise Collection. 'Tis hard to name a Word which will not be a clear Instance of this. *Life* is a Term none more familiar. Any one almost would take it for an Affront, to be asked what he meant by it. And yet if it comes in Question, whether a Plant, that lies ready formed in the Seed, have Life ; whether the Embrio of an Egg before Incubation, or a Man in a Swound without Sense or Motion, be alive, or no ? It is easy to perceive, that a clear distinct

settled *Idea* does not always accompany the Use of
so known a Word, as that of *Life* is. Some gross
and confused Conceptions Men indeed ordinarily
have, to which they apply the common Words of
their Language, and such a loose use of their Words
serves them well enough in their ordinary Discourses
or Affairs. But this is not sufficient for Philosophical
Enquiries. Knowledg and Reasoning require precise
determinate *Ideas*. And though Men will not be so
importunately dull, as not to understand what others
say, without demanding an Explication of their
Terms ; nor so troublesomely critical, as to correct
others in the use of the Words they receive from
them : yet where Truth and Knowledg are concerned
in the Case, I know not what Fault it can be to
desire the Explication of Words, whose Sense seems
dubious ; or why a Man should be ashamed to own
his Ignorance, in what Sense another Man uses his
Words, since he has no other way of certainly knowing it, but by being informed. This Abuse of taking
Words upon Trust, has no where spread so far, nor
with so ill Effects, as amongst Men of Letters. The
Multiplication and Obstinacy of Disputes, which has
so laid waste the intellectual World, is owing to
nothing more than to this ill use of Words. For
though it be generally believed, that there is great
Diversity of Opinions in the Volumes and Variety of

Controversies, the World is distracted with ; yet the most I can find, that the contending learned Men of different Parties do, in their Arguings one with another, is, that they speak different Languages. For I apt to imagine, that when any of them quitting Terms, think upon Things, and know what they think, they think all the same : Though perhaps what they would have, be different.

§ 23. To conclude this Consideration of the Imperfection and Abuse of Language ; the *The ends of Language : First to convey our* Ideas. ends of Language in our Discourse with others being chiefly these three : *First, To make known* one Man's Thoughts or *Ideas* to another. *Secondly,* To do it *with* as much ease and *quickness* as is possible ; and *Thirdly,* Thereby *to convey* the *Knowledg* of Things : Language is either abused, or deficient, when it fails of any of these Three.

First, Words fail in the first of these Ends, and lay not open one Man's *Ideas* to another's view. *First,* When Men have Names in their Mouths without any determined *Ideas* in their Minds, whereof they are the Signs : or *Secondly,* When they apply the common received Names of any Language to *Ideas,* to which the common use of that Language does not apply them : or *Thirdly,* When they apply them very unsteddily, making them stand now for one, and by and by for another *Idea.*

§ 24. *Secondly*, Men fail of conveying their Thoughts, with all the quickness and ease that may be, when they have complex *Ideas*, without having distinct Names for them. *Secondly, to do it with quickness.* This is sometimes the Fault of the Language it self, which has not in it a Sound yet apply'd to such a Signification ; and sometimes the Fault of the Man, who has not yet learned the Name for that *Idea* he would shew another.

§ 25. *Thirdly*, There is no Knowledg of Things, conveyed by Mens Words, when their *Ideas* agree not to the Reality of Things. *Thirdly, Therewith to convey the Knowledg of Things.* Tho' it be a Defect, that has its Original in our *Ideas*, which are not so conformable to the Nature of Things, as Attention, Study, and Application might make them ; yet it fails not to extend it self to our Words too, when we use them as Signs of real Beings, which yet never had any Reality or Existence.

.§ 26. *First*, He that hath Words of any Language, without distinct *Ideas* in his Mind, to which he applies them, does, so far as he uses them in Discourse, only make a *How Mens Words fail in all these.* Noise without any Sense or Signification ; and how learned soever he may seem by the use of hard Words, or learned Terms, is not much more advanced thereby in Knowledg, than he would be in Learning,

who had nothing in his Study but the bare Titles of
Books, without possessing the Contents of them.
For all such Words, however put into Discourse,
according to the right Construction of Grammatical
Rules, or the Harmony of well turned Periods, do
yet amount to nothing but bare Sounds, and nothing
else.

§ 27. *Secondly*, He that has complex *Ideas*, without
particular Names for them, would be in no better
a Case than a Bookseller, who had in his Ware house
Volumes that lay there unbound, and without Titles ;
which he could therefore make known to others, only
by shewing the loose Sheets, and communicate them
only by Tale.   This Man is hindred in his Discourse,
for want of Words to communicate his complex
Ideas, which he is therefore forced to make known
by an Enumeration of the simple ones that compose
them ; and so is fain often to use twenty Words to
express what another Man signifies in one.

§ 28. *Thirdly*, He that puts not constantly the
same Sign for the same *Idea,* but uses the same
Words sometimes in one, and sometimes in another
Signification, ought to pass in the Schools and Conversation for as fair a Man, as he does in the Market
and Exchange, who sells several Things under the
same Name.

§ 29. *Fourthly*, He that applies the Words of any

Language to *Ideas*, different from those to which the common use of that Country applies them, however his own Understanding may be filled with Truth and Light, will not by such Words be able to convey much of it to others, without defining his Terms. For however the Sounds are such as are familiarly known, and easily enter the Ears of those who are accustomed to 'em ; yet standing for other *Ideas* than those they usually are annexed to, and are wont to excite in the mind of the Hearers, they cannot make known the Thoughts of him who thus uses 'em.

§ 30. *Fifthly,* He that hath imagined to himself Substances such as never have been, and filled his Head with *Ideas* which have not any correspondence with the real Nature of Things, to which yet he gives settled and defined Names, may fill his Discourse, and perhaps another Man's Head, with the fantastical Imaginations of his own Brain, but will be very far from advancing thereby one jot in real and true Knowledg.

§ 31. He that hath Names without *Ideas*, wants meaning in his Words, and speaks only empty Sounds. He that hath complex *Ideas* without Names for them, wants Liberty and Dispatch in his Expressions, and is necessitated to use Periphrases. He that uses his Words loosly and unsteddily, will either be not minded, or not understood. He that applies his Names to *Ideas*, different from their common use, wants Propriety in his Language, and speaks Gibberish. And he that hath *Ideas* of Substances, disagreeing with the real Existence of Things, so far wants the Materials of true Knowledg in his Understanding, and hath instead thereof *Chimera's*.

§ 32. In our Notions concerning Substances we *How in Sub-* are liable to all the former Inconveni-*stances.* ences: *v. g.* He that uses the word *Tarantula*, without having any Imagination or *Idea* of what it stand for, pronounces a good Word ; but so long means nothing at all by it. 2. He that in a new-discovered Country shall see several sorts of Animals and Vegetables, unknown to him before, may have as true *Ideas* of them, as of a Horse, or a Stag ; but can speak of them only by a Description, till he shall either take the Names the Natives call them by, or give them Names himself. 3. He that uses the word *Body* sometimes for pure Extension and sometimes for Extension and Solidity together, will talk very fallaciously. 4. He that gives the Name *Horse*, to that *Idea* which common Usage calls *Mule*, talks improperly, and will not be understood. 5. He that thinks the Name *Centaur* stands for some real Being, imposes on himself, and mistakes Words for Things.

§ 33. In Modes and Relations generally we are liable only to the Four first of these Inconveniences, (*viz.*) 1. I may have in my Memory the Names of Modes, as *Gratitude*, or *Charity*, and yet not have any precise *Ideas* annexed in my Thoughts to those Names. 2. I may have *Ideas*, and not know the Names that belong to them; *v. g.* I may have the *Idea* of a Man's drinking, till his Colour and Humour be altered, till his Tongue trips, and his Eyes look red, and his Feet fail him, and yet not know, that it is to be called *Drunkenness*. 3. I may have the *Ideas* of Vertues or Vices, and Names also, but apply them amiss: *v. g.* When I apply the name *Frugality* to that *Idea* which others call and signify by this Sound, *Covetousness.* 4. I may use any of those Names with inconstancy. 5. But in Modes and Relations, I cannot have *Ideas* disagreeing to the Existence of Things: for Modes being complex *Ideas*, made by the Mind at pleasure; and Relation being but my way of considering or comparing two Things together, and so also an *Idea* of my own making, these *Ideas* can scarce be found to disagree with any thing existing; since they are not in the Mind, as the Copies of Things regularly made by Nature, nor as Properties inseparably flowing from the internal Constitution or Essence of any Substance; but, as it

How in Modes and Relations.

were, Patterns lodged in my Memory, with Names
annexed to them, to denominate Actions and Relations by, as they come to exist.   But the mistake is
commonly in my giving a wrong Name to my Conceptions ; and so using Words in a different Sense
from other People, I am not understood, but am
thought to have wrong *Ideas* of them, when I give
wrong Names to them.   Only if I put in my *Ideas*
of mixed Modes or Relations, any inconsistent *Ideas*
together, I fill my Head also with *Chimæra's* ; since
such *Ideas*, if well examined, cannot so much as
exist in the Mind, much less any real Being be ever
denominated from them.

§ 34. Since Wit and Fancy finds easier entertain-
Seventhly,   ment in the World, than dry Truth, and
Figurative   real Knowledg, *figurative Speeches*, and
Speech   also
an Abuse of allusion in Language, will hardly be
Language.   admitted, as *an* Imperfection or *Abuse*
of it.   I confess in Discourses, where we seek rather
Pleasure and Delight than Information and Improvement, such Ornaments as are borrowed from them,
can scarce pass for Faults.   But yet, if we would
speak of Things as they are, we must allow, that all
the Art of Rhetorick, besides Order and Clearness,
all the artificial and figurative Application of Words
Eloquence hath invented, are for nothing else but to
insinuate wrong *Ideas*, move the Passions, and thereby

mislead the Judgment, and so indeed are perfect
cheat : And therefore however laudable or allowable
Oratory may render them in Harangues and popular
Addresses, they are certainly, in all Discourses that
pretend to inform or instruct, wholly to be avoided ;
and where Truth and Knowledg are concerned,
cannot but be thought a great Fault, either of the
Language or Person that makes use of them. What,
and how various they are, will be superfluous here to
take Notice ; the Books of Rhetorick which abound
in the World, will instruct those who want to be
informed. Only I cannot but observe, how little the
Preservation and Improvement of Truth and Knowledg, is the Care and Concern of Mankind ; since
the Arts of Fallacy are endowed and prefered. 'Tis
evident how much Men love to deceive, and be
deceived, since Rhetorick, that powerful Instrument
of Error and Deceit, has its established Professors,
is publickly taught, and has always been had in great
Reputation : And I doubt not but it will be thought
great boldness, if not Brutality in me to have said
thus much against it. *Eloquence*, like the fair Sex,
has too prevailing Beauties in it, to suffer it self ever
to be spoken against. And 'tis in vain to find Fault
with those Arts of Deceiving, wherein Men find
pleasure to be Deceived.

Q

CHAPTER XI.

OF THE REMEDIES OF THE FOREGOING IMPER-
FECTIONS AND ABUSES.

§ 1. The natural and improved Imperfections of

They are worth seek-ing. Languages, we have seen above at large; and Speech being the great Bond that holds Society together, and the common Conduit, whereby the Improvements of Knowledg are conveyed from one Man, and one Generation to another, it would well deserve our most serious Thoughts, to consider what *Remedies* are to be found for *these Inconveniences* above-mentioned.

§ 2. I am not so vain to think, that any one can

Are not easy. pretend to attempt the perfect *Reform-ing* the *Languages* of the World, no not so much as of his own Country, without rendring himself ridiculous. To require that Men should use their Words constantly in the same Sense, and for none but determined and uniform *Ideas*, would be to think, that all Men should have the same Notions, and should talk of nothing but what they have clear and distinct *Ideas* of. Which is not to be expected

by any one, who hath not Vanity enough to imagine
he can prevail with Men to be very knowing or very
silent. And he must be very little skilled in the
World, who thinks that a voluble Tongue shall
accompany only a good Understanding; or that
Mens talking much or little, shall hold Proportion
only to their Knowledg.

§ 3. But though the Market and Exchange must
be left to their own ways of Talking, *But yet ne-*
and Gossippings not be robbed of their *cessary to*
antient Priviledg; though the Schools, *Philosophy.*
and Men of Argument would perhaps take it amiss
to have anything offered, to abate the length, or
lessen the number of their Disputes; yet, methinks,
those *who* pretend *seriously* to *search after* or maintain *Truth*, should think themselves obliged to
study how they might deliver themselves without
Obscurity, Doubtfulness, or Equivocation to which
Mens Words are naturally liable, if care be not
taken.

§ 4. For he that shall well consider the *Errors* and
Obscurity, the Mistakes and Confusion,
that are *spread in the World by an ill* *Misuse of*
use of Words, will find some Reason to *Words the*
cause of great
doubt, whether Language, as it has been *Errors.*
employ'd, has contributed more to the Improvement
or Hindrance of Knowledg amongst Mankind. How

many are there, that when they would think on things, fix their Thoughts only on Words, especially when they would apply their Minds to Moral Matters? And who then can wonder, if the result of such Contemplations and Reasonings, about little more than Sounds, whilst the *Ideas* they annexed to them, are very confused, or very unsteddy, or perhaps none at all; who can wonder, I say, that such Thoughts and Reasonings end in nothing but Obscurity and Mistake, without any clear Judgment or Knowledge?

§ 5. This Inconvenience, in an ill use of Words, *Obstinacy.* Men suffer in their own private Meditations; but much more manifest are the Diorders which follow from it, in Conversation, Discourse, and Arguings with others. For Language being the great Conduit, whereby Men convey their Discoveries, Reasonings, and Knowledg, from one to another, he that makes an ill use of it, though he does not corrupt the Fountains of Knowledg, which are in Things themselves; yet he does, as much as in him lies, break or stop the Pipes, whereby it is distributed to the publick use and advantage of Mankind. He that uses Words without any clear and steddy meaning, What does he but lead himself and others into Errors? And he that designedly does it, ought to be looked on as an Enemy to Truth and Knowledg. And yet who can wonder, that all the Sciences and Parts of Knowledg, have been so over-charged with obscure and equivocal Terms, and insignificant and doubtful Expressions, capable to make the most attentive or quicksighted, very little or not at all the more Knowing or Orthodox ; since Subtilty in those who make Profession to teach or defend Truth, hath passed so much for a Vertue. A Vertue, indeed, which consisting for the most part, in nothing but the fallacious and illusory use of *obscure* or *deceitful Terms*, is only fit to *make Men* more *conceited* in their Ignorance, and *obstinate* in their Errors.

§ 6. Let us look into the Books of Controversy of any kind, there we shall see, that the *And Wrang-*
effect of obscure, unsteddy or equivocal *ling.*
Terms, is nothing but noise and wrangling about Sounds, without convincing or bettering a Man's Understanding. For if the *Idea* be not agreed on, betwixt the Speaker and Hearer, for which the Words stand, the Argument is not about Things, but Names. As often as such a Word, whose Signification is not ascertained betwixt them, comes in use, their Understandings have no other Object wherein they agree, but barely the Sound, the Things that they think on at that time as expressed by that Word, being quite different.

§ 7. Whether a *Bat* be a *Bird*, or no, is not a

Instance, Bat Question ; whether a *Bat* be another
and Bird.   thing than indeed it is, or have other
Qualities than indeed it has, for that would be extremely absurd to doubt of : But the Question is,
1. Either between those that acknowledged themselves to have but imperfect *Ideas* of one or both of
those sorts of Things, for which these Names are
supposed to stand ; and then it is a real Enquiry
concerning the Nature of a *Bird*, or a *Bat*, to make
their yet imperfect *Ideas* of it more compleat, by
examining, whether all the simple *Ideas*, to which,
combined together, they both give the Name *Bird*,
be all to be found in a *Bat* : But this is a Question
only of Enquirers, (not Disputers) who neither affirm,
nor deny, but examine : Or, 2. It is a Question
between Disputants, whereof the one affirms, and the
other denies, that a *Bat* is a *Bird*. And then the
Question is barely about the Signification of one, or
both these Words ; in that they not having both the
same complex *Ideas*, to which they give these two
Names ; one holds, and t'other denies, that these two
Names may be affirmed one of another. Were they
agreed in the Signification of these two Names, it
were impossible they should dispute about them.
For they would presently and clearly see, (were that
adjusted between them,) whether all the simple *Ideas*,

of the more general Name *Bird*, were found in the
complex *Idea* of a *Bat*, or no ; and so there could be
no doubt, whether a *Bat* were a *Bird* or no. And
here I desire it may be considered, and carefully.
examined, whether the greatest part of the Disputes
in the World are not merely Verbal, and about the
Signification of Words ; and whether if the Terms
they are made in, were defined, and reduced in their
Signification (as they must be where they signify
any thing) to determined Collections of the simple
Ideas they do or should stand for, those Disputes
would not end of themselves, and immediately vanish.
I leave it then to be considered, what the learning
of Disputation is, and how well they are employ'd
for the Advantage of themselves, or others, whose
Business is only the vain Ostentation of Sounds,
i. e. those who spend their Lives in Disputes and
Controversies. When I shall see any of those
Combatants strip all his Terms of Ambiguity and
Obscurity (which every one may do in the Words
he uses himself) I shall think him a Champion for
Knowledg, Truth, and Peace, and not the Slave of
Vain-Glory, Ambition, or a Party.

§ 8. *To Remedy the Defects of Speech* *First, Remedy*
to use no
before-mentioned, to some degree, and *Word with-*
to prevent the Inconveniences that *out an* Idea.
follow from them, I imagine the Observation of these

following Rules may be of use, till some Body better able shall judge it worth his while, to think more maturely on this Matter, and oblige the World with his Thoughts on it.

First, A Man should take care *to use no word without a Signification,* no Name without an *Idea* for which he makes it stand. This Rule will not seem altogether needless, to any one who shall take the Pains to recollect how often he has met with such Words ; as *Instinct, Sympathy,* and *Antipathy, &c.* in the Discourse of others, so made use of, as he might easily conclude, that those that used them had no *Ideas* in their Minds to which they apply'd them ; but spoke them only as Sounds, which usually served instead of Reasons, on the like Occasions. Not but that these Words, and the like, have very proper Significations in which they may be used ; but there being no natural Connection between any Words, and any *Ideas,* these, and any other, may be learned by rote, and pronounced or writ by Men who have no *Ideas* in their Minds, to which they have annexed them, and for which they make them stand ; which is necessary they should, if Men would speak intelligibly even to themselves alone.

§ 9. *Secondly,* 'Tis not enough a Man *uses* his *Words as Signs of* some *Ideas,* those *Ideas* he annexes them to, if they be *simple,* must be clear and distinct; if *complex*, must be *determinate, i. e.* the precise Collection of simple *Ideas* set- *Secondly, to* tled in the Mind, with that Sound an- *have distinct* nexed to it, as the Sign of that precise Ideas *annex'd* *to them in* determined Collection, and no other. *Modes.* This is very necessary in Names of Modes, and especially moral Words; which having no settled Objects in Nature, from whence their *Ideas* are taken, as from their Original, are apt to be very confused. *Justice* is a Word in every Man's Mouth, but most commonly with a very undetermined loose Signification : Which will always be so, unless a Man has in his Mind a distinct Comprehension of the component Parts, that complex *Idea* consists of; and if it be decompounded, must be able to resolve it still on, till he at last comes to the simple *Ideas* that make it up : And unless this be done, a Man makes an ill use of the Word, let it be *Justice*, for example, or any other. I do not say, a Man need stand to recollect, and make this Analysis at large every time the word *Justice* comes in his way : But this, at least, is necessary, that he have so examined the Signification of that Name, and settled the *Idea* of all its Parts in his Mind, that he can do it when he pleases. If one who makes his complex *Idea* of *Justice*, to be such a treatment of the Person or Goods of another, as is according to Law, hath not a clear and distinct *Idea* what *Law* is, which makes a part of his complex *Idea* of Justice, 'tis plain, his *Idea* of Justice it self will be confused and imperfect. This exactness will, perhaps, be judged very troublesome; and therefore most Men will think they may be excused from settling the complex *Ideas* of mixed Modes so precisely in their Minds. But yet I must say, till this be done, it must not be wondred, that they have a great deal of Obscurity and Confusion in their own Minds, and a great deal of wrangling in their Discourses with others.

§ 10. In the Names of *Substances*, for a right use of them, something more is required *And conformable in* than barely *determined Ideas*: In these *Substances.* the Names must also be conformable to *Things*, as they exist: But of this, I shall have occasion to speak more at large by and by. This Exactness is absolutely necessary in Enquiries after Philosophical Knowledg, and in Controversies about Truth. And though it would be well too, if it extended it self to common Conversation, and the ordinary Affairs of Life; yet I think that is scarce to be expected. Vulgar Notions suit Vulgar Discourses; and both, though confused enough, yet serve pretty well the Market, and the Wake. Merchants and Lovers, Cooks and Taylors, have Words wherewithal to dispatch their ordinary Affairs; and so, I. think, might Philosophers and Disputants too, if they had a Mind to understand, and to be clearly understood.

§ 11. *Thirdly,* 'Tis not enough that Men have *Ideas,* determined *Ideas,* for which they make these Signs stand ; but they *must* *Thirdly,* *Propriety.* also take care to *apply their Words,* as near as may be,· *to such* Ideas *as common use has annexed them to.* For Words, especially of Languages already framed, being no Man's private Possession, but the common Measure of Commerce and Communication, 'tis not for any one, at Pleasure, to change the Stamp they are current in ; nor alter the *Ideas* they are affixed to ; or at least when there is a Necessity to do so, he is bound to give Notice of it. Men's Intentions in speaking are, or at least should be, to be understood ; which cannot be without frequent Explanations, Demands, and other the like incommodious Interruptions, where Men do not follow common Use. Propriety of Speech, is that which gives our Thoughts entrance into other Men's Minds with the greatest Ease and Advantage: and therefore deserves some part of our Care and Study, especially in the Names of moral Words. The proper Signification and Use of Terms is best to be learned from those, who in their Writings and Discourses, appear to have had the clearest Notions, and apply'd to them their Terms

with the exactest choice and fitness. This way
of using a Man's Words, according to the Propriety of the Language, tho' it have not always
the good Fortune to be understood ; yet most
commonly leaves the blame of it on him, who is
so unskilful in the Language he speaks as not
to understand it, when made use of as it ought
to be.

§ 12. *Fourthly,* But because common use has not

Fourthly, to make known their mean-ing. so visibly annexed any Signification to
Words, as to make Men know always
certainly what they precisely stand for :
And because Men in the Improvement of their
Knowledg, come to have *Ideas* different from the
vulgar and ordinary received ones, for which they
must either make new Words, (which Men seldom
venture to do, for fear of being thought guilty of
Affectation or Novelty,) or else must use old ones,
in a new Signification. Therefore after the Obser-·
vation of the foregoing Rules, it is sometimes
necessary for the ascertaining the Signification of
Words, to *declare their Meaning*; where either
common Use has left it uncertain and loose (as it
has in most Names of very complex *Ideas*) or where
the Term, being very material in the Discourse, and
that upon which it chiefly turns, is liable to any
Doubtfulness or Mistake.

§ 13. As the *Ideas*, Mens Words stand for, are of different sorts; so the way of making *And that three ways.* known the *Ideas*, they stand for, when there is Occasion, is also different. For though defining be thought the proper *way to make known the proper Signification of Words*; yet there are some Words that will not be defined, as there are others, whose precise Meaning cannot be made known, but by Definition; and, perhaps, a third, which partake somewhat of both the other, as we shall see in the Names of simple *Ideas*, Modes and Substances.

§ 14. *First*, When a Man makes use of the *Name* of *any simple* Idea, which he perceives is *First, In simple* Ideas *by synony-* not understood, or is in danger to be *mous terms, or shewing.* mistaken, he is obliged by the Laws of Ingenuity, and the end of Speech, to declare his meaning, and make known what *Idea* he makes it stand for. This, as has been shewn, cannot be done by Definition; and, therefore, when a synonymous Word fails to do it, there is but one of these ways left. *First*, Sometimes the *naming the Subject, wherein that simple* Idea *is* to be found, will make its Name be understood by those, who are acquainted with that Subject, and know it by that Name. So to make a Country-man understand what *Fucillemorte* Colour signifies, it may suffice to tell him, 'tis the Colour of withered Leaves falling in *Autumn.* *Secondly,* But, the only sure way of making known the Signification of the Name of any simple *Idea,* is *by presenting to his Senses that Subject, which may produce it in his Mind,* and make him actually have the *Idea* that Word stands for.

§ 15. *Secondly, Mixed Modes,* especially those belonging to Morality, being most of them such Combinations of *Ideas,* as the Mind puts together of its own choice; and whereof there are not always standing Patterns to be found existing; the Signification of their Names cannot be made known, as those of simple *Ideas,* by any shewing; but in recompence thereof, may be perfectly and exactly *defined.* For they being Combinations of several *Ideas,* that the Mind of Man has arbitrarily put together, without reference to any Archetypes, Men may, if they please, exactly know the *Ideas* that go to each Composition, and so both use these Words in a certain and undoubted Signification, and perfectly declare, when there is Occasion, what they stand for. This, if well considered, would lay great blame on those, who make not their Discourses about moral Things very clear and distinct. For since the precise Signification of the Names of mixed Modes, or which is all one, the real Essence of each Species, is to be known,

Secondly, in mixed Modes, by Definition.

they being not of Nature's, but Man's making, it is a
great Negligence and Perverseness, to Discourse of
moral Things with Uncertainty and Obscurity, which
is more pardonable in treating of natural Substances,
where doubtful Terms are hardly to be avoided, for
a quite contrary Reason, as we shall see by and by.

§ 16. Upon this ground it is, that I am bold to
think, that *Morality is capable of De-*
monstration, as well as Mathematicks:
Since the precise real Essence of the

Morality ca-
pable of De-
monstration.

Things moral Words stand for, may be perfectly
known ; and so the Congruity, or Incongruity of the
Things themselves be certainly discovered, in which
consists perfect Knowledg. Nor let any one object,
that the Names of Substances are often to be made
use of in Morality, as well as those of Modes, from
which will arise Obscurity. For as to Substances,
when concerned in moral Discourses, their divers
Natures are not so much enquired into, as supposed ;
v. g. when we say that *Man is subject to Law*: We
mean nothing by *Man,* but a corporeal rational Creature : What the real Essence or other Qualities of
that Creature are in this Case, is no way considered.
And therefore, whether a Child or Changeling be a
Man in a physical Sense, may amongst the Naturalists be as disputable as it will, it concerns not at
all the *moral Man,* as I may call him, which is this

immoveable unchangable *Idea, a corporeal rational Being.* For were there a Monkey, or any other Creature to be found, that had the use of Reason, to such a degree, as to be able to understand general Signs, and to deduce Consequences about general *Ideas,* he would no doubt be subject to Law, and in that Sense be a *Man,* how much soever he differed in Shape from others of that Name. The Names of Substances, if they be used in them, as they should, can no more disturb Moral, than they do Mathematical Discourses: Where, if the Mathematician speaks of a *Cube* or *Globe* of *Gold,* or any other Body, he has his clear settled *Idea* which varies not, though it may by mistake be applied to a particular Body to which it belongs not.

§ 17. This I have here mention'd by the bye, to shew of what Consequence it is for Men, in their Names of mixed Modes, and consequently, in all their moral Discourses, to define their Words when there is Occasion: Since thereby. moral Knowledg may be brought to so great Clearness and Certainty. And it must be great want of Ingenuity, (to say no worse of it) to refuse to do it: Since a *Definition is the only way, whereby the precise Meaning of moral Words can be known ;* and yet a way, whereby their Meaning may be known *certainly,* and without having

Definitions can make moral Discourses clear.

any room for any contest about it. And therefore
the Negligence or Perverseness of Mankind cannot
be excused, if their Discourses in Morality be not
much more clear, than those in Natural Philosophy :
since they are about *Ideas* in the Mind, which are
none of them false or disproportionate ; they having
no external Beings for the *Archetypes* which they are
referr'd to and must correspond with. It is far easier
for Men to frame in their Minds an *Idea*, which shall
be the Standard to which they will give the Name
Justice, with which Pattern so made all Actions that
agree shall pass under that Denomination, than,
having seen *Aristides*, to frame an *Idea* that shall in
all Things be exactly like him, who is as he is, let
Men make what *Idea* they please of him. For the
one, they need but know the Combination of *Ideas*
that are put together in their own Minds ; for the
other, they must enquire into the whole Nature, and
abstruse hidden Constitution, and various Qualities
of a thing existing without them.

§ 18. Another Reason that makes the *defining of
mix'd Modes* so necessary, *especially of*   *And is the
moral Words*, is what I mentioned a *only way.*
little before, *viz.* That it is *the only way whereby the
Signification of the most of* them can be known with
Certainty. For the *Ideas* they stand for, being for
the most part such, whose component Parts no where

R

exist together, but scattered and mingled with others, it is the Mind alone that collects them, and gives them the Union of one *Idea*: and it is only by Words, enumerating the several simple *Ideas* which the Mind has united, that we can make known to others what their Names stand for; the Assistance of the Senses in this Case not helping us, by the Proposal of sensible Objects, to shew the *Ideas*, which our Names of this kind stand for, as it does often in the Names of sensible simple *Ideas,* and also to some Degree in those of Substances.

§ 19. *Thirdly, For the explaining* the Signification of *the Names of Substances* as they

Thirdly, in Substances, by shewing and defining.
stand for the *Ideas* we have of their distinct Species, both the fore-mentioned ways, *viz.* of *shewing and defining, are requisite,* in many Cases, to be made use of. For there being ordinarily in each sort some leading Qualities, to which we suppose the other *Ideas,* which make up our complex *Idea* of that Species, annexed, we forwardly give the specifick Name to that thing, wherein that characteristical Mark is found, which we take to be the most distinguishing *Idea* of that Species. These leading or characteristical (as I may so call them) *Ideas,* in the sorts of Animals and Vegetables, is (as has been before remarked, *Ch.* VI. § 29. and *Ch.* IX. § 15.) mostly

Figure, and in inanimate Bodies Colour, and in some both together. Now,

§ 20. These *leading sensible Qualities*, are those which make *the chief Ingredients of our specifick Ideas*, and consequently the most observable and unvariable part in the Definitions of our specifick Names, as attributed to Sorts *of Substances* coming under our Knowledg.

Ideas of the leading Qualities of Substances, are best got by shewing.

For though the Sound *Man*, in its own Nature, be as apt to signify a complex *Idea* made up of Animality and Rationality, united in the same Subject, as to signify any other Combination ; yet used as a Mark to stand for a sort of Creatures we count of our own kind, perhaps the outward Shape is as necessary to be taken into our complex *Idea*, signified by the Word *Man*, as any other we find in it ; and therefore why *Plato's Animal implume Bipes latis unguibus*, should not be as good a Definition of the Name *Man*, standing for that sort of Creatures, will not be easy to shew: for 'tis the Shape, as the leading Quality, that seems more to determine that Species, than a Faculty of Reasoning, which appears not at first, and in some never. And if this be not allowed to be so, I do not know how they can be excused from Murder, who kill monstrous Births, (as we call them,) because of an unordinary Shape, without knowing whether they have a rational Soul, or no; which can be no more discerned in a well formed, than ill shaped Infant, as soon as born. And who is it has informed us, that a rational Soul can inhabit no Tenement, unless it has just such a sort of Frontispiece, or can join it self to, and inform no sort of Body but one that is just of such an outward Structure?

§ 21. Now *these leading Qualities are best made known by shewing*, and can hardly be made known otherwise. For the Shape of an *Horse*, or *Cassuary*, will be but rudely and imperfectly imprinted on the Mind by Words, the sight of the Animals doth it a thousand times better: And the *Idea* of the particular Colour of *Gold* is not to be got by any Description of it, but only by the frequent Exercise of the Eyes about it, as is evident in those who are used to this Metal, who will frequently distinguish true from counterfeit, pure from adulterate, by the Sight, where others (who have as good Eyes, but yet, by use, have not got the precise nice *Idea* of that peculiar Yellow) shall not perceive any difference. The like may be said of those other simple *Ideas* peculiar in their kind to any Substance; for which precise *Ideas* there are no peculiar Names. The particular Ringing Sound there is in *Gold*, distinct from the Sound of other Bodies, has no particular

Ideas of the leading Qualities of Substances, are best got by shewing.

Name annex'd to it, no more than the particular Yellow that belongs to that Metal.

§ 22. But because many of the simple *Ideas* that make up our specifick *Ideas* of Substances, are Powers which lye not obvious to our Senses in the Things as they ordinarily appear ; therefore, in the *The* Ideas *of their Powers best by Definition.* Signification of our *Names of Substances some part of the Signification will be better made known by enumerating those simple* Ideas, *than in shewing the Substance it self.* For he that, to the yellow shining Colour of *Gold* got by sight, shall, from my enumerating them, have the *Ideas* of great Ductility, Fusibility, Fixedness, and Solubility in *Aq. Regia*, will have a perfecter *Idea* of *Gold,* than he can have by seeing a piece of *Gold,* and thereby imprinting in his Mind only its obvious Qualities. But if the formal Constitution of this shining heavy, ductil thing (from whence all these its Properties flow) lay open to our Senses, as the formal Constitution, or Essence of a Triangle does, the Signification of the Word *Gold* might as easily be ascertained as that of *Triangle*.

§ 23. Hence we may take Notice, how much the Foundation of all *our Knowledg of corporeal Things lies in our Senses.* For how Spirits, separate from Bodies, (whose Knowledg and *Ideas* of these *A Reflection on the Knowledg of Spirits.*

Things, are certainly much more perfect than ours) know them, we have no Notion, no *Idea* at all. The whole extent of our Knowledg, or Imagination, reaches not beyond our own *Ideas*, limited to our ways of Perception. Though yet it be not to be doubted, that Spirits of a higher rank than those immersed in Flesh may have as clear *Ideas* of the radical Constitution of Substances, as we have of a Triangle, and so perceive how all their Properties and Operations flow from thence : but the manner how they come by that Knowledg exceeds our Conceptions.

§ 24. But though Definitions will serve to explain the Names of Substances, as they stand *Ideas also of* for our *Ideas* ; yet they leave them not *Substances must be conformable to* without great Imperfection, as they *Things.* stand for Things. For our Names of Substances being not put barely for our *Ideas*, but being made use of ultimately to represent Things, and are so put in their Place, their Signification must agree with the Truth of Things, as well as with Mens *Ideas.* And therefore in Substances, we are not always to rest in the ordinary complex *Idea*, commonly received as the Signification of that Word, but must go a little farther, and enquire into the Nature and Properties of the Things themselves, and thereby perfect, as much as we can, our *Ideas* of their distinct Species; or else learn them from such as are used to that sort of Things, and are experienced in them. For since 'tis intended their Names should stand for such Collections of simple *Ideas*, as do really exist in Things themselves, as well as for the complex *Idea* in other Mens Minds, which in their ordinary Acceptation they stand for: therefore *to define their Names right, natural History is to be enquired into*; and their Properties are, with Care and Examination, to be found out. For it is not enough, for the avoiding Inconveniences in Discourses and Arguings about natural Bodies and substantial Things, to have learned from the Propriety of the Language, the common but confused, or very imperfect *Idea*, to which each Word is applied, and to keep them to that *Idea* in our use of them: but we must, by acquainting our selves with the History of that sort of things rectify and settle our complex *Idea*, belonging to each specifick Name; and in Discourse with others, (if we find them mistake us) we ought to tell what the complex *Idea* is that we make such a Name stand for. This is the more necessary to be done by all those who search after Knowledg, and Philosophical Verity, in that Children being taught Words whilst they have but imperfect Notions of Things, apply them at Random, and without much thinking, and seldom frame determined *Ideas* to be

signified by them. Which Custom, (it being easy,
and serving well enough for the ordinary Affairs of
Life and Conversation) they are apt to continue,
when they are Men: And so begin at the wrong
end, learning Words first, and perfectly, but make
the Notions to which they apply those Words afterwards, very overtly. By this means it come to pass,
that Men speaking the proper Language of their
Country, *i. e.* according to Grammar-Rules of that
Language, do yet speak very improperly of Things
themselves; and by their arguing one with another,
make but small Progress in the Discoveries of useful
Truths, and the Knowledg of Things, as they are to
be found in themselves, and not in our Imaginations;
and it matters not much, for the Improvement of
our Knowledg, how they are called.

§ 25. It were therefore to be wish'd, That Men,
Not easy to versed in Physical Enquiries, and ac-
be made so. quainted with the several sorts of
natural Bodies, would set down those simple *Ideas,*
wherein they observe the Individuals of each sort
constantly to agree. This would remedy a great
deal of that Confusion which comes from several
Persons, applying the same Name to a Collection of
a smaller or greater number of sensible Qualities,
proportionably as they have been more or less
acquainted with, or accurate in examining the Quali-

ties of any sort of Things, which come under one Denomination. But a Dictionary of this sort, containing, as it were, a Natural History, requires too many Hands, as well as too much Time, Cost, Pains and Sagacity, ever to be hoped for; and till that be done, we must content our selves with such Definitions of the Names of Substances, as explain the sense Men use them in. And 'twould be well, where there is Occasion, if they would afford us so much. This yet is not usually done; but Men talk to one another, and dispute in Words, whose meaning is not agreed between them, out of a mistake, that the Signification of common Words are certainly established, and the precise *Ideas*, they stand for, perfectly known; and that it is a shame to be ignorant of them. Both which Suppositions are false: no Names of complex *Ideas* having so settled determined Significations, that they are constantly used for the same precise *Ideas*. Nor is it a shame for a Man not to have a certain Knowledg of any thing, but by the necessary ways of attaining it; and so it is no discredit not to know what precise *Idea* any Sound stands for in another Man's Mind, without he declare it to me by some other way than barely using that Sound, there being no other way, without such a Declaration, certainly to know it. Indeed, the necessity of Communication by Language, brings

Men to an Agreement in the Signification of common Words, within some tolerable Latitude, that may serve for ordinary Conversation : and so a Man cannot be supposed wholly ignorant of the *Ideas*, which are annexed to Words by common Use, in a Language familiar to him. But common Use being but a very uncertain Rule, which reduces it self at last to the *Ideas* of particular Men, proves often but a very variable Standard. But tho' such a Dictionary, as I have above-mention'd, will require too much Time, Cost and Pains, to be hop'd for in this Age ; yet, methinks, it is not unreasonable to propose, that Words standing for Things, which are known and distinguish'd by their outward shapes, should be expressed by little Draughts and Prints made of 'em. A Vocabulary made after this Fashion, would, perhaps with more ease, and in less time, teach the true Signification of many Terms, especially in Languages of remote Countries or Ages, and settle truer *Ideas* in Mens Minds of several Things, whereof we read the Names in ancient Authors, than all the large and laborious Comments of learned Criticks. Naturalists, that treat of Plants and Animals, have found the Benefit of this way : And he that has had occasion to consult them, will have reason to confess, that he has a clear *Idea* of *Apium*, or *Ibex*, from a little Print of that Herb, or

Beast, than he could have from a long Definition of the Names of either of them. And so no doubt, he would have of *Strigil* and *Sistrum,* if instead of a *Curry comb* and *Cymbal,* which are the English Names Dictionaries render them by, he could see stamp'd in the Margin, small Pictures of these Instruments, as they were in use amongst the Antients. *Toga, Tunica, Pallium,* are Words easily translated by *Gown, Coat,* and *Cloak;* but we have thereby no more true *Ideas* of the Fashion of those Habits amongst the *Romans,* then we have of the Faces of the Taylors who made 'em. Such things as these which the Eye distinguishes by their Shapes, would be best let into the Mind by Draughts made of 'em, and more determine the Signification of such Words, than any other Words set for 'em, or made use of to define 'em. But this only by the bye.

§ 26. *Fifthly,* If Men will not be at the Pains to declare the meaning of their Words, and Definitions of their Terms are not to be had; yet this is the least that can be expected that in all Discourses, *Fifthly, By Constancy in their Signification.* wherein one Man pretends to instruct or convince another, he should *use the same Word constantly in the same Sense:* If this were done, (which no Body can refuse without great Disingenuity) many of the Books extant might be spared; many of the Controversies in Dispute would be at an end, several of those great Volumes, swollen with ambiguous Words, now used in one Sense, and by and by in another, would shrink into a very narrow compass ; and many of the Philosophers (to mention no other,) as well as Poets Works, might be contained in a Nut-shell.

§ 27. But after all, the Provision of Words is so scanty in respect of that infinite variety of Thoughts that Men, wanting Terms to suit their precise Notions will, notwithstanding their utmost caution, be forced often to use the same Word, in somewhat different Senses. And though in the Continuation of a Discourse, or the pursuit of an Argument, there be hardly room to digress into a particular Definition, as often as a Man varies the Signification of any Term ; yet the import of the Discourse will, for the most part, if there be no designed Fallacy, sufficiently lead candid and intelligent Readers into the true meaning of it : but where that is not sufficient to guide the Reader, there it concerns the Writer to explain his meaning, and shew in what Sense he there uses that Term.

When the Variation is to be explained.

LOCKE'S ESSAY.

BOOK III.—NOTES.

"*And lastly, let us consider the false appearances that are imposed upon us by words, which are framed and applied according to the conceit and capacities of the vulgar sort: and although we think we govern our words, and prescribe it well* loquendum ut vulgus sentiendum ut sapientes; *yet certain it is that words, as a Tartar's bow, do shoot back upon the understanding of the wisest and mightily entangle and pervert the judgment. So as it is almost necessary, in all controversies and disputations to imitate the wisdom of the mathematicians, in setting down in the very beginning the definitions of our words and terms, that others may know how we accept and understand them, and whether they concur with us or no. For it cometh to pass for want of this, that we are sure to end there where we ought to have begun, which is, in questions and differences about words.*"—BACON, Advancement of Learning, Book II. Chap. xiv. Sec. ii.

LOCKE'S ESSAY.

NOTES.

pp. 33, 34.

CHAPTER I.

§ 2. *Signs of internal conceptions.*—On Locke's view that words are only signs of the speaker's own ideas, compare note to Chap. ii. sec. 2.

§ 3. *General terms* are names which apply to all the members of a class. Thus *dog* is the name of all those things which resemble each other in a certain way. They are thus equivalent to common nouns in grammar. On the *origin* of general terms see note to Chap. iii. sec. 4.

§ 4. *Ideas simple or complex.*—See Introduction, p. 14.

Privative words.—Logicians often apply the term privative to a name which implies (1) the absence of certain attributes, and (2) that their presence might have been expected. *E.g. blind,* which not only implies the absence of sight, but that the thing denoted can usually or normally see. But Locke uses the term as equivalent to negative ; and in point of fact no clear line can be drawn between the two classes of words.

Relate to positive ideas.—If negative terms simply signified negation, and did not imply any positive qualities whose presence is denied, they would be absolutely without distinct meaning.

§ 5. *Original,* origin. Cf. Shakspere, " It hath its original from much grief." (2 Henry IV. i. 2, 131.)

Sensible ideas.—See Introduction, p. 12.

Imagine, from *imago,* an image ; *apprehend, comprehend,* from *prehendo,* to lay hold of ; *adhere,* from *haereo,* to stick ; *conceive,* from *capio,* to take ; *instil,* from *stillo,* to drop ; *disturbance,* from *turba,* a crowd ; *tranquillity,* probably connected with *quiesco,* to be still ; *spirit,* from *spiro,* to breathe ; *angel,* from ἄγγελος, a messenger. " It does not follow that a word as we use it now bears a gross, narrow, or natural sense, because the root to which we can refer it had a limited meaning, and was connected with matter." (Thomson, Laws of Thought, p. 8.) " In point of fact the obligation is not entirely on one side. While as regards attributes and phenomena, the language of mental science has mostly been borrowed from that of sensation ; in all that relates to the notions of cause or force, as has been well remarked by Maine de Biran, the language properly belonging to the mental fact has been transferred by analogy to the physical. As the basis of a theory, the fact is of no great value ; but its weight, such as it is, should at least be acknowledged to bear on both sides of the question." (Mansel, Prolegomena Logica, p. 168.)

The first beginners of languages.—Locke and his contemporaries were inclined to look on language, law, and religion as arbitrary and artificial products, due to agreements and contracts entered into by men. Modern theories tend to regard them as natural products growing up almost unconsciously, and not as the result of convention consciously agreed upon. We may allow that " language is based upon general agreement, if we give our assent to its use every day by hearing and answering it, just as truly as if the view of Maupertuis were correct,

pp. 36, 37.

that language was originally formed by a session of learned societies." (Thomson, Laws of Thought, p. 38. Cf. also Sayce, Introduction to the Science of Language, vol ii. Chap, x. ; Donaldson, New Cratylus, Chap. iii.) Locke, however, guards against the error in his Thoughts concerning Education, sec. 168, " Languages were made not by rules of art but by accident and the common use of the people."

Ideas of sensation.—See Introduction, p. 12.

Operations they experimented in themselves, operations they experienced in themselves ; *i.e.,* mental activities of which they were themselves conscious.

Agreed, agreed upon.

§ 6. *Species and genera.*—A genus means in logic any superior class, including under it a lower class or species. Thus the genus Animal includes the species Dog. (Cf. note to Chap. iii. sec. 10.)

Propositions, and those most commonly universal ones.— Knowledge, according to Locke, consists in the " perception of the agreement or disagreement of two ideas " ; this agreement or disagreement, expressed in words, is what we call a proposition. A universal proposition is one in which the subject is " distributed" ; that is, one in which *all* the things signified by the term which forms the subject are referred to. " *All* men are mortal," is a universal proposition ; " *Some* men are mortal," is a particular proposition. It is the chief object of science and practical experience to establish universal propositions ; since, while we only have particular propositions, we can never be sure whether any given instance comes under them. If I only know " *Some* men are mortal," I cannot be *sure* whether A, B, or C be mortal.

CHAPTER II.

§ 1. *Sensible,* perceptible by the senses.

By a voluntary imposition.—Locke's view of the artificial origin of language is prominent here. Cf. note to Chap. i. sec. 5. As it has been said, to invent language already presupposes language. At the same time, Locke is no doubt right in ascribing the predominance of articulate language to the variety and quickness with which this special sort of symbols can be produced. Cf. Spencer, Principles of Psychology, vol. ii. pp. 122-5, on the connection between names and things.

§ 2. *The use men have of these marks.*—Locke omits another important use of language, viz., its symbolic use as a mechanical aid to thought. "A highly complex notion [*e.g.,* happiness, the state, etc.] is seldom fully realized ; seldom other than symbolical. Here, then, is a further use of names ; they serve to abbreviate the process of thought." (Thomson, Laws of Thought, p. 37 ; Mill, Logic, ii. pp. 264, *et seq.*)

Nothing but the ideas in the mind of him that uses them.— "But seeing names . . . are signs of our conceptions, it is manifest they are not signs of the things themselves ; for that the sound of this word *stone* should be the sign of a stone cannot be understood in any sense but this, that he that hears it collects that he that pronounces it thinks of a stone." (Hobbes, Computation or Logic, Chap. ii. sec. 5.) Locke does not seem to go so far as this. He puts in the qualifications "primary," "proper and immediate." Still, he lays down that words are, strictly speaking, the signs of ideas ; and that to make them stand for "the reality of things" is to misuse them. (Cf. sec. 5.) Compare Mill : "If it be merely meant that the conception alone, and not the thing itself, is recalled by the name or imparted to the hearer, this of course cannot be denied. Nevertheless, there seems good reason for adhering to the common usage, and calling the word *sun* the name of the sun, and not the name of our idea of the sun. For names are not intended only to make the hearer conceive what we conceive, but also to inform him what we believe. Now when I use a name for the purpose of expressing a belief, it is a belief concerning the thing itself, not concerning my idea of it. When I say, ' the sun is the cause of day,' I do not mean that my idea of the sun causes, or excites in me the idea of day ; or, in other words, that thinking of the sun makes me think of day. I mean that a certain physical fact, which is called the sun's presence (and which in the ultimate analysis resolves itself into sensations, not ideas), causes another physical fact, which is called day." (Logic, i. pp. 23-4.) But this view was not logically open to Locke, who held that we only know our own ideas, and nothing beside or beyond them. This denial, in spite of frequent incon-sistencies, real or apparant, underlies the whole of the Essay. The question is fully discussed in Prof. Green's admirable Intro-duction to Hume's Treatise of Human Nature.

§ 5. *Barely of their own imaginations,* merely about their own fancies and thoughts.

Simple ideas.—See Introduction, p. 14.

§ 7. *Words often used without signification.*—Cf. note to sec. 2 of this chapter.

Several.—Divers, many.

§ 8. *Peculiar ideas.*—Their own ideas.

The great Augustus himself.—The reference is possibly to Suetonius, Vita Tiber., Cap. 71.

CHAPTER III.

§ 2. *Some generals.*—Cf. Pliny, Hist. Nat., Bk. VII. Chap. xxiv., who relates this of Cyrus the elder. Xenophon's account in Cyropædia, Bk. V. Chap. iii. 46-50, is less astonishing, but much more credible.

§ 4. *Enlarges itself by general views.*—Knowledge is essentially general, and its growth is always, when we take a wide survey, from particular cases to universal laws. (Compare the note to Chap. i. sec. 6.) In this lies the chief importance of general names. " If they only served, by mutually limiting each other, to afford a designation for such individual objects as have no names of their own, they could · only be ranked among contrivances for economizing the use of language. But it is evident that this is not their sole function. It is by their means that we are enabled to assert *general* propositions ; to affirm or deny any predicate of an indefinite number of things at once." (Mill, Logic, i. p. 27.)

And therefore in these, i.e., in general names.

§ 5. *Bucephalus.*—The famous horse of Alexander the Great, which carried him in his Asiatic Expedition.

Jockeys, horsedealers, those who have to do with horses, not merely, as now-a-days, riders of racehorses. The word is a diminutive of Jack.

§ 6. *By this way of abstraction.*—General ideas arise by separating the points of agreement of a group of things from the points of difference. The mind abstracts (*abstrahere =* draw off) its attention from the latter, in order to dwell on the former. Hence Locke rightly calls all general ideas *abstract*. There is another side of- the question, since abstraction seems to involve the power of forming general ideas. (See Mansel,

Prolegomena Logica, pp. 34-6.) Compare below note to Chap. viii., sec. 1, and also Introduction, p. 14.

§ 8. *Extension.*—By the "extension" of a name logicians mean the various individual things to which the name applies. This is often called the "denotation." By the "comprehension," "intention," or "connotation" of a name is meant the attributes which the name implies. Locke here tells us that if we diminish the connotation by leaving out of sight some of the attributes implied, we increase the denotation. There are more *animals* than *men*, because the term *animal* implies fewer qualities than the term *man*. (Compare Thomson, Laws of Thought, p. 79.)

§ 10. *Genus and differentia.*—A genus is a superior class ; a species is a class comprehended under the genus. The additional attributes implied by the genus *man* over and above those implied by the species *animal* is called the *differentia*. It is obviously a shorter way to define by genus and differentia than by enumerating all the attributes implied by the general name. If we define *man* as a *rational animal*, *rational* being the differentia, we save ourselves the trouble of separately naming all the attributes implied by the term *animal*.

§ 11. *Signs, whether words or ideas.*—Locke calls ideas "signs," because he considers them as being in many cases (*e.g.*, simple ideas and ideas of substances) representative or symbolic of external realities. (Cf. Essay, Bk. II. Chap. xxxi. especially sec. 12–13.)

That rest, that remain.—Compare Shakspere :
> "What *resteth* more,
> But that I seek occasion how to rise."
> 3 *Henry VI.*, i. 2, 44.

Creatures of our own making.—External things, says Locke, are all individual existences ; there is no general essence shared in common by all the things ranked in a given class. But nature makes things resemble each other in different ways, and we group them into classes according to the number and importance of the resemblances. (See Introduction, p. 22.)

§ 12. *A sort of things,* class of things. Compare Shakspere :

> " There are a *sort* of men, whose visages
> Do cream and mantle like a standing pond."
> *Merchant of Venice,* i. 1, 88-9.

Are nothing but these abstract ideas.—Locke attacks the Realistic theory of the meaning of general names. In the middle ages one of the most vexed questions of philosophy was that of the "nature of universals." What is it which is really shared in common by all the members of a class? Apart from subtleties which could hardly be explained here, we may say that two answers were suggested as early as the ninth or tenth century. (i.) That there is a real common nature which each member of the class possesses, an essence of the species actually present in each of the individual things belonging to the species. This *substantial form* (cf. note to Chap. vi. sec. 10) is really existent, apart from the minds of men, in the individuals included in the class. *Humanity* is a real something, objectively present in all *men;* and it is this which constitutes them men. The "universal," according to this theory, called Realism, is *in re.* (ii.) The other answer, the theory of Nominalism, asserted that the universal character, the bond between individuals of the same kind, was not to be found in the individual things, but in the mind itself, derived from a perception of the things, and therefore *post rem.* Classes of things are made by the mind, which forms a conception of the points wherein a number of things agree, and fixes it by giving a general name. Of this theory two distinct forms were developed. According to one, Conceptualism, the conception of a class is a general idea, not an individual representative of one of the things contained in the class, but a general though imperfect representative of all. The Conceptualists say that I can conceive the idea of Man in general, as opposed to individual ideas of Tom, Dick, and Harry. This is what Locke held. The other modification of the anti-realistic theory denies that we can form a general conception, what Locke calls "the abstract idea for which a name stands," and holds that we can only form conceptions of individuals, Tom, Dick, Harry. What is universal is the *name* of the class, not the idea of the class. "There is nothing universal but names," says Hobbes. The name Nominalism is now generally reserved in order to denote this extreme form of the theory. Both forms agree in denying that the "universal" general nature is to be found in things themselves apart from our minds; but Conceptualism says that it is a concept or general idea, while (ultra-) Nominalism says that it is a word or general name. (Compare Thomson, Laws of Thought, pp. 95–106.)

Essence of the species, the universal, or general fact, the presence of which constitutes a class, whether it be name, idea, or self-existing entity. According to Locke, it is "conformity to the abstract idea" which makes us place things in this or that class; and this abstract or general idea is termed by him the *Nominal Essence*, as opposed to the *Real Essence*, the fundamental constitution or essential attribute of a thing. (See note to next section.)

§ 13. *Classis*, class.—"Class" does not seem to have been used in the singular during the seventeenth century, though the plural form frequently occurs.

Jack, here probably a "bottle-jack," used for roasting meat.

Real essence of substances, the real but unknowable constitution of things, upon which their knowable qualities depend. This, as he points out, is quite distinct from the "abstract idea" of the species, which he calls the *nominal essence*. His objection to the Realist doctrine is, that it confuses the two things.

For two species may be one, etc.—In other words, it is just as absurd to suppose the nominal essence and the real essence both to be the essence of the species, as it would be to suppose that two different classes of things are the same class. There can no more be two essences to one class, than one class for two essences. The internal constitution of the individual and the "abstract idea" of the class cannot both be the fact which constitutes the class. But we know that "conformity to the abstract idea" does distinguish things into classes. Therefore, the internal constitution does not.

Alterations may or may not be.—The relative is omitted : "*which* may or may not." Compare Shakspere : " In war was never lion raged more fierce.—*Richard II.,* ii. 1, 173.

In determining the species of things.—We can easily decide whether a given thing belongs to a class if only the "essence of the species," the fact which constitutes the class, is our "abstract idea" ; because we can come to an agreement that the "abstract idea" (connotation of the class name) shall contain just such and such attributes, and no others. If the given thing possesses just those attributes, it belongs to the class ; if not, not. But if we make participation in the same real essence the test of belonging to a class, we shall never be certain whether a given thing belongs to the class or not ; because we can never be certain what amount of external likeness implies the possession of the same internal constitution, or real essence.

§ 16. By *nominal essence* Locke means the connotation of the class-name, the group of attributes implied by the name : for instance, animality, rationality, a given shape, etc., in the case of Man. Hence, of course, the name *Man* will be applied where this group of attributes is found.

§ 17. *The one.*—This is the doctrine of Realism, described above, note to sec. 12.

§ 18. *Parcel*, a small part or portion. French, *parcelle*, from Latin *particula*, the diminutive of *pars*. (Compare the word *parcel gilt;* and A. V., Genesis xxxiii. 19.)

Insensible parts.—The parts not perceptible by the senses. (Cf. Bacon, Novum Organum, Lib. ii. sec. 7.)

Fixedness.—Locke explains this elsewhere as "a power to remain in the fire unconsumed." Fixed means not volatile, not capable of being evaporated.

§ 19. *Ingenerable*, cannot be generated or produced. Aristotle lays down that Form or Essence is ingenerable in Bk. VI. of the Metaphysics ; what is produced in any given case is the embodiment of the Form in Matter. Locke's argument in this section brings into relief the half-concealed distinction between what is Aristotle's meaning of Form or Essence, and that current in Locke's time, which he denotes by the term Real Essence. " Real Essence," according to Locke, is, after all, material ; it is " a structure " or " inward constitution," of things ; whereas Aristotle intended to express by the words Form or Essence the exact opposite of Matter—the formative principle not yet embodied in Matter.

Besides the Author, except the Author ; not, of course, as well as the Author.

As perhaps that figure exists not anywhere exactly marked out.—" There exist no real things exactly conformable to the definitions [of Geometry]. There exist no points without magnitude ; no lines without breadth, nor perfectly straight ; no circles with all their radii exactly equal, nor squares with all their angles perfectly right." (Mill, Logic, i. p. 259.) Compare Henry More, Antidote against Atheism. (Appendix ; p. 147, Edit. 1662.) " The exact idea of a circle or triangle is rather hinted to us from those described in matter, than taught us by them."

CHAPTER IV.

§ 2. *Intimate real existence.*—The simple idea *red*, and the idea of the substance *gold*, have each a real or archetype pattern, of which they are ectypes or copies. This external reality is supposed to exist independently of the ideas, although we can have no knowledge of it, save by means of them.

§ 4. *Capable of being defined.*—Descartes had already pointed out that we must distinguish between what has to be defined before it is understood and what can be clearly known in itself. He preceded Locke in asserting that names of " simple ideas," as Locke termed them, are indefinable. So, too, the writers of the Port Royal Logic, published in 1662, see Part I. Chap. xiii. Sir W. Hamilton says that the observation had been made " by Aristotle, and after him by many others ; while subsequent to Descartes, and *previous to Locke*, Pascal and the Port Royal Logicians, to say nothing of a paper by Leibnitz, in 1684, had reduced it to a matter of commonplace." (Reid's Works, p. 220, note.)

§ 6. *What a definition is.*—Locke's account of the term definition, although agreeing with ordinary use, is much vaguer than that given by most logicians. He includes, for instance, what they call descriptions, as well as definitions proper. (Compare Mill, Logic, vol. i. pp. 155-160.)

§ 7. *Incapable of being defined.*—Compare the Port Royal Logic. " It would be impossible to define all words ; for in order to define a word we must of necessity have others which may designate the idea to which we may wish to attach that word ; and if we still wish to define the words which we have employed for the explication of it, we should still have need of others, and so on to infinity. It, therefore, is necessary

that we stop at some primitive terms which cannot be defined ;
and it would be as great a fault to wish to define too much as
not to define enough, because by one or the other we should
fall into that confusion which we pretend to avoid." (Professor
T. S. Baynes' transl. p. 85.)

Several terms, several ideas, different, distinct, individual.
(Cf. A. V., 2 Kings, xv. 5 ; Rev. xxi. 21.) Below, in this
section, the word is used in its more recent and ordinary sense.
(Cf. note to Chap. ii. sec. 7.)

§ 8. *Act of a being in power, etc.*—"Who is there that ever
comprehended the nature of motion better through this definition—*Actus entis in potentia quatenus in potentia ?* Is not
the idea which nature gives us of it a hundred times more
clear than this? And who is there that has ever learned from
it any of the properties of motion ? " (Port Royal Logic,
p. 168.) The seventeenth-century opponents of Scholasticism
constantly strove to throw ridicule on the definitions given by
Aristotle, especially those of Motion, Light (compare sec. 10
of this chapter), and the Soul. These definitions were, indeed,
expressed in strictly technical terms, and of technical terms
the new schools had a great horror. It is clear that "the
man of very ordinary capacity" would derive no practical information from such definitions. But the mistake made was
to suppose that the definitions were ever intended to afford
useful information to such a person. All strictly scientific definitions, such as those of Geometry, are open to the same
objections, and can be defended on the same grounds, as those
of Aristotle. They aim at showing us the relation borne by
the thing defined to the whole system of the science. Their
purpose, as Mill says (Logic, i. p. 59), is "to serve as the land-
marks of scientific classification " ; to point out the position
some one thing occupies in reference to an arrangement of
things in general. Given a comprehension of what Aristotle
means by Act, Power, etc., given his view of what are the

ultimate realities of the universe, and then the definitions are anything but "exquisite jargon." Mr. Spencer's dennition of Evolution as "an integration of matter and concomitant dissipation of motion; during which the matter passes from an indefinite, incoherent homogeneity to a definite, coherent heterogeneity, and during which the retained motion undergoes a parallel transformation," might fairly "puzzle any rational man," until he took the trouble to find out what was meant by such terms as *integration, homogeneity, heterogeneity,* etc. ; but this would be no argument against its value or validity. But, in addition to this, we must remember that Locke and Aristotle often (as here) mean quite different things by Definition. The former means by it an "analysis of the subjective impression," which the thing defined produces in the mind ; while the latter means by it an account of the objective cause of the phenomenon. And, although we cannot analyze the simple idea which Light or Motion produces in us, we can assign the cause of Light or Motion, the essential conditions which invariably accompany it or produce it. (Compare Mansel, Appendix to Aldrich, C.)

It is difficult to explain in a few words the real meaning of Aristotle's definition of motion (ἡ τοῦ δυνατοῦ ᾖ δυνατόν ἐντελέχεια κίνησίς ἐστιν, Phys. I. iii), as that would involve a further explanation of one of the fundamental points of his Metaphysics. *Actus* (ἐνέργεια) and *potentia* (δύναμις) are with him primary conceptions, in reality simpler than that of Motion, Light, etc., though acquired by us long after these latter. What he undertakes to do is to express Motion in terms of these. But, in the first place, Aristotle regards Motion (κίνησις) as almost equivalent to Change (μεταβολή). He defines it as the energy or activity of a thing only potentially real ; in other words, as the becoming real of a thing which is not at present real. Change is realization. A house is being built ; a heap of bricks is being changed into a house. The house is at first potentially present in the bricks ; it is present *in potentia*, ἐν δυνάμει. After a time it is really and actually present ; present

pp. 70, 71.

in actu, ἐν ἐνεργείᾳ. In the interim there is Change or Motion, *κίνησις,* and at any given moment the change is an actualization of what was already potentially present. When the house is built change ceases, because actualization is complete. The very notion of realization involves that the subject of it should be as yet unrealized, incomplete. This is what is meant by *quatenus in potentia,* "as far forth as in power." There is only *κίνησις* in so far as the reality is yet *in potentia.* (Cf. Aristotle, Metaphysics, x. 9.)

Jargon.—This word, which plays an important part in seventeenth-century attacks on Aristotle, comes from the French ; its origin is not certain. Chaucer and Gower used it in the sense of chatter :—

> " He was al coltish, ful of ragerie,
> And ful of jargon as a flecked pie."—
> Merchant's Tale, v. 9722.

Beweeginge. — Beweeging is the Dutch for movement, motion (German, Bewegung). Locke had lived in Holland from 1683 to 1689 on terms of intimate friendship with Limborch and other learned Dutchmen.

§ 9. *Atomists.*—The followers of Democritus and Epicurus, who held that the ultimate constituents of the universe were indivisible atoms, moving in empty space. (Cf. note to Chap. x. sec. 14.) This view had been revived by Gassendi, a French philosopher (1592-1655), and his followers, who formed a rival school to that of Descartes, and is to some extent confirmed by modern science.

Passage from one place to another.—This definition of motion was given by Epicurus (μετάβασις ἀπὸ τόπου εἰς τόπου). It is discussed and adopted by Gassendi in his Physics. sec. I, v. i.

Cartesians.—The followers of René Descartes. On the use of the name Cartesian, see Prof. Mahaffy's Descartes, p. 7.

Successive application of the parts of the superficies, etc.

I have not been able to trace this definition in any of the early Cartesians. Descartes' own definition of motion is " the action by which a body passes from one place to another," or, more fully, "the transporting of one part of matter or of one body from the vicinity of those bodies that are in immediate contact with it, or which we regard as at rest, to the vicinity of other bodies." (Princ. Philos. part ii. sec. 25.)

§ 10. *The act of perspicuous, etc.*—Aristotle gives this definition of Light in the De Animâ, II. vii. (φῶς δέ ἐστιν ἡ τούτου ἐνέργεια τοῦ διαφανοῦς ᾗ διαφανές.) There exists in air, water, and such other things as transmit light, a common nature or quality, which makes them able so to transmit it; this is termed by Aristotle the Diaphanous, or, as Locke translates, the Perspicuous. It is thrown into a state of activity by coloured objects or fire, and this state of activity constitutes Light. Light is thus the energy or activity of the light-transmitting medium, while darkness is its state of mere potentiality when not actualized. That Light is due to the proper activity of the medium is shown by the fact that if we place a coloured object on the eye itself we do not see it; a transmitting medium is necessary. Since, however, the medium might be in activity without producing light, Aristotle adds to his definition the words, " in so far as light-transmitting" (" as far forth as perspicuous"). Aristotle's explanation is not fairly open to Locke's criticism, any more than is the modern theory, which makes Light due to the undulations of Ether. Neither professes to do more than explain the nature of the physical cause, or antecedent, of the sensation we call Light; not at all to describe the sensation itself in terms belonging to the language of physical science. There is an ambiguity in such words as Light, Sound, etc., which are used to mean (1) the physical antecedent or external cause of sensation; and (2) the sensation or state of consciousness itself.

pp. 72, 73.

It is unfair to object to an account of (1) that it does not also describe (2). Nothing is more certain than that it is quite impossible to describe states of feeling in terms of matter and motion ; so that no explanation of the physical nature of light could possibly "make the meaning of the word 'light' understood by a blind man."

Perspicuous, literally, translucent, letting light through. For instance, in Sir John Beaumont's Bosworth Field (1629) :—

> "At his command an angel swiftly flies
> From sacred truth's perspicuous gate, to bring
> A crystal vision on his golden wing."

It is now obsolete in this literal sense, and is only used metaphorically to mean clear, intelligible, etc.

Those who tell us that light, etc.—"The extremities of the optic nerves, comprising the coat in the eyes called the retina, are not moved by the air nor by any terrestrial bodies, but only by the globules of the second element" [a kind of extremely rarefied matter, answering in some degree to our modern idea of ether] "whence arises the sense of light and colours." Descartes' Princ. Phil., Pt. IV. sec. 195 (Latin version, which differs slightly from the French). Cf. also Pt. III. sec. 55 ; and Dioptrics, Chap. i.

Gutta serena.—The disease now called *amaurosis,* arising from paralysis of the optic nerve, without injury to the eye itself. Cf. Milton,—

> "So thick a drop serene hath quenched their orbs."—
> Paradise Lost, iii. 25.

§ 11. *Faculty to see Dulcinea by hearsay.*—Don Quixote, Part II. Chap. ix. "Take no heed, sir," said the squire, "for the fact is, her message and the sight of her too were both by hearsay, and I can no more tell who the Lady Dulcinea is than I can buffet the moon."

By applying to his senses the proper object.—Sir W. Hamilton quotes an "old saying," *Omnis intuitiva notitia est definitio.* This way of explaining the meaning of words does not apply to the names of all "simple ideas." Locke overlooks the case of "simple ideas" derived from "reflection." I may in this way make known exactly what I mean by the word *red*, or *extension*, but hardly what is meant by the word *pleasure* or *consciousness*. The impossibility of making our own mental state directly perceptible to others is one of the great obstacles in the science of psychology.

Studious blind man.—That Aristotle was himself aware of the necessity for the direct presentation of "simple ideas" may be seen from his remark that a blind man may talk about colours, but forms no idea of the things which his words denote. (Cf. Physics, Bk. II. Chap. i. sec. 11.)

§ 14. *In no case whatsoever.*—This is not exactly true. We may, as Mill says, define the term whiteness as the power of exciting in us the sensation of white. We cannot define the name of the simple feeling itself, but we can define the name of the attribute which produces it, and the name of the object to which the attribute belongs. "The only names which are unsusceptible of definition, because their meaning is unsusceptible of analysis, are the names of the simple feelings themselves." (Logic, vol. i. p. 155.)

§ 15. *The names of simple ideas least doubtful.*—Bacon takes a very different view. He considers that the words least liable to error are names of substances; then come names of actions, included under Locke's names of modes; and then, most uncertain of all, the names of qualities (excepting the immediate objects of the senses), such as heavy, light, thin, thick, etc. Now these last, which Bacon regards as specially uncertain, are Locke's names of simple ideas. (Novum Organum, Bk. I., Aphorism 60.) Compare Bacon's discussion of the term *damp* in the same aphorism.

pp. 79, 80.

Will not be apt to misapply the word.—"As we should define whiteness in vain to a blind man, while one who can see a white object wants nothing further ; so to know what doubting is, and what thinking is, it is only necessary to doubt and think." (Descartes, edit. Cousin, vol. xi. p. 369. Cf. Port Royal Logic, Pt. I. Chap. xiii.)

§ 16. *Ascents in lineâ predicamentali.*—As a rule, any class of things is included under a higher class, which embraces it together with other classes. Thus the class Animal includes the class Man, and also the classes Lion, Dog, etc. But the class Animal is itself included under the class Organized Body, together with the class Plant. The highest possible class to which we can refer anything is called the *summum genus;* the lowest, the *infima species.* The classes thus arranged form a series or hierarchy ; and the line which connects an *infima species* with its *summum genus,* passing through a succession of intermediate classes, is the *linea predicamentalis.* Thus the "ascents" from Man to Animal, Organized Body, and so on up to Substance (the *summum genus*), are ascents *in lineâ predicamentali.* By the term predicament or category, recent logicians denote the highest class under which any object can be placed. (Cf. note to Chap. x. sec. 14.) But the older logicians meant by the terms not only the *summum genus* itself, but the subclasses contained under it, orderly arranged. Thus Smiglecius tells us that " Praedicamentem est series et dispositio generum ac specierum, sub uno summo genere. Quare praedicamentum non significat summum genus, sed multa genera et species co-ordinatas sub uno genere summo, ipsum vero summum genus non est Praedicamentum sed genus Praedicamenti." (Logica, edit. 1618, vol. ii., Disputatio VII. p. 517.) So, too, Burgersdyk, Ramus, Sanderson, Crackanthorp, Keckermann, &c. To quote only one of them, Burgersdyk says, " Categoria est series rerum sub eodem summo genere gradatim depositarum." The point is rather an interesting one, because it would seem that most modern logicians assert that

T

their predecessors meant by a category what Smiglecius expressly tells us they did not mean.

[For the material of this note, the editor is indebted to the learning and kindness of Mr. Venn.]

CHAPTER V.

§ 2. *Made by the understanding.*—On the other hand, simple ideas are beyond the power of the mind to frame. They come to us only by sensation, or reflection, and are, as it were, given from outside the mind. (Cf. Essay, Bk. II. Chap. ii. sec. 2.)

§ 3. *Very arbitrarily.*—Locke lays stress on the arbitrary character of those complex ideas called Mixed Modes. (See Introduction, p. 16). But care should be taken to remember that he means only (i.) that the mind disregards some groups of ideas which occur to it, while it retains others ; and (ii.) that the groups are not derived from physical objects or referred to them. He perhaps would not deny that the ideas thus grouped have certain logical relations, and that the groups are therefore not entirely arbitrary in formation. The mind cannot put together absolutely contradictory ideas. And he specially calls attention to the fact that "convenience" determines the formation of these Mixed Modes, which is another reason why they cannot be entirely arbitrary. As he elsewhere observes, "I do not say this is done without reason . . . . . but this I say, that it is done by the free choice of the mind pursuing its own ends." (Compare Essay, Bk. II. Chap. xxii.)

Archetype and specific idea.—The type of the class, in conformity with which things are placed in the class. It does not alter the clearness snd logical validity of this conception, even if no such combination of events and states of consciousness ever existed.

§ 5. *The resurrection* (of Christ).—Men had put together that group of ideas which we signify by the word Resurrection before any one had actually risen from the dead, thinks Locke ; and this complex idea would be " right " and " true " (cf. sec. 3) even before the real event occurred.

§ 8. *The Caribee or Westoe tongues.*—The Carib language was spoken in the lower basin of the Orinoco, and along all the coast known as " Tierra Fiome," including Venezuela, as well as in most parts of the West India Islands. There were many dialects. Mr. Clements Markham, who kindly gave me this information, thinks that " Westoe " must be a misprint ; the *W* is certainly an impossible letter for any American language as written by Spaniards. The nearest thing to Westoe that I have yet come across is Witcheka, the name of a tribe of Indians in N. Texas, mentioned by Ludewig, Literature of American Aboriginal Languages.

Versura.—Since Roman debts had to be paid within a fixed time determined by law (a year), it was a common practice to borrow money of a new creditor in order to pay the former one within the legal term. This was called *versura.* Hence the proverbial expression *versurâ solves,* you pay by borrowing —get out of one hole by getting into another. (Terence, Phormio, 5, 2, 15.)

Corban, by its etymological derivation, means (my friend Mr. Jacobs informs me) "something brought near," hence "an offering ;" and thus in its special sense an " offering to God," a " sacrifice." The last word, from our familiarity with its use in the Old Testament, is as accurate a translation as any one English word can be of a foreign one ; and the example seems

T 2

therefore, not a very fortunate one for Locke. He seems to have been led to it by the use of the Hebrew word, as being untranslatable, in Mark, vii. 11, " It is Corban, that is to say, a gift,"—" gift " being the Septuagint version of " Corban," and the Greek word δῶρον in a transliterated form being actually used in the Talmud for a sacrifice, and explained from the analogy of a gift to a king. (Talm., Bab. Sebachim, 7b.)

Hora.—The Roman *hora* was not like our *hour*, a fixed period of time, but varied in length according to the season. The space between sunrise and sunset was divided into twelve equal parts (*horae*), each of which was of course longer in summer than in winter.

Pes.—The probable length of the Roman foot is 11·65 inches English.

Libra contained twelve Roman ounces, or 11 ounces and 237·5 grains, avoirdupois.

Sensible here means evident, obvious.

§ 9. *Constantly*, permanently, unchangeably.

§ 10. *Triumphus.*—The military procession of a victorious Roman general. (See Smith, Dict. of Classical Antiquities.)

§ 12. *Anything existing*, that is, any concrete, external thing.

Notions.—Notion, Lat. *notio*, comes from the verb *nosco*, to get a knowledge of. The old root, *gno* or *gna*, makes its appearance in most of the Indo-European languages with the guttural retained (cf. in English, knowledge, *ken*). Locke seems to think that the word is derived from the Greek νόος or νοῦς, mind, understanding (cf. Essay II. xxii. 2): "And hence I think it is that these ideas [of Mixed Modes] are called ' notions ;' as if they had their original and constant existence more in the thoughts of men than in the reality of things." Locke appears to use the word notion to mean what is called now a conception, whereas he uses the word idea to cover both conceptions and perceptions. In Bp. Stillingfleet's criticisms on the Essay, and Locke's reply (Second Letter), there is a passage of arms about the use of the word *idea*. The Bishop seems to prefer the word *notion;* and Locke says, in his somewhat casual way, " For that ' notion ' will not stand for every immediate object of the mind in thinking, as ' idea ' does, I have, as I guess, somewhere given a reason in my book, by showing that the term ' notion ' is more peculiarly appropriated to a certain sort of those objects, which I call ' mixed modes ;' and I think it would not sound altogether so well to say, ' the *notion* of red,' and ' the *notion* of a horse,' as ' the *idea* of red ' and ' the *idea* of a horse.' . But if any one thinks it will, I contend not ; for I have no fondness for, no antipathy to, any particular articulate sounds ; nor do I think there is any spell or fascination in any of them."

§ 13. *Bundle*, bind.—Cf. Goldsmith, Vicar of Wakefield, " Their trains bundled up in a heap behind." (Chap. iv.)

§ 14. *Barely*, merely, simply.

See hereafter.—Essay, Bk. IV. Chap. iv. sec. 4–9. Knowledge, according to Locke, consists in the perception of the agreement or disagreement of our ideas. If the ideas have no reference to external objects, as is the case with Mixed Modes, we can, with care, make sure that our knowledge respecting them is certain. "That which is not designed to represent anything but itself, can never be capable of a wrong representation, nor mislead us from the true apprehension of anything by its dislikeness to it ; and such, excepting those of substances, are all our complex ideas. . . . . So that we cannot but be infallibly certain that all the knowledge we attain concerning these ideas is real." Hence it arises that Mathematical truths are so certain ; and for the same reason the truths of Morality are susceptible of absolute proof.

pp. 97—101.

§ 15. *As it happens,* as it may happen.

§ 16. *Pudder,* another form of pother or bother. (Compare the two forms murder and murther.) In this case the form in *d* is perhaps the earlier one. It is connected with the verb put; and is thus not derived from the French *poudre,* dust, as has been suggested, says Mr. Skeat, who however thinks that bother and pother are quite unconnected. The original meaning of pudder is probably to stir about ; hence turmoil, confusion.

Huffing, swelling, arrogant. Perhaps connected with *heave.* Huff, huffer, huffing, etc., are common words in Butler.

> " There's but the twinkling of a star
> Between a man of peace and war,
> A thief and justice, fool and knave,
> A huffing officer and a slave."
>
> Hudibras, Pt. II. canto iii.

CHAPTER VI.

§ 1. *Who think there are.*—" And, first, because every fixed star is supposed by astronomers to be of the same nature with our sun, and each may very possibly have planets about them though, by reason of their vast distance, they be invisible to us," etc. Bentley, Confutation of Atheism, published in 1693. Cf. Gassendi, Phys , sec. 2, Lib. I. cap. iii. (Edit. 1658, vol. i. p. 512.)

pp. 102—108.

§ 3. *Clock at Strasburg.*—One of the most famous clocks in the world. Originally erected about 1352, it showed the planetary movements, while various figures, such as angels and saints, struck the hours. A golden cock crowed and flapped its wings at every hour. The clock was remodelled in 1570 by Conrad Dasypodius, a mathematician, aided by the Halvechts, two young and skilful clockmakers, and by David Wolkenstein. It worked from 1574 to 1789. There is an account of the clock in the Saturday Magazine for 1833, vol. III. p. 156. See also Piton, Strasbourg illustré.

§ 4. *Essential* is used throughout this section to denote what Locke calls the *nominal essence,* that is, what is necessarily implied by a general name. "Nothing is essential to individuals," because *as* individuals their names can have no meaning; they are merely arbitrary marks or signs. It is only when an individual is regarded as a member of a class that we regard certain qualities as "essential" to it. Proper names, for instance, do not (except, perhaps, in abnormal cases) imply the possession of any attribute ; but common names, the use of which necessarily "ranks things into sorts," connote the presence of certain attributes.

§ 6. *Essence even in this sense refers to a sort.*—Locke seems to contradict himself here. But compare Mansel, Prolegomena Logica, pp. 70 *seq.,* which perhaps gives a clue to his meaning.

Aqua regia, a mixture of muriatic (hydrochloric) and nitric acids, used for dissolving the precious metals.

§ 8. *Not according to the precise, distinct, real essences in them.*—The ranking of substances into classes under different general names is not of course an arbitrary matter ; but it is independent of the "real essence," or internal constitution, of the things classified. The classes into which we rank objects are certainly determined by the qualities of things, but by the qualities known to us, and not by the unknowable "real essence." (Cf. note to sec. 30.)

Chymists especially, etc.—The "parcels" of (say) sulphur varied because they were not pure. Locke argues that the different "parcels" could not have had the same real essence because the "sensible" qualities differed. They were classed together as specimens of the same substance on account of their general and apparent resemblance. On investigation they turned out, really, to be different substances (sulphur combined with various impurities), and thus no longer deserved the name sulphur, although in the then state of chemical knowledge they would probably retain it. Strictly speaking, the different "parcels" were not "bodies of the same species having the same nominal essence," and thus Locke's argument fails. Things bearing the same name may differ ; but not things having exactly the same attributes.

§ 9. *Than a collection of those sensible ideas, etc.*—That is, all that our minds can do is to discover and enumerate those attributes of things which can be perceived by the senses. This is only true in the sense that our knowledge of things can, ultimately, only consist of facts which could be perceived by our senses if they were strengthened to an indefinite degree.

Cassiowary.—From the Malay word *kassuwaris*. Locke, we may remark, seems to have taken considerable interest in this bird, for he several times alludes to it. (Cf. sec. 34 below.) According to Buffon, it was first brought into Europe by the Dutch, from Java, on their return from their first East Indian voyage, 1597.

Querechinchio.—The Reverend C. Swainson has kindly furnished the following quotation :—"In provinciâ Cujo [in Chile] et multi reperiuntur lepores, quorum quidam, qui appellantur Quiriquincios, carnem habent qualem porcelli

p. 111.

lactentes." George Marcgraff, Historiæ Rerum Naturalium Brasiliæ, Libri Octo (Leyden and Amsterdam, 1648), p. 292. The "Observationes" on Chile, from which the above is taken, were, however, written by Father Alonso d'Ouaglie, or d'Ovalle, of the Society of Jesus, and added to Marcgraff's work by the editor, De Laet. Locke was a diligent reader of works of travel and natural history ; see Fox Bourne's Life, *passim*.

§ 10. *Substantial forms.*—The distinction between *form* (εἶδος) and matter (ὕλη) lies at the root of Aristotle's philosophy. (Cf. especially Metaphysics, Bk. VI. *passim :* also Phyiscs, Bk. I. Chap. viii.) To take his own favourite illustration, a statue is the result of two distinct elements or factors —the material of which it is composed, say brass, and the ideal form which has been given to the matter, say that of a man. Each factor is strictly relative to the other, and in itself has no independent existence. Reality only comes as the product of the two together. There is no such thing as pure form, shape by itself, apart from something shaped ; so, also, there is no such thing as mere matter, without any form, since all matter necessarily wears some shape. At the same time we can logically distinguish between form and matter. Each successive combination of form and matter serves as a matter (*materia formata*) to be once more combined with form. A log of wood is a concrete substance, a combination of form and matter, looked at from one point of view ; but it serves as matter to receive a new form, if we make it into the leg of a table. Form or essence, however, implies much more than mere external shape. It is equivalent to quality, attribute, determination : the form of anything is what gives it its definite qualities and attributes, hence what makes it real. It is the formative principle which makes a thing to be what it is. The soul, for instance, is the form of the body. It thus may answer roughly to what Locke calls the *real essence ;* though by no means exactly, since Locke seems to conceive of the

real essence as an arrangement of material particles, hence as
a concrete combination of matter and form, and not as pure
form or essence. (Cf. note to Chap. iii. sec. 19.) The Port Royal
Logic, Part III. Chap. xviii., has the following account :—
"The Form is that which renders a thing what it is, and
distinguishes it from others, whether it be a thing really distinguished from the Matter, according to the opinion of the
schools, or simply the arrangement of parts." The new
schools of philosophy which strove to supplant scholasticism,
held as a rule the modern view, that the particular nature of
each individual thing depends on the nature and arrangement
(or, on the supposition that the ultimate atoms are all of the
same kind, simply the arrangement) of its material particles.
On the other hand, the scholastics, following Aristotle and
developing his views, asserted that in addition to the matter
and its arrangement, there is in all natural objects a real,
though immaterial principle, which gives them their definite
characters, and thus distinguishes them from one another.
This is the *substantial form.* It is distinguished from what
was called the *accidental form*, which latter is simply a principle of determination in addition to the substantial form, or
source of some attribute over and above the essential attributes
which are due to the substantial form.

Substantial forms were a constant target for the ridicule of
the new schools of philosophy. Thus the Port Royal Logic
speaks of "those sorts of substances which are discovered
neither by the senses nor by the mind, and of which we know
nothing further than that they are called substantial forms."
(Prof. Bayne's transl., p. 249.) The fullest discussion of the
scholastic doctrine will be found in Fr. Harper's Metaphysics
of the school, i. pp. 385, *seq.*

Cf. note to Chap. x. sec. 15, on *Matter.*

§ 11. *Notion we have of God.*—This metaphysical conception
of God as the most real and most perfect Being, borrowed
from Descartes and the scholastics, was got at by putting

pp. 112—114.

together all positive attributes and raising them to an infinite degree. (Cf. Essay, Bk. II. Chap. xxiii. secs. 33–5.) On the curious use of this idea in order to prove that God exists, cf. Descartes, Meditations, III. ; Princ. Phil. I. 14.

Different species of angels.—Theologians, following the teaching of the pseudo-Dionysius the Areopagite (De Coelesti Hierarchia, Chap. vi.-ix.), have generally recognized nine orders of Angels, adding to the Angels, Archangels, Seraphim and Cherubim, the Thrones, Dominions, Principalities and Powers spoken of in St. Paul's Epistle to the Colossians, i. 16, and the Virtues (δύναμις, translated Might, in 1611) mentioned in Ephesians, i. 21. The grades of angels are discussed in St. Thomas Aquinas, who recognizes the continuity spoken of by Locke, in sec. 12 below. (Summa Theologiæ, Pt. I. Qu. cviii.)

Conceit, conception, idea, notion. Cf. Bacon, " Those whose conceits are beyond popular opinions have a double labour ; the one to make themselves conceived, and the other to prove and demonstrate." (Advancement of Learning, II. xviii. 10. Cf. also Shakspere, *Othello,* iii. 1, 115.)

§ 12. *We see no chasms or gaps.*—This argument is based on what is called the Principle of Continuity. *In mundo non datur hiatus,* or as it is otherwise expressed, *Natura non agit per saltum.* It has been of enormous importance in suggesting scientific discoveries.

Whose blood is as cold as fishes'.—The blood of birds is as a rule warmer than that of other vertebrates. Prof. Newton has kindly furnished me with the following information :—It is of course altogether a mistake to suppose that there are any birds "whose blood is as cold as fishes'," but it is quite true that there are birds which are (or were) allowed to be eaten on " fish days." Chief among the latter are what are known in

France as " Macreuses." Curiously enough this name is applied to two different kinds of birds. In the south the name is given to what we call the Coot, and in the north to what is known among us as the Scoter. Ray, Locke's contemporary, seems to have been much exercised by the account of the Macreuse published at Caen in 1680 ; and, after obtaining skins from France, found them to be what we now call the Scoter (*Œdemia nigra*), a kind of duck. He subsequently gave an account of them in the Philos. Trans. (vol. xv. p. 1041). It was this bird that Locke in all probability had in his mind.

Blood and entrails of a hog.—The Porpoises belong to the mammalian order *Cetacea*, and possess the same general characteristics as the mammals which live on land. Ray speaks of " the Porpoise, which as his English name Porpesse, *i.e.* Porcpiscese, imports, resembles the hog both in the strength of his snout and also in the manner of getting his food by rooting." (Discourses on the Creation, p. 122, Edit. 1827.)

Lowest of one and highest of the other.—In point of fact the animal and vegetable kingdoms most nearly approach each other in their lowest forms. There is little resemblance between a rose and the very undeveloped animals classed as Protozoa, but there is a considerable resemblance between the simplest plants (Algae) and the Protozoa. It is often uncertain whether a particular species should be ranked in the vegetable or animal kingdoms. Haeckel has suggested the formation of an intermediate " kingdom," in which to place these doubtful intermediate forms. With higher development comes divergence.

§ 14. *Substantial beings,*—" Substances," concrete things.

For if it should stand here, etc.—Locke seems to mean, that it would be nonsense to say, " we can never know what are the precise number of properties depending on " the *nominal* essence of *gold*, because the nominal essence is simply the group of attributes implied by the name, when used

(as it generally is) as a common noun. In his example Locke
seems to be using the term *gold* as a proper noun, a mere
arbitrary mark to designate this individual given piece of
matter, and as not implying the existence of known attributes.
The real essence of this individual fragment of matter, he
says, we do not know ; therefore, we do not know all the
properties depending on it ; and hence we cannot place it in
the class to which it belongs by nature, supposing such a class
to exist. But the last two or three sentences in the section
are not quite clear.

§ 21. *As by examination we find to be united together.*—This
shows that Locke felt that the classification and definition of
"substances" was not entirely "arbitrary." (Cf. Introduction,
p. 25.)

Specific essence, essence of the species. Cf. note to Chap
iii. sec. 12.

There be that say.—For the omission of the demonstrative
pronoun, compare Shakspere, *Othello,* iii. 3, 157.

The Cartesians are meant. Descartes and his followers
held that the essence of body lies in extension ; that what we
mean by body is, in the ultimate analysis, occupation of space.
Locke, on the other hand, maintained that, in addition to extension, the idea of body involves "solidity," that is, impenetrability and resistance to compression. "Solidity is so
inseparable an idea from body that upon that depends its
filling of space, its contact, impulse, and communication of
motion from impulse . . . Body and extension, it is evident,
are two distinct ideas." (Essay, Bk. II. Chap. xiii. sec. 11.)
The Cartesians so completely identified extension with body,
that they held that no such thing as a perfect vacuum, positively
empty space, can exist ; there cannot be extension without
body. (Cf. Descartes, Princ. Philos., Pt. II. secs. 11-12, 16-18.)

Putting the essence of anything for the thing itself.—We can

---

substitute the attributes implied by the class name (nominal essence) for the name itself, and a proposition in which it occurs will still remain true. If the proposition does not remain true it will show that our own assumed connotation is not the correct one, it is not the true " specific essence," though it is our own " nominal essence," the " essence in respect of us." Locke here means by " specific essence" the true " nominal essence," such a connotation of the class name as a being gifted with perfect knowledge would give it. Locke has no right to assume such an objective specific essence, since on his principles all species are equally arbitrary. Yet he here and elsewhere recognizes, to some extent, an appeal to an external standard, " by which we may at least try the truth of these nominal essences." (Cf. Introduction, p. 25.)

§ 22. *Creatures in the world.*—Ourangs, &c.

Naturals, idiots. Cf. Shakspere : " For this drivelling love is like a great natural." (*Romeo and Juliet*, ii. 4, 95 seq.)

Have hairy tails.—See Marco Polo, Bk. III. Chap. xv., with Marsden's note, p. 613 of his edition. Pliny, Hist. Nat., Bk. VII. Chap. ii. Even quite recently it has been several times asserted that tails are common among the Niam-Niams in Central Africa. (Cf. the curious note on page 216, vol. ix. Series II. of the Dictionnaire encyclopédique des Sciences médicales, edited by Dr. Dechambre.)

Males have no beards.—This is not unusual. (Cf. the work just cited, vol. viii. Series I., article Barbe.)

Females have.—For a learned and interesting note on the very unusual growth of beards on women, cf. the Lancet, 1852, vol. i. p. 421. Aristotle tells us that certain priestesses in Caria had beards (Hist. Anim., Bk. III. Chap. x. sec. 7) ; and Lambert Daneau, in his commentary on St. Augustine's book, De

pp. 121, 122.

Haeresibus (Cap. 97, p. 240, original edit., 1578), tells us that among the Georgians the women were similarly decorated.

No part of that going into our specific idea.—Our ideas of things are simply compounded of groups of attributes, and we know nothing of the real essence which gives rise to the attributes.

Changeling, an idiot.—The literal meaning is that of a child changed at birth, especially by the fairies, who were supposed to take away mortal children to be their servants. (Cf. Shakspere, *Mids. Night's Dream*—

> " She, as her attendant, hath
> A lovely boy stol'n from an Indian king ;
> She never had so sweet a changeling."
> ii. 1, 21 *seq.*)

Locke often refers to facts connected with idiocy, etc., and is one of the earliest writers on mental science who have appealed to abnormal or pathological cases. (Cf. Essay, Bk. IV. Chap. iv. secs. 13–15.)

Drill.—Some African species of monkey. The origin of the word is uncertain. Richardson connects it with " drivel," an idiot. But in all probability it is of African origin. Buffon, in two foot-notes, kindly pointed out to me by Prof. Newton, speaks of " mandrill " as a term used by the English living on the coast of Guinea, but one of which they could give no explanation ; and adds a very wild suggestion of his own as to its origin. (Cf. his Hist. Nat., Quadrupèdes, tom. vii. [Paris, 1788], pp. 97 and 99.) Buffon identifies the mandrill, or drill (he seems to consider the latter word an abbreviation of the former) with the orang-outang.

§ 23. *Women have conceived by drills.* Cf. Licetus, De Monstrorum Causis, Bk. II. Chap. lxviii.

Jumart.—This is a French word; origin uncertain, according to Littré.

pp. 123—127.

Issue of a cat and a rat.—" This cannot be true ; but if it were ? Are there, therefore, no mere cats and no mere rats ?" (Hallam, Hist. of Literature, iv. p. 147, note referring to this passage.)

§ 25. *Have been established long before sciences.*—This, however, does not prevent us from correcting the use of general names by inquiry. Such a correction is, indeed, always going on. (Cf. Mill, Logic, i. pp. 171–6 ; ii. p. 217 *seq.*) "Language, as Sir J. Mackintosh used to say of government, is not made, but grows A name is not imposed at once and by previous purpose upon a *class* of objects, but is first applied to one thing, and then extended by a series of transitions to another and another." (Ib. i. 173.)

§ 26. *Animal rationale.*—This, the "sacred definition" of the Aristotelians, is found in Porphyrii Isagoge, Cap. iii. Duval's edition of Aristotle (1629), vol. i. p. 6. Compare Aristotle's Politics, Lib. I. Cap. 2, p. 1253, sec. 10, λόγον δὲ μόνον ἄνθρωπος ἔχει τῶν ζῴων.

Animal implume, etc.—" Plato having defined a man to be an animal with two legs, without feathers, and having gained great applause thereby, he [Diogenes, the Cynic] stript a cock, and brought him into his school, and said, ' Here is Plato's man for you': which occasioned him to add to his definition, with broad nails." (Diogenes Laertius, Bk. VI., transl., 1688, i. p. 414.)

Acted, driven, moved, animated. "If I shall be told that I am *acted* by prejudice, I am sure it is an honest prejudice."— *Spectator,* No. 287.

Menage.—Giles Menage (1613–1692), advocate, and afterwards priest, a well-known writer on language. His chief work was Les Origines de la Langue Françoise, published in 1650. But he is perhaps still better known by the collection of anecdotes,

table talk, etc., called "Menagiana, ou les Bons-mots et
Remarques critiques, historiques, morales, et d'erudition de
Monsieur Menage, recueillées par ses Amis." The reference
to *l'Abbé Malotru* occurs on p. 95, vol. ii. of the Edition of 1729
(Paris).

And yet there can be no reason. Cf. Essay, Bk. IV. Chap.
iv. secs. 15–16.

§ 27. *Amongst men.*—Locke possibly says "amongst men"
in order not to deny too positively the existence of species
"made by nature," but not known to men as such. (Cf. Introduction, p. 25.)

Licetus.—Fortunio Liceti, an Italian physician (died 1657),
author of De Ortu Animae Humanae, De Novis Astris, and
other scientific works. Locke's reference is to his Book De
Monstrorum Causis: the editions of 1634 and 1668, both
published at Padua, contain engravings of this wonderful and
certainly fabulous monster. (Cf. Lib. II. Cap. lxviii. of the
same work.) On the subject of "Monsters," cf. the article by
C. Davaine in the Dictionnaire encyclopédique des Sciences
médicales, vol. ix. Series II.

As to make but one idea.—The ideas which compose the
signification of the word, its connotation, must be capable of
being "united in a possible object of intuition." There must
be no impediment to our putting together the various elements ;
such as would happen if the component ideas were in expressed or implied contradiction, or had no conceivable connection. (Cf. Mansel, Prolegomena Logica, pp. 23 *seq.*) In
forming an idea of a class of natural things we are spared this
difficulty because the several elements of our idea (*e.g.* shape,
colour, etc.), have been already actually united in the thing
itself, and thus can be united again. But Locke in the next
section admits that we may suppose elements to co-exist which
do not actually co-exist.

` *Be exactly the same*, should not differ from time to time. Locke does not discuss this requirement at length, as he does the first.

Serve to, serve for.—*To* and *for* are often interchanged. In Elizabethan English, and still in the northern counties, the question would run, " What will you have *to* dinner ? " (Cf. St. Matthew, iii. 9. Abbot, Shakspearian Grammar, sec. 186.)

Be not some way answering, do not in some way answer to, etc.

Babel.—Cf. Genesis, xi. 1–9.

§ 29. *Various*, varying.

Fancy, probably means imagination. The word has now a stronger suggestion of arbitrariness or unreasonableness than it used to have when it was employed simply to denote the faculty of imagination or representation. Fancy is Phantasy, misspelled, (φαντασία, from φαντάζω, to show, make visible).

Balaam's ass.—Cf. Numbers, xxii. 28 *seq.*

In a good picture, etc.—A bad instance for Locke, since we do not really suppose the other qualities are present. When we say, This is a lion, we mean, This represents a lion. But the general statement is nevertheless true. All recognition of objects is really rapid and unconscious inference from the presence of one or two attributes to the presence of the object itself with the rest of the attributes. (Cf. Mill, Logic, ii. 186–8.)

§ 30. *It requires much time, pains, and skill.*—Here we have another admission from Locke that species are not entirely "arbitrary." (Cf. Chap. ix. sec. 11 ; Chap. xi. sec. 24.)

§ 32. *Lowest species.*—A Lowest Species (*infima species*) is the narrowest Real kind to which an individual thing can be referred. Thus Napoleon is a man, he is an animal, and he is an organized creature. Man is the lowest species, because no other real kind can be found to place between this and the individual Napoleon. If we divide up the class Man, we divide it not into other classes but into separate individuals. The Lowest Species is thus a species which cannot become a genus. (Cf. Thomson, Laws of Thought, pp. 77–8.)

To that purpose.—For that purpose. (Cf. note to sec. 28.)

§ 34. *In St. James's Park.*—Allusions to the collection of strange animals in St. James's Park occur several times in the diaries of Pepys and Evelyn. (Cf. Evelyn, i. pp. 389–90; iii. p. 136 [Ed. 1852]; Pepys, ii. p. 9 [Ed. 1849].)

Spanish broom.—*Spartium junceum;* belonging to the order Leguminosæ, grows in Southern Europe; its coarse fibres are used for making rope, rough cloth, etc.

Knew probably as much.—Locke means that on his learning the name of the birds, newly imported into the language, he learned nothing fresh about the birds themselves. When he first saw the birds he knew as much about them as most Englishmen do of birds whose names they are well acquainted with. In both cases the knowledge came from observation.

§ 38. *Shock and a hound.*—A shock, or shough, was a rough-coated kind of dog. The name is perhaps connected with shag, which means rough: and we find the compound *shag-dog.* A hound is a hunting-dog; and Dr. Caius, in his treatise Of English Dogs, absurdly derives "hound" from "hunt." "It signifieth such a dog only as serveth to hunt, and therefore it is called a hound." (Cf. also *Macbeth*, iii. 1, 93 *seq.*)

§ 39. *Strings and physics.*—The latter word stands probably for *fusee*, the name of the cone round which the chain, or "string," is wound. It is the French *fusée*, a spindle.

§ 42. *The greatest part of mixed modes being actions.*—Thus virtue, glory, murder, are the names of actions, evanescent events, or can be ultimately resolved into them, while the moving causes of the events are men, who are " substances " or " concrete things."

§ 44. *Kinneah and niouph.*—See next section.

Lamech, Adah.—Cf. Genesis, iv. 18 *seq.*   .

§ 45. *Which I think answer.*—Mr. Jacobs tells me that Locke's prehistoric philology is somewhat at fault here.   In their original meaning both *kinneah* and *niouph* express physiological processes ; the former, *e.g.*, meaning " getting red in the face from excitement," which may be of almost any kind :— jealousy, as in Cant. viii. 6 ; rivalry, as Eccles. iv. 4 ; zeal, as Isaiah, ix. 6 ; or anger, Ps. lxxix. 5.   " Jealousy," therefore, scarcely " answers " *kinneah*, though " adultery " does *niouph*, so far as it is used in the Old Testament.

§ 46. *Being to represent,* having to represent.   For this use of *to be*, where we should employ *to have*, cf. Shakspere :

> " What stuff 'tis made of, whereof it is born
>   I *am* to learn."   *Merchant of Venice,* i. 1, 5.

§ 49. *They have supposed a real essence.*—Locke, perhaps, does not mean that they consciously and knowingly assumed a real essence ; though the general tendency of philosophy at his time was to mistake natural and unconscious inferences for deliberate and conscious ones.

§ 50. *All gold is fixed* may mean, says Locke, (1) that the idea *fixed* is a part of the complex idea *gold;* or (2) that the property of *fixedness* belongs to the concrete something we call *gold*, the something which has a given internal constitution, or real essence quite unknowable by us.   This latter statement,

pp. 156—160.

thinks Locke, though intelligible after a fashion, is of no use. We cannot know *gold* as a concrete thing apart from the mind, but only as a group of ideas in the mind. We cannot tell whether this particular piece of matter has a certain real essence, viz., that of gold ; we can only tell whether this particular group of ideas, to which we give the name *gold*, does or does not include the idea of *fixedness* as a part of it.

This passage shows as clearly as any in Locke how completely his theory of knowledge, as the perception of agreement or disagreement between our ideas, shut him off from making affirmations about real things, and confined his propositions to statements about the relations between ideas. (Cf. Introduction, p. 17 ; and note to Chap. x. sec. 17.)

CHAPTER VII.

§ 2. *In train*, coherently, connectedly.

§ 3. *Discoursing*, reasoning. Discourse is seldom used as a verb in this sense, though often (in sixteenth and seventeenth century writers) as a noun. Cf. Shakspere :

> " Sure, he that made us with such large discourse,
> Looking before and after, gave us not
> That capability and god-like reason
> To fust in us unused."

> *(Hamlet*, iv. 4, 36 *seq.)*

§ 4. *Intimation*, suggestion.

pp. 160—162.

Stands, halting-places.   Cf. Shakspere :

> " Like Romans, neither foolish in our stands
> Nor cowardly in retire."
>
> > *(Coriolanus*, i. 6, 2.)

In the Hebrew tongue there is a particle.—This may be either the particle *b'* " in," or *l'* " to," each of which is prefixed to Hebrew words, and is analyzed by Gesenius into some forty variations of meaning, and has been made the subject of a separate treatise by German scholars.

§ 5. *Discretive*, disjunctive.

Minor of a syllogism.—The syllogism is a formal way of stating our reasoning so as to exhibit clearly the premises, or ground of the conclusion.   There are always two premises ; the first, called the major, makes some general statement, while the second, the minor, brings a particular case under it.   (See Thomson, Laws of Thought, pp. 143–5.)

§ 6. *Other significations.*—On the use of *but* cf. Earle, Philology of the English Tongue, sec. 549.

Explication, explanation.

In this one, in the case of this one sign.   Cf. Shakspere :

> " Almost all
> Repent *in* their election."
>
> > *(Coriolanus*, ii. 3, 263.)

Cf. Abbot, Shakespearian Grammar, sec. 162.

pp. 163—165.

CHAPTER VIII.

§ 1. *Abstract and concrete terms.*—A concrete term is the name of a thing ; an abstract term is the name of an attribute of a thing. Thus *child* is a concrete, *childhood* an abstract, term. Adjectives are properly concrete terms ; they are names applicable to all the *things* of a certain sort ; "snow is white," means that snow is a white thing. But they are sometimes used to signify a quality instead of a thing, as, for instance, " white (= whiteness) is the prevailing colour in the arctic regions ;" they are then abstract. An abstract term is not the name of an "abstract idea." An abstract idea (in Locke) is a general idea, the name of which is called a *general* term, and includes both concrete and abstract terms. (See Introduction, p. 14.)

Intuitive knowledge.—Direct knowledge got by merely looking at (*intueor*) a thing, as opposed to knowledge got by inference or reasoning. "For if we will reflect on our ways of thinking, we shall find that sometimes the mind perceives the agreement or disagreement of two ideas immediately by themselves, without the intervention of any other : and this, I think, we may call 'intuitive knowledge.'" (Essay, Bk. IV. Chap. ii. sec. 1.)

Allowed, approved, recognized. Bacon, "And surely I do best *allow* of a division of that kind, though in more familiar and scholastical terms." (Advancement of Learning, Bk. II. Chap. vii. sec. 1 ; see also Prayer Book Psalms, xi. 6.)

All our affirmations then are only in concrete. Cf. Mansel, Prolegomena Logica, p. 67.

§ 2. *The Schools.*—The " Schools," here used metaphorically for the teachers of the scholastic philosophy. The name Schoolmen (*scholastici*) was originally applied to those who taught in the schools instituted by Charlemagne ; it was after-

pp. 165—168.

wards extended to all those who taught and developed the system of philosophy professed in these monastic schools. (See notes to Chap. x. secs. 2, 6.) The term Schools is still used at Oxford and Cambridge to denote the University lecture rooms, and also certain exercises held there. There was nothing necessarily ridiculous in this attempt to coin abstract terms for purely logical and metaphysical purposes. Of course such words sounded uncouth, but this is a common fault of all purely technical terms. We speak of *quality* and *quantity,* why should we laugh at *quiddity?* Amongst curious examples is the famous term *haecceity*, abstract of the demonstrative pronoun, equivalent to *thisness.* And even proper names furnished corresponding abstracts ; *e.g.*, *Petreity*, from Peter.

Consciousness to themselves.—Consciousness, or self-consciousness. (Cf. the Latin expression, *conscius sibi.*)

Humanitas, says Locke, meant the state or condition of being humane, as *humanity* does with us ; not the state or condition of being a man. This, however, is a mistake, since it is often used in the latter sense, *e.g.*, by Cicero, in De Oratore, Bk. I. Chap. xii., and in many other places.

CHAPTER IX.

§ 2. *Indifferent.*—That is, not in their nature attached to particular ideas. The word " Horse " would serve just as well as the word " Man " to signify what we mean by the latter.

§ 3. *Commerce,* intercourse, not necessarily by way of trade.

§ 4. *Arbitrary imposition.* — Words, however, were not connected with ideas by mere exercise of self-will on the part of men ; some sort of *reason* led to the use of a particular sound to signify a particular idea. (Cf. note to Chap. i. sec. 5. See also Mill, Logic, ii. pp. 239 *seq.*; Thomson, Laws of Thought, pp. 38-45.)

§ 5. *Naturally*, of their own nature.

§ 7. *The word "sham," "wheedle," or "banter."*—Apparently none of these occur before the second half of the seventeenth century. In the *Tatler*, Number 230, "sham" and "banter" are ironically described as "modern terms of art." North, in his Examen, gives the following improbable account of the former :—" The word *sham* is true cant of the Newmarket breed. It is contracted of *ashamed.* The native signification is—a town lady of diversion in countryman's clothes, who, to make good her disguise, pretends to be so *'sham'd:* thence, it became proverbial" . . . . The word *wheedle* is to be found in Butler's Hudibras, Part III. Canto i. 760, where he speaks of reasons,

> " Which ralliers, in their wit and drink,
> Do rather wheedle with than think."

This was published in 1678. It is also to be found in Blunt's Glossographia, Edit. 1661:—" Whead or Wheadle is a late word of fancy, and signifies to draw one in, by fair words or subtile insinuation, to act anything of disadvantage or reproof." In the later editions he gives a wildly improbable etymology. Swift says of *banter :* " This polite word of theirs was first borrowed from the bullies in White Friars, then fell among the footmen, and at last retired to the pedants, by whom it is as properly applied to the production of wit, as if I should apply it to Sir Isaac Newton's mathematics." (Tale of a Tub, Author's Apology.)

pp. 174—181.

§ 9. *Moral words.*—Words signifying ideas belonging to Ethics and the other "moral" sciences.

§ 11. *Characteristical notes.*—We cannot, says Locke, put together arbitrary collections of ideas to be types of classes of external things. We must in this case "accommodate our complex ideas to real existences." (Cf. note to Chap. vi. sec. 30.)

§ 13. *Ideas that are found to coexist.*—Practically, *idea* in this and similar passages is equivalent to *attribute.* (Introduction, p. 11.) Locke means that the name of a concrete thing, *e.g.,* Dog, simply signifies the various attributes implied by the name ; in other words, the *nominal essence.* It cannot possibly signify, or bring before the mind, the unknown internal constitution which is the cause and origin of the various qualities, and which he calls the *real essence.*

Powers.—By powers is meant "the aptness . . . in any substance to give or receive such alterations of primary qualities as that the substance so altered should produce in us different ideas from what it did before." "Powers, therefore, make a great part of our complex ideas of substances. . . For, to speak truly, yellowness is not actually in gold ; but is a power in gold to produce that idea in us by our eyes when placed in a due light." (Essay, Bk. II. Chap. xxiii. secs. 9-10.)

§ 14. *Who shall determine in this case.*—Locke means to point out that there is no authority to decide on the exact connotation of the names of concrete things. Each individual thing has a vast number of different attributes ; the class name cannot signify *all* of these, because no two things are alike in every particular. A selection has to be made ; but who is to select the attributes which the name is to be understood to imply ? In practice, as we have said (note to Chap. vi. sec. 30), the name connotes different selections of attributes, according to the occasion of its use. A human being possesses an almost infinite number of attributes. But when the word Man is used by a sculptor or biologist, it connotes chiefly, or merely, physical attributes ; when, on the other hand, it is used by a theologian or moralist, it connotes chiefly, or merely, moral attributes.

§ 15. *Known seminal propagation*, known to be propagated by seed.

§ 16. *Determined*, determinate, fixed, settled.

Ingenious had in the seventeenth century a stronger meaning than it has now, viz., possessed of genius.

Main.—The main point. We still use *main* as a noun-substantive to denote an ocean.

§ 17. *Straitly*, strictly.—Strait, straight, strict, stretch, and strain, are all connected, though, of course, not by way of direct derivation. The primary idea is to strain, or stretch tight.

Property.—An attribute not connoted by the name of a thing, but always found in conjunction with the attributes so implied, is called a property (*proprium*). It thus forms no part of the nominal essence. The attribute of having equal angles is a property of equilateral triangles ; it is not contained in the definition, but is, nevertheless, always found along with the possession of equal sides.

§ 18. *But barely that perception they immediately signify.*— The names of simple ideas are never supposed to signify anything beyond that simple attribute denoted by them ; the word "red" means the colour *red*, and nothing else. Whereas the names of substances are constantly supposed to refer, not to the collection of attributes (nominal essence) which they really do signify, but to their unknowable inner constitution (real essence). (Cf. Chap. vi. sec. 49.)

§ 21. *Exception*, objection.

This discourse of the understanding. (*sc.* the Essay.)

The preposition *of* was often used (till late in the eighteenth century) where we use *on :* compare, *e.g.*, the title of Hume's work, the Treatise of Human Nature, and the titles of chapters in the Essay. Even now we say "dependent on," but "independent *of.*"

The first two books of the Essay deal with the origin of our ideas, "the ways whereby the understanding comes to be furnished with them," and analyze compound ideas into their simple elements. The fourth, and last, book deals with the nature and reality of knowledge. Locke tells us here, and elsewhere (cf. Bk. II. Chap. xxiii. sec. 19), that when he had finished the first part of his inquiry, contained in Bks. I. and II., he found that an inquiry into "the nature, use, and signification of language" was necessary before he proceeded to the matters treated of in Bk. IV. ; for though his inquiry was not to be a merely grammatical one, but "terminated in things," yet, as words are the means of registering and expressing our thoughts, it became necessary to consider them separately. He accordingly devotes Bk. III. to this subject. (Cf. Mr. Fox Bourne, Life of Locke, ii. pp. 101-2, who thinks that Locke had actually begun Bk. IV. before he found it necessary to write what is now Bk. III.)

§ 22. *The Greek authors.*—Locke, like Bacon, has the profoundest contempt for ancient and mediæval philosophers, and seldom loses an opportunity of throwing a stone at them. The present charge cannot be confined to "Greek authors," but must in fairness be brought against all philosophers. As Locke says afterwards, "There is scarce any sect in philosophy has not a distinct set of terms that others understand not." (Chap. x. sec. 14.) Every original writer is obliged to attach his special meaning to the technical terms he uses. Definitions of terms, though placed first, are the results, rather than the causes, of

pp. 191—193,

divergence of views. Thus Locke's special use of the words *substance, essence,* etc., differs from the use of preceding writers, the schoolmen, Cartesians, etc. (Cf. note to Chap. x. sec. 2.)

CHAPTER X.

On the subject of this chapter it may be worth while to quote the following section from Locke's Conduct of the Under-standing :—

" I have copiously enough spoken of the abuse of words in another place, and therefore shall upon this reflection, that the sciences are full of them, warn those that would conduct their understandings right not to take any term, however authorized by the language of the schools, to stand for anything till they have an idea of it. A word may be of frequent use and great credit with several authors, and be by them made use of, as if it stood for some real being ; but yet if he that reads cannot frame any distinct idea of that being, it is certainly to him a mere empty sound without a meaning, and he learns no more by all that is said of it or attributed to it than if it were affirmed only of that bare empty sound. They who would advance in knowledge, and not deceive and swell themselves with a little articulated air, should lay down this as a funda-mental rule, not to take words for things, nor suppose that names in books signify real entities in nature, till they can frame clear and distinct ideas of those entities. It will not, perhaps, be allowed if I should set down *substantial forms* and *intentional species,* as such that may justly be suspected to be of this kind of insignificant terms. But this, I am sure, to

p. 193.

one that can form no determined ideas of what they stand for, they signify nothing at all; and all that he thinks he knows about them is to him so much knowledge about nothing, and amounts at most but to a learned ignorance. It is not without all reason supposed that there are many such empty terms to be found in some learned writers, to which they had recourse to etch out their systems where their understandings could not furnish them with conceptions from things. But yet I believe the supposing of some realities in nature, answering those and the like words, have perplexed some and quite misled others in the study of nature. That which in any discourse signifies *I know not what,* should be considered *I know not when.* Where men have any conceptions, they can, if they are ever so abstruse or abstracted, explain them, and the terms they use for them. For our conceptions being nothing but ideas, which are all made up of simple ones, if they cannot give us the ideas their words stand for, it is plain they have none. To what purpose can it be to hunt after his conceptions who has none, or none distinct? He that knew not what he himself meant by a learned term, cannot make us know anything by his use of it, let us beat our heads about it ever so long. Whether we are able to comprehend all the operations of nature and the manners of them, it matters not to enquire; but this is certain, that we can comprehend no more of them than we can distinctly conceive; and, therefore, to obtrude terms where we have no distinct conceptions, as if they did contain, or rather conceal, something, is but an artifice of learned vanity, to cover a defect in a hypothesis or our understandings. Words are not made to conceal, but to declare and show something; where they are by those, who pretend to instruct, otherwise used, they conceal indeed something, but that which they conceal is nothing but the ignorance, error, or sophistry of the talker, for there is, in truth, nothing else under them." (Section 28, *Words.*)

§ 2. *In this kind,* that is, in the class of "wilful faults and neglects."

pp. 193, 194.

Clear and distinct ideas.—"As a clear idea is that whereof the mind has such a full and evident perception as it does receive from an outward object operating duly on a well-disposed organ, so a distinct idea is that wherein the mind perceives a difference from all other." (Essay, Bk. II. Chap. xxix. sec. 4.) In the Epistle to the Reader, prefixed to the Essay, Locke explains that he means by the expression "clear and distinct," *determinate*, that is fixed and settled. But his explanation is rather confused, and may for our purposes be neglected.

Two sorts.—"The idols imposed by words on the understanding are of two kinds. They are either names of things which do not exist (for as there are things left unnamed through lack of observation, so likewise are there names which result from fantastic suppositions, and to which nothing in reality corresponds), or they are names of things which exist, but yet confused and ill-defined, and hastily and irregularly derived from realities. Of the former kind are Fortune, the Prime Mover [*Primum Mobile*], Planetary Orbits, Element of Fire, and like fictions which owe their origin to false and idle theories. And this class of idols is more easily expelled, because to get rid of them it is only necessary that all theories should be steadily rejected and dismissed as obsolete." (Bacon, Novum Organum, Bk. I. Aphorism 60 ; Spedding's transl.)

Either affecting something singular.—But, as Locke afterwards allows, when "men in the improvement of their knowledge come to have ideas different from the vulgar and ordinary received ones," it is necessary either to invent new words, or else use old ones in a new signification. (Cf. Chap. xi. sec. 12.) And the latter course is open to special dangers, as the history of the sciences of Ethics and Political Economy shows. "So long as the pedantic objection to the introduction of new technical terms continues, accurate thinkers on moral and political subjects are limited to a very scanty vocabulary for the expression of their ideas." (Mill, Unsettled Questions, p. 75.) This "pedantic objection" dates back to the

pp. 194, 195.

Renascence, when writers became absolutely fanatical about the purity of their Latin style. Locke, however, in no way exaggerates the importance of affixing definite meanings to such new terms ; and his contempt for those who use political, scientific, or theological catchwords without attaching distinct ideas to them is not a bit too strong.

Insignificant, that is, without signification.

Mint Masters.—The Master of the Mint is the title of the official who has the nominal superintendence of the Royal Mint. This is now usually the Chancellor of the Exchequer.

Locke's friend, Sir Isaac Newton, was Master of the Mint from 1695 till his death.

The Schoolmen.—The mediæval philosophers who taught in the monastic "schools" (Cf. note to Chap. viii. sec. 2), or followed the doctrines current there, are known as the School-men or Scholastics. Their systems were all, in the main, based on Aristotle, though they introduced modifications from Platonic, Arabian, and Jewish sources. Aristotelian doctrines were at first regarded with disfavour by the ecclesiastical authorities ; some of them were forbidden by a synod at Paris in 1209, and so late as 1231 the Physics and other treatises of Aristotle were censured by Pope Gregory IX.* Nevertheless Aristotelianism, in a slightly modified form, became the dominant, and at length the exclusive, doctrine of the Schools ; and was gradually recognized as the orthodox philosophy in the Roman Catholic Church. In 1629 the Parliament of Paris decreed that to contradict Aristotle was to contradict the Church. The present Pope, Leo XIII., has recently issued an encyclical in which he strongly advocates the revived study of the works of St. Thomas Aquinas (d. 1274), the greatest of the

---

* It is perhaps open to question how far these ecclesiastical censures were due to the pantheistic interpretations and interpolations of the Arabic philosophers through whose translations Aristotle was made known to western Europe.

Scholastics. Besides St. Thomas (the "Angelic Doctor"), may be mentioned St. Anselm, Archbishop of Canterbury (d. 1109); Abelard (d. 1142); Alexander of Hales, the "Irrefragable Doctor" (d. 1245); Albert the Great, the "Universal Doctor" (d. 1280); Duns Scotus, the "Subtle Doctor" (d. 1308); and William of Occam, the "Invincible Doctor" (d. 1347). At the Renascence, Platonic, Epicurean, and other ancient systems of philosophy were revived; and as Aristotelianism became more and more sterile, and seemed incapable of any further development, it gradually succumbed to the attacks made on it from all sides, such as those of Giordano Bruno (burned, 1600), Bacon (d. 1626), Descartes (d. 1650), Gassendi (d. 1655), and Hobbes (d. 1679.) Though with little else in common, all these thinkers agreed in their contempt for the philosophy of the Schools, which had become firmly bound up with a rigid orthodoxy in religion, and opposition to the new scientific ideas. However, it lingered on at the Universities, both Catholic and Protestant, after a partial reversion to Aristotle himself, in place of his commentators. Melancthon had been the means of its adoption by the Protestants. Oxford was formally pledged by the University Statutes to follow Aristotle; a fine of five shillings was imposed on Bachelors or Masters of Arts who contradicted him. Locke's Essay was long regarded with suspicion and dislike by the academic authorities; and, even when its use had become general, passages such as the present, in which the old system was ridiculed, seem to have been omitted by tutors.

In the seventeenth century the modified Scholasticism held its position only by sheer force of prejudice and the conservatism natural to Universities. But we ought not to overlook the fact that Scholasticism had not always been equally barren. It had once been an earnest, and not altogether unsuccessful, attempt to give a thorough, complete, and systematic account of God, the universe, and man. Modern writers have done something towards modifying the harsh judgments of the pioneers of newer methods, whose position of antagonism

X

made them unfair critics of the system they were attacking. To speak only of Englishmen, writers so divergent as Coleridge, Hamilton and Mill, for instance, invariably speak with respect of the acuteness, clearness, and subtlety of the Schoolmen.

A readable, but superficial and not very reliable, account of the struggle with Aristotelianism will be found in Lewes, History of Philosophy, vol. ii. (See also Hallam, History of Literature, i. pp. 389 *seq.* ; ii. pp. 100 *seq.*)

§ 5. *It is plain cheat and abuse.*—Locke of course exaggerates. He himself is by no means consistent in his use even of technical terms. As he tells us later on, " But after all the provision of words is so scanty in respect of that infinite variety of thoughts that men wanting terms to suit their precise notion will, notwithstanding their utmost caution, be forced often to use the same word in somewhat different senses." (Chap. xi. sec. 27.)

Presently, at once, immediately. So, generally, in Shakspere, *e.g.*, *Hamlet* ii., 2, 170, 620.

The two names, knave and fool.

Constantly, always, ever.

Wit had in Locke's time a wider and more serious signification than it has now. It meant intelligence, acuteness.

" Would steer too nigh the sands to boast his wit."
　　　　　(Dryden, *Absalom and Achitophel*, i. 162.

Misplacings of counters.—Counters were used on a board (abacus) for the purposes of easy calculation. In Shakspere's Winter's Tale the clown says, "Fifteen hundred shorn, what comes the wool to ?—I cannot do it without counters." (iv. 3, 38.)

§ 6. *The peripatetic philosophy.*—" Hermippus relates that Ximocrates was head of the Academic school, when Aristotle was deputed by the Athenians ambassador to Philip ; but returning home and finding that the school was still in other hands than his own, he made choice of a place to walk in, in the Lyceum, where he accustomed himself so much to walk to and fro, while he instructed his disciples, that he was from thence called the Peripatetic, or the Walker." (Diogenes Laertius, transl. of 1688, i. pp. 322-3.) More probably the name comes directly from περίπατοι, the shady walks of the Lyceum where Aristotle lectured, and thus *indirectly* from περιπατέω.

"*Body*" *and* "*extension*."—The Cartesians held that the essence of body is extension. (Cf. note to Chap. vi. sec. 21.) The idea of body, according to Locke, however, includes the idea of extension and of "solidity" besides; hence, while we can speak of the extension of body, we cannot speak of the body of extension, because the former word implies impenetrability, which the latter excludes.

Art of disputing.—Academic exercises throughout the middle ages, and indeed until the present century, usually took the form of public disputations, in which a thesis was maintained by the candidate for a degree against appointed Examiners (as we should now call them), or against any who chose to enter the lists. "The schools, having made disputation the touchstone of men's abilities, and the criterion of knowledge, adjudged victory to him that kept the field; and he that had the last word was concluded to have the better of the argument, if not of the cause." (Essay, Bk. IV. Chap. vii. sec. 11.) "Something may be said in favour of that art of disputation against which so much eloquence has been expended. It was doubtless carried to a dangerous and ridiculous excess, and seems utterly worthless and wearisome now. Yet it was to the athletes of the Middle Ages what parliamentary debate has been to the English—a good, though by no means an unmixed good, and far from the best. We may admit that the art was ineffectual as an instrument of research, and was so far injurious that it withdrew men's energies from patient contemplation of phenomena, and employed them in the easy but illusory

pp. 199, 200.

manipulation of formulas, thus rearing curious exotics sterile
of all flowers and fruit. Nevertheless in those days any intellectual activity which could escape on the one hand from the
oppression of barbarian indifference, and on the other from
theological dictation, was of value." (Lewes, History of Philosophy, ii. p. 8. Cf. also Sir W. Hamilton's favourable opinion
in his Discussions, pp. 679 *seq.* and note.) Details with respect
to the scholastic disputations may be found in Mr. J. Bass
Mullinger's University of Cambridge from the Earliest Times
to 1535, Chap. iv.

§ 7. *Parts*, talents.

§ 8. *Such as Lucian wittily and with reason taxes.*—The
satirist, Lucian of Samosata (died about 190 A.D.), is constantly
attacking the philosophers of his day, and Locke probably has
no particular passage in his mind. (Cf. for instance, Vitarum
auctio, or the Sale of the Philosophers, etc.)

Admiration, wonder.
"It seemeth the reprehension of Saint Paul was not only
proper for those times, but prophetical for the times following;
and not only respective to divinity, but extensive to all knowledge : *Devita profanas vocum novitates, et oppositiones falsi
nominis scientiae.* [1 Timothy vi. 20.] For he assigneth two
marks and badges of suspected and falsified science : the one,
the novelty and strangeness of terms ; the other, the strictness
of positions which of necessity doth induce oppositions, and so
questions and altercations. Surely, like as many substances in
nature which are solid do putrify and corrupt into worms ; so it
is the property of good and sound knowledge to putrify and
dissolve into a number of subtle, idle, unwholesome, and (as I
may term them) verniculate questions, which have indeed a
kind of quickness and life of spirit, but no soundness of matter
or goodness of quality. This kind of degenerate learning did
chiefly reign amongst the schoolmen who, having sharp and

strong wits and abundance of leisure, and small variety of reading, but their wits being shut up in the cells of a few authors (chiefly Aristotle, their dictator), as their persons were shut up in the cells of monasteries and colleges, and knowing little history either of nature or time, did out of no great quantity of matter and infinite agitation of wit spin out unto us those laborious webs of learning which are extant in their books."—Bacon, Advancement of Learning, Bk. I. Chap iv. sec. 5.

Small advantage to human life.—It is worth while to remember, that "as an engine of science, an instrument of discovery, logic never, even by the schoolmen, was proposed." (Sir W. Hamilton, Reid's Works, note p. 701. Compare Bacon, Novum Organum, Bk. I. Aphorisms, 11 *seq.*)

§ 9. *Gibberish.* Gibber is another form of *jabber* and *gabble.* (Cf. *Hamlet*, i. 1, 116.)

This, like "jargon," is another of Locke's "question-begging epithets." It is perhaps worth while to remember, "that there are scarcely any advocates who do not accuse each other of delaying the process, and concealing the truth by artifices of speech." (Cf. Port Royal Logic, Pt. III. Chap. xx. sec. 5, Bayne's transl., p. 271.)

§ 10. *Inform*, to put form into anything, to give a shape to anything, hence, to instruct. To *inform* the mind thus implies something else besides filling it with disconnected scraps of knowledge. (Cf. note to sec. 15.)

> "The god of soldiers,
> With the consent of supreme Jove, *inform*
> Thy thoughts with nobleness."
> (Shakspere, *Coriolanus*, v. 3., 71.)

To prove that snow was black.—This was Anaxagoras, who contended that snow was black—that is, dark, as well as white— since water, of which it consists, is so. This paradoxical statement was advanced to show that the senses are fallible and easily deceived. The mind assures us that the snow is not white, while the senses assure us it is ; and it is obvious that the former must be right. (See Cicero, Academica, Lib. II. Cap. xxiii. sec. 72, and Cap. xxxi. sec. 100.)

§ 12. *A man of very ordinary capacity.*—Another example of Locke's dislike for theologians and lawyers. All the earlier opponents of Scholasticism, overwhelmed with the immense extent of its literature—chiefly commentaries and glosses, and summaries of commentaries and glosses—laid stress on the natural power of the mind, which, if only freed from the bonds of the old system and furnished with the new Method (of Bacon, Descartes, or of whomever it might be), would easily attain to philosophical truth. In the same way, the Reformers believed that any "plain man," if left to study the Bible without note or comment, would necessarily arrive at what they severally considered theological truth, so long as he refrained from obscuring and confusing his ideas by consulting Catholic divines.

"Every man carries about him a touchstone, if he will make use of it, to distinguish substantial gold from superficial glitterings, truth from appearances. And indeed the use and benefit of this touchstone, which is natural reason, is spoiled and lost only by assumed prejudices, overweening presumption, and narrowing our minds." (Locke, Conduct of the Understanding, sec. 3. Cf. Descartes, Discourse on Method, Pt. I. Cf. also Locke's prefatory, "Essay for the Understanding of St. Paul's Epistles by consulting St. Paul himself.")

§ 13. *By-interests*, side interests, selfish interests. "[Truth] is rigid and inflexible to any by-interests." (Locke, Conduct of the Understanding, sec. 14.)

§ 14. *The ten predicaments*, or Categories, of Aristotle were, it is usually said, an enumeration of the highest classes to which we can refer things ; a classification of the assertions

we can make about anything ; or, to put it in another way, they
are an analysis of the different questions which can be asked
concerning anything. But the older logicians seem to have
understood by Predicament not merely the *summum genus,* to
which anything belongs, but an orderly arrangement of the
lower classes contained under it, together with the highest
class itself. (Cf. note to Chap. iv. sec. 16.) The ten predicaments were Substance or Being in itself (οὐσία), Quantity
(ποσόν), Quality (ποιόν), Relation (πρόςτι), Action (ποιεῖν),
Passion (πάσχειν), Place (ποῦ), Time (πότε), Position (κεῖσθαι),
Habit (ἔχειν).

"These are the ten categories of Aristotle, about which there
has been so much mystery, although they are in themselves of
very little use . . . . but are often very injurious, for two reasons, which it is important to remark. The first is :—That we
regard the categories as something founded on reason and
truth, whereas they are altogether arbitrary, and are founded
only in the imagination of a man who had no authority to prescribe a law to others, who have as much right as he to arrange
after another manner the objects of their thoughts, each
according to his own method of philosophising. . . . The second
reason which renders the study of the categories dangerous
is, that it accustoms men to satisfy themselves with words, and
to imagine they know all things when they know only arbitrary
names, which form in the mind no clear and distinct idea of
the things." (Port Royal Logic, Pt. I. Chap. iii. Bayne's transl.,
40.) This objection to what may be called pigeon-holing
Nature, by trying to regard things only according to a somewhat artificial and superficial classification, is constantly found
in seventeenth-century antagonists of Aristotle. (Cf. Bacon,
Novum Organum, Bk. I. Aph. 63.)

Substantial forms. (Cf. note to Chap. vi. sec. 10.)

Vegetative souls.—By the nutrient or vegetative soul was
meant the "vital principle," or source of life in animals and
plants. Aristotle recognized different kinds, or rather stages of

development, of souls. The lowest of these is the Nutrient Soul, shared by all organized bodies. It is the "form" (Note to Chap. vi. sec. 10) of the organism, building it up, preserving it against the forces of external nature, and reproducing it. When the faculty of sensation is added, this soul becomes the Sentient Soul; and this stage of development is characteristic of all animal life. In man the Sentient Soul has become Noëtic, or Intelligent, by the addition of fresh powers. (Aristotle, De Anima, Bk. II. Chap. ii. *seq.*)

Abhorrence of a vacuum.—This phrase was the explanation commonly put forward to account for the phenomena of suction, the rise of water in a pump, the mercurial barometer, etc. In point of fact it is no *explanation* at all, but only a figurative, though convenient, description of the observed facts. An imaginary principle, adopted on insufficient evidence, it was conclusively disproved by showing that a vacuum can be produced by water in a tube over thirty-four feet high, and by heavier fluids in shorter tubes, as was done by Torricelli about 1643. This doctrine of Nature's horror of a vacuum "was *unphilosophical*, because it introduced the notion of an emotion, horror, as an account of physical facts; it was *imperfect*, because it was at best only a law of phenomena, not pointing out any physical cause; and it was *wrong*, because it gave an unlimited extent to the effect." (Whewell, Hist. of Inductive Sciences, ii. p. 65.) Or, as the writers of the Port Royal Logic put it, "There are some who assign chimerical causes for chimerical effects, as those who maintain that Nature abhors a vacuum, and that she exerts herself to avoid it (which is an imaginary effect, for Nature abhors nothing, but all the effects which are attributed to that horror depend on the weight of the air alone), and are continually advancing for that imaginary horror reasons which are still more imaginary. . . . . It is a kind of science, which proves the non-existent by means of the existent." (Part III. Chap. xix.)

Intentional species.—The knowledge of external objects was supposed to be due to the appropriation by the mind of certain images or *species* thrown off by the things. In one form or other this doctrine of perception was common to nearly all the ancient and mediæval philosophers ; it is to be found in its grossest and most materialistic form among the Epicureans, and in its most refined and metaphysical shape among the scholastics. "But the philosophy schools through all the universities of Christendom, grounded upon certain texts of Aristotle, say, for the cause of vision, that the thing seen sendeth forth on every side a visible species — in English, a visible show, apparition, or aspect, or a being seen, the receiving whereof in the eye is seeing ; and for the cause of hearing, that the thing heard sendeth forth an audible species—that is, an audible aspect, which, entering at the ear, maketh hearing; nay, for the cause of understanding also, they say the thing understood sendeth forth an intelligible species, which, coming into the understanding, makes us understand." (Hobbes, Leviathan, Pt. I. Chap. i.) Descartes also opposes the doctrine, and speaks ironically of "those little images flying through the air, called *intentional species*, which so wonderfully exercise the imagination of philosophers." (Dioptrics, Chap. i. sec. 5.) Why these *species*, or images, were called *intentional* is not very clear ; although several explanations are quoted by Sir W. Hamilton in his edition of Reid, Note M. p. 952 ; *e.g.*, because they have only a relative and incomplete reality, the full reality being in the object from which they are derived, or because they require *intentio*—that is, attention— on the part of our minds in order to apprehend them.

Soul of the world.—In the Timæus Plato speaks of the soul of the world, which he seems to conceive of as bearing the same relation to the universe as the soul of man does to his body. It is the expression of the form and order of the universe, created by God before the material universe itself. It is the source of the movement of the heavens, and is the highest and best of created things. All this is described in a

pp. 205, 206.

mystical fashion ; Plato's tone seeming here to be half-way between that of mythical tradition and philosophical speculation. (Cf. Cudworth, Works, i. p. 702 *seq.;* Edit. 1837.)

Endeavour towards motion in their atoms when at rest. —The Epicureans and their seventeenth-century followers held that the ultimate realities of the universe were atoms and empty space. All things, on analysis, could be resolved into combinations of atoms. These possessed only shape, size, and weight ; they were, as the name implies, indivisible, and also indestructible. They had a constant motion downwards, and also an infinitesimally small swerving from this particular movement, which sufficed to bring them into collision with each other, and thus to set up aggregation. This swerving is brought about, according to Lucretius, by a spontaneous impulse in the atoms themselves. (Cf. De Rerum Natura, Lib. II. 216 *seq.*, 251–93.) Gassendi lays down that there is in atoms a " native, inherent, etc., endeavour towards motion (*ad motum propensio*), a spontaneous effort and impulse (*ab intrinseco propulsio*)." (Physics, Sec. I. Lib. III. Cap. vii.) Descartes uses the expression *propensio ad motum, e.g.,* Dioptrics, Chap. i. sec. 8. Diogenes Laertius, one of the principal authorities for the opinions of Epicurus, says that he taught that "Atoms are in continual motion. . . . Some are also far distant from one another ; others retain the same agitation, when they are inclined of themselves to embrace each other, or detained by those that are violently hurried close together in order to some composition." (Bk. X. transl. 1688–96.)

Aërial and etherial vehicles.—The later Platonists, Plotinus, Porphyry, etc., taught that the disembodied soul was attached to a body of air or ether, called its vehicle. " Now from these passages, cited from Philoponus, it further appeareth, that the ancient assertors of the soul's immortality did not suppose human souls, after death, to be stripped stark naked from all body ; but that the generality of souls had then a certain spirituous, vaporous, or airy body accompanying them, though

in different degrees of purity and impurity respectively to themselves. . . . . . Nevertheless the same Philoponus there addeth,
that according to these ancients, besides the terrestrial body,
and this spirituous and airy body too, there is yet a third kind
of body, of a higher rank than either of the former (peculiarly
belonging to such souls after death as are purged and cleansed
of corporeal affections, lusts, and passions), called by them
σῶμα αὐγοειδὲς, and οὐράνιον, and αἰθέριον, etc., a luciform and
celestial and etherial body." (Cudworth, Works, ii. pp. 222-3;
Edit. 1837.) This doctrine had also been advocated by Henry
More, another contemporary of Locke's, in his book on the
Immortality of the Soul, from which may be quoted the following :—"The Platonists do chiefly take notice of three kinds
of vehicles, aetherial, aërial, and terrestrial ; in every one of
which there may be several degrees of purity and impurity,
which yet need not amount to a new species. . . . . Wherefore
not letting go that more orderly conceit of the Platonists ; I
shall make bold to assert that the soul may live and act in an
aërial vehicle as well as in the aetherial ; and that there are
very few that arrive at that high happiness, as to acquire a
celestial vehicle immediately upon their quitting the terrestrial
one : that heavenly chariot necessarily carrying us in triumph
to the greatest happiness the soul of man is capable of: which
would arrive to all men indifferently, good and bad, if the
parting with this earthly body would suddenly mount us into
the heavenly. Wherefore, by a just Nemesis, the souls of men
that are not very heroically virtuous will find themselves re-
strained within the compass of that caliginous air, as both reason itself will suggest, and the Platonists have unanimously
determined." (Bk. II. Chap. xiv. secs. 1 and 6.)

Scarce any sect in philosophy has not.—Compare Chap. ix.
sec. 22, and note. For the omission of the relative pronoun
"[which] has not," see Abbot, Shakespearian Grammar, secs.
244 *seq.*

Peripatetic forms.—See note to Chap. vi. sec. 10, on *Substantial forms.*

pp. 206—208.

§ 15. *Instance in one; i.e.,* I shall give an instance in one case only.

Matter.—See note to Chap. vi. sec. 10, on *Form.* " The [Aristotelian] notion of matter is entirely different from what we now-a-days understand by 'matter.' . . . . We conceive of matter as a corporeal thing distributed universally, save where there is a vacuum, and of an essentially uniform nature, although subject to certain modifications. In Aristotle the notion of matter is *relative;* it is matter in relation to that which is to result from it through the accession of form . . . . as we see there is no question whatever of an independent corporeal substrate of things." (Lange, Hist. of Materialism, Eng. transl., i. p. 193.) Mere matter was to Aristotle only potentiality; it was only a possibility of receiving form; it had no attributes. (Cf. Harper, Metaphysics of the School, ii. p. 189 *seq.*) What matter is to a modern philosopher can be seen by looking at Mr. Spencer's Principles of Psychology, i. pp. 616–624. This ideal matter, absolutely devoid of form, and not supposed to really exist, is called by Aristotle *materia prima* (ὑλη πρώτη). (Physics, Bk. I. Chap. viii.) It signifies, as Hobbes says, " body in general, that is, body considered universally, not as *having* neither form or accident" [since all actual matter possesses some form], "but in which no form or other accident but quantity are *at all considered.*" (Philosophy, Part II. Chap. viii. sec. 24.) It is evident that material for endless disputes was laid up in the natural confusion between the new scientific conception of Matter, due to the revived Epicurean (Atomistic) philosophy, and the old metaphysical conception of Matter due to Aristotle. What the new philosophers called Matter was to the older school a combination of Matter and Form.

§ 16. *None of the least causes that men are so hardly drawn, etc.*; that is, not one of the least reasons why men are drawn with so much difficulty to leave their errors, etc.

§ 17. *Whereof the nominal essences are only known to us.*—
(Cf. note to Chap. ii. sec. 2.) The present passage is unsatisfactory, because it is difficult to see whether Locke considers that
the true subject of the proposition, " Gold is malleable," is—(1)
an external *thing*, recognized by us as possessing certain attributes, though not as possessing a given real essence ; or (2) a
complex *idea*, composed of the simple ideas of those same attributes ; or (3) a *word*, the sound ' gold.' The second meaning
would be that most consistent with the general drift of Locke's
philosophy ; but it by no means follows that it was the one
really in his mind.

§ 18. *v.g.*, verbi gratiâ, for example.

§ 19. *Chance-medley*, according to Cowell, Law Dictionary,
" signifies the casual killing of a man not altogether without the
killer's fault, though without an evil intent." Strictly, it was
homicide in self-defence on the part of a man who had been
assaulted in a sudden brawl. The word is an instance of what
has been called double etymology. It really comes from *chaude
mêlée*, an " affray in hot blood " ; but another derivation has
been forced upon it in consequence of a similarity of sound.
(See Trench, English, Past and Present, Lect. VIII. p. 306.)

Manslaughter is the unlawful killing of another, without
malice expressed or implied, but from sudden passion.

Murder differs from Manslaughter in the presence of
"malice aforethought," expressed or implied ; that is, clearly
proved or inferrible from the circumstances of the case. (Cf.
Chap. v. sec. 6.)

The real as well as the nominal essence.—Cf. Chap. v. sec. 14.

In that called gold.—The same difficulty as that referred to
in the note to sec. 17 recurs.

Certain precise essences; i.e., "real essence."

§ 22. *Same just precise collection.*—"Just" means exact.

Ill use of words.—This is of course an exaggeration. The "different languages" spoken by philosophers and theologians are often forced on them as the results of their disputes instead of causing them. (Note to Chap. ix. sec. 22.) But, making every allowance for this, there is no doubt a vast amount of controversy which is purely verbal due to misunderstanding, unconscious or wilful, of the language of opponents. The difficulty is to see when a controversy is really of this charac-ter. Nothing is more usual than for a modern disputant to assure the world that it is only a contention about words, a mere logomachy, with the implied assertion, that his use of words is right and that of his antagonist wrong.

§ 27. *By tale*, by number. Cf. Milton's often misunderstood line :—

> And every shepherd tells his *tale.*—*L'Allegro.*

§ 29. *Without defining his terms.*—Important instances of this truth are to be found in Political Economy. Thus the terms Wealth, Price, Rent, Productive, etc., have all to be most carefully defined, and the greatest care taken lest the associa-tions of ordinary use should mislead in the employment of them. "We ought, when we are restricted to the employment of old words, to endeavour as far as possible that it shall not be necessary to struggle against the old associations with those words. We should, if possible, give the words such a meaning that the propositions in which people are accustomed to use them, shall as far as possible still be true ; and that the feelings habitually excited by them shall be such as the things to which we mean to appropriate them ought to excite." (Mill Unsettled Questions, p. 80.)

§ 31. *Not minded*, not attended to.

§ 32. *Tarantula*, the old name of a species of spider found in

pp. 224—228.

Sicily, whose bite produced a state of extreme nervous excitement, only, it is said, to be cured by music.

§ 34. *Arts of fallacy*, rhetoric.

Preferred, exalted, promoted.

Rhetoric, that powerful instrument of error and deceit.—An interesting, though inaccurate, account of the reaction in favour of the "affectionate study of eloquence" will be found in Bacon, Advancement of Learning, Bk. I. Chap. iv. secs. 2-4. (See also Bk. II. Chap. xviii. secs. 1-5.) Bacon, with more moderation than Locke, allows, " But yet, notwithstanding it is a thing not hastily to be condemned, to clothe and adorn the obscurity even of philosophy itself with sensible and plausible elocution." The Port Royal Logic (Part. III. Chap. xx. sec. 2) is more stringent; *e.g.*, " How many false thoughts has the desire of making a good point produced? How many have been led into falsehood for the sake of a rhyme?" " It is true that precision renders the style more dry and less pompous; but it also renders it clearer, more vigorous, more serious, and more worthy of an honourable man." (Cf. also Locke's Thoughts concerning Education, sec. 189, and the Essay, Bk. II. Chap. xi. sec. 2.)

CHAPTER XI.

§ 4. *On hinderance of knowledge.*—Of course not serious. Language is, practically speaking, *necessary* to thought. (Note to Chap. ii. sec. 2. See also Mansel, Prolegomena Logica, pp. 17, *seq.*)

§ 7. *Is not a question.*—Locke means to say that we cannot discuss the question whether a bat is just the same thing as a bird, because this would, of course, imply that it is not a *bat :* if A is B, it cannot be A. This, however, is a distortion of the ordinary meaning of predication ; and so far as true is a highly metaphysical subtlety. Locke implies that affirmation cannot involve negation, which is certainly not true. (Cf. Caird, Philos. of Kant, Part II. Chap. vi. espec. pp. 298–304.)

Where they agree, etc.—In so far as they agree in the connotation of the names, they must agree in the denotation (application) of them ; they must see whether the one class of things is, or is not, included in the other. (But cf. Mill, Logic, vol. i. pp. 171 *seq.*)

§ 9. *In modes,* in the case of modes.

Especially in moral words.—Although this is no doubt a consummation devoutly to be wished, the difficulty is to do it. As examples, we may refer to the discussion on the meaning of the word *Justice* in Plato's Republic, Bks. I.-II. ; and Mr. Sidgwick's still more refined analysis in his Methods of Ethics, Bk. III. Chap. v. Locke speaks as though the definition was a matter only a little " troublesome " at the worst. He overlooks the fact that in fixing the meaning or connotation of a word more strictly, we shall disarrange its denotation. We may settle that a word shall imply just such and such attributes ; but in doing so we almost always make many of the propositions in which it is to be found either untrue or absurd. (See Mill, Logic, i. pp. 171–6 ; ii. pp. 217–51.)

§ 10. *I shall have occasion to speak.* Cf. sec. 24.

§ 11. *To such ideas as common use has annexed them to.* Cf. Port Royal Logic, Part I. Chap. xiii. " We must not change definitions already received when we have nothing to complain of in them. . . . . When we are to define a word, we ought as far as possible to accommodate ourselves to custom, in not giving to words a sense altogether removed from that which they have, and which might be even contrary to their etymology." (Prof. Bayne's transl. p. 85. See also Mill, Logic, ii. pp. 220 *seq.*) " It would be a complete misunderstanding of the proper office of a logician in dealing with terms already in use, if we were to think that because a name has not at present an ascertained connotation, it is competent to any one to give it such a connotation at his own choice. The meaning of a term actually in use is not an arbitrary quantity to be fixed, but an unknown quantity to be sought."

§ 12. *Come to have ideas different from the vulgar.*—" We thus see that to frame a good definition of a name already in use, is not a matter of choice but of discussion, and discussion not merely respecting the usage of language, but respecting the properties of things, and even the origin of those properties. And hence every enlargement of our knowledge of the objects to which the name is applied, is liable to suggest an improvement in the definition. It is impossible to frame a perfect set of definitions on any subject, until the theory of the subject is perfect ; and as science makes progress, its definitions are also progressive." (Mill, Logic, ii. p. 222.)

§ 14. *Ingenuity*, candour, ingenuousness.

" If a child when questioned for anything directly confess, you must commend his *ingenuity*, and pardon the fault, be it what it will." (Locke, Some Thoughts concerning Education, sec. 132.)

§ 15. *Arbitrarily put together.* (Cf. note to Chap. v. sec. 3 ; and to sec. 9 of this Chap.)

§ 16. *Morality is capable of demonstration.*—" The idea of a Supreme Being, infinite in power, goodness, and wisdom, whose

workmanship we are, and on whom we depend ; and the idea
of ourselves as understanding, rational beings, being such
[ideas] as are clear in us, would I suppose if duly considered
and pursued, afford such foundations of our duty and rules of
action as might place morality amongst the sciences capable of
demonstration : wherein I doubt not, but from self-evident
propositions, as incontestable as those in mathematics, the
measures of right and wrong might be made out, to any one
that will apply himself with the same indifferency and attention
to the one as he does to the other of these sciences." (Essay,
Bk. IV. Chap. iii. sec. 18 ; cf. Chap. iv. sec. 7, and Chap. xii.
sec. 8 of the same book.) These passages show the thoroughly
Cartesian reliance on deductions from axioms "clearly and
distinctly" conceived, and the same tendency to assimilate
ethics, etc., to mathematics, which reached its culminating point
in the great Cartesian, Spinoza. They are important to show
that Locke's indebtedness to Descartes was more than a
matter of terms and phrases, and was, in truth, fundamental.

§ 17. *Disproportionate*, that is, not in keeping with reality

§ 19. *Forwardly*, quickly, rashly.

§ 20. *Such a sort of frontispiece*, a countenance of some particular kind. "Where now, I ask, will be the just measure of
the utmost bounds of that shape which carries with it a human
soul?" (Essay, Bk. IV. chap. iv. sec. 16. Cf. above, chap.
vi. sec. 26.)

Inform.—The soul was conceived of by the Aristotelians as
the *form* of the body, that is, as the formative principle which
gives a definite constitution to the body. It was thus regarded
as the source of the organizing or vital activities of the body,
as well as the agent of thought. (Cf. notes to Chap. x. sec. 10,
and sec. 14.)

" While life informs these limbs."—Pope, Odyssey.

§ 21. *Nice*, exact, precise.

§ 22. *Formal constitution*, same as *substantial form.* (Cf. notes to Chap. vi. sec. 10, and to Chap. x. sec. 14.)

§ 24. *With the history of that sort of things.*—We must, says Locke, actually observe the things themselves, we must know their "history" (*i.e.* natural history). This passage is one of those in which Locke allows that the boundaries of species are not by any means wholly arbitrary.

Very overtly, consciously, with full knowledge.

§ 25. *Draughts*, drawings, pictures. Locke's plan had been already carried into practice in the Orbis Sensualium Picture of the great educational reformer, John Amos Commenius (Kommensky). An English edition of this was published in 1659 by "Charles Hoole, Teacher of a Private Grammar-School in Lothbury, London. For the use of young Latine Scholars." It professed to be a "Picture and Nomenclature of all the Chief Things that are in the World ; and of Mens Employments therein. A work newly written by the author in Latine and High Dutch." Other English editions were published in 1777 and in 1810 (New York). An account of the theories of Commenius will be found in Prof. Laurie's monograph.

Apium was, in classical Latin, the name of some plant ; the precise species has not been determined. Probably wild parsley, or wild celery.

Ibex, a kind of goat, capra ibex (Linnæus).

Strigil, a scraper of horn or metal, bent in shape, with a sharp edge, used after a warm bath by Greeks and Romans. Very different from the modern curry-comb to which Locke refers.

pp. 251, 252.

Sistrum, a kind of rattle, used by the Egyptians in religious ceremonies. No resemblance to a cymbal.

Toga, the chief outer garment ordinarily used by Roman gentlemen, shaped like a large semi-circular cloak, but falling into voluminous folds when worn.

Tunica, an under-garment worn by both sexes among the Romans, beneath the *toga* or *pallium* in the case of men, beneath the *stola* in the case of women.

Pallium, the most common outer garment, a mere square of undyed cloth used as a cloak over the tunic, or even alone in the case of poor people.

§ 27. *To explain his meaning.*—As a matter of fact, it is to a large extent due to this scanty provision of words that definition is at once so necessary and so difficult. If we had a name for everything there would be less temptation to extend, and consequently change, the meaning of terms.

Woodfall and Kinder, Printers, Milford Lane, Strand, London, W.C.